THE DAWNING OF A TROUBLED NEW AGE

"It's time for a new day in Ilia, Granddaughter. I see change coming—and not all of it good. It's just as well the city has a young queen to deal with it!"

Sivell felt cold rising in her veins. "What change do you mean? What do you see?"

"I don't think peace will hold with the Ganus for very much longer," the old woman replied. "Didn't you notice at the Proving ceremony? In other times, the Ganus brought gifts to the new queen—flamestones to adorn her neck and fingers, gold coins for her purse! And what did they bring today? Empty hands, sullen eyes and insolent speech, that's what."

Unease prickled along her spine. Sivell turned to her brother, who had been quiet all through the banquet. "Parvey, what do you think of this? You'll help me face whatever it is, surely?"

Instead of answering, he shrugged. He lifted his crystal wine goblet, studying it, as if the future was displayed within. "Remember you're queen now, Sivell. A queen needs no one."

"I'll remember that I'm deeply in your debt," she said. "If you ever need me, Parvey, I shall count it an honor to repay."

Suddenly Parvey pushed his chair back and rose from the table. "Promises are light to make. Let's hope neither of us has occasion to break them."

"Moving and thought provoking, and a good story besides, with characters who linger in the mind even after the story is ended. I liked it. I liked it a lot."

—Judith Tarr, author of
The Hound and the Falcon Trilogy

THE
GARDEN
OF THE
SHAPED

Sheila Finch

BANTAM BOOKS
NEW YORK · TORONTO · LONDON · SYDNEY · AUCKLAND

THE GARDEN OF THE SHAPED

A Bantam Spectra Book / September 1987
2nd printing / July 1989

ISBN 0-553-26801-5

Published simultaneously in the United States and Canada

Bantam Books are published by Bantam Books, a division of Bantam Doubleday Dell Publishing Group, Inc. Its trademark, consisting of the words "Bantam Books" and the portrayal of a rooster, is Registered in U.S. Patent and Trademark Office and in other countries. Marca Registrada. Bantam Books, 666 Fifth Avenue, New York, New York 10103.

PRINTED IN THE UNITED STATES OF AMERICA

O   11 10 9 8 7 6 5 4 3 2

for Morris L. Thomas,
this book's godfather

CHAPTER ONE

(PROLOGUE, EARTHDATE: 2087)

Robocams picked the tiny world out of the background clutter of dust particles, asteroids, and assorted debris hurtling around *Beta Orbis* and displayed it on the large vidscreen above the navconsole on board the *Shakespeare*. Data flowed across a neighboring, smaller screen. Scientists and crew members—sympathizers who'd chosen to go into exile with them—gathered to gaze at their new home.

Anger burned vividly in Elena Tagak's veins, as it had in the days of the infamous trial of the geneticists of Venn Labs. *Damn,* she thought, *damn!* The judges had known what they were doing. Death would've been preferable to this knowledge of a life wasted. She had to find a way past grief. The others seemed to have done this; why couldn't she? But her eyes closed against a sudden rush of tears. All of it lost. The promise of so much goodness betrayed. Well, then, let the sanctimonious citizens of Earth rot in their own biblical prison, she thought fiercely. Edward Venn would have made them angels, and the fools thought that a sin.

She slid gracefully in zero-grav through the group toward John Askar, Venn's closest colleague and scientific heir. "Looks like we can start our new lives as farmers and tillers of the soil any day now!"

1

A warning bell pinged, and a screen displayed the message "ENTERING PLANETARY ORBIT." The crew dispersed, gliding away with varying degrees of deftness to their stations.

Miranda Illing looked up at them from the screen where she'd been studying the planet. "We're going to have a *long* time to make friends with the local fauna."

John Askar shrugged irritably. "Some of us have bigger ambitions than that! Ed's dream deserves to live."

Ed's dream. They'd all shared it at one time. The dream of creating a perfect race—birth defects unknown, no more ugliness or ungainliness, no splotches, stains or awkward contours, no crooked teeth or crossed eyes, disease resistant—living in a perfect society. They'd argued late into the night over what that society should be like: Marxist or Hobbesian, Mill's enlightened egoists or Kant's duty-bound followers. Personally, Elena had leaned toward the theories of her husband, Alexei Rhodarivich Tagak, author of the definitive work on the development of strong human society under adverse environmental conditions. She'd never see Alexei again, or their twelve-year-old daughter she'd left in his care. She wondered if forever was a long enough time to get used to the loss.

"They'll have the champagne bulbs open in a minute! I saw the crates being smuggled aboard when Security wasn't looking," Miranda said. "I almost thought of that myself, but I spent all my credits on a music library. You know, we'll have to find a better name for this planet than *Beta Orbis IV* if we're going to live here forever."

Forever was an ominous word, Elena thought, doubly so when you were denied your life's work with which to fill it. Venn's last gift to his followers was the vaccine he'd worked on in secret, long after he'd turned over the routine of genetic experimentation to the others. It was a gift that threatened now to become a curse: the so-called immortality drug.

"How about something from Shakespeare?" Miranda said thoughtfully. "That would be appropriate. How does the line go? 'What country is this?' 'This is Illyria, Lady.'

There: Illyria. That's from *Twelfth Night*, I think. Or maybe it's from *The Tempest*—"

"I had something else in mind," John said. "Not all of us came unprepared on this little expedition. Some of us brought more valuable cargo along than champagne. I saved something important out of Ed's lab, just before the mob got to it."

Elena wondered if she could ever forget that night when the Biblists came for the blood of the "devil" geneticists.

"Ed's notecubes?" Miranda wondered aloud. "But even so—"

He lowered his voice. "Human germ plasm."

Elena stared at him. "EarthGov would've executed you if they'd known! Why take such a risk?"

"Because I share Ed's dreams!" he said passionately. "The shaping of a *new*, perfect human being—not just patching up an old, tired race!"

"It's tempting," Miranda said. "Really tempting to think we could continue the beloved work. I have such wonderful ideas! But we've lost so much ground. There'd be so much to do even to get back to where we were before Ed was killed. We have no labs—no equipment—"

"We'll cannibalize the ship. We've got some good people who can adapt the computers to our purposes—Donald, for instance. We could turn this—what did you call it, Miranda?—'Ilia'—into a garden of Eden, a perfect world, filled with a perfect race."

Miranda Illing started to say something, then changed her mind. Instead, she said thoughtfully, "You know, I really do have a few ideas about a new race. While we were modifying genes for strength and longevity, the ability to work at high altitudes or underwater without artificial breathing aids, and so on, I did some thinking about adding a few *exciting* changes. Something really exotic."

"A coherent philosophy is a prerequisite," Elena said. "What we'd teach them to believe is—"

"Yes!" Miranda agreed. "First we'll have to invent the time of myths and legends for them."

"And for us," John put in. "How will our creations see us?"

"Oh, it'll be wonderful," Miranda said, executing a graceful, backward arc, like a dancer in slow-motion. "A magnificent enterprise."

"We'll need to be careful," Elena said. "There could be consequences we don't foresee."

"We'll observe the whole history of human progress in miniature," Miranda said. "Altered, of course, as we alter their flesh."

"Something bothers me," Elena began. "Before we tamper with human evolution, we should—"

The door of the bridge slid open, admitting a slim little boy, his fair hair and graceful movements wrenching Elena's heart with memories—the lurid, flickering night sky above the wreckage that had once been the classic white buildings of Venn Labs, Inc., flames devouring the equipment and the datacubes, the screams of trapped lab animals mixed with the animal howl of the Biblist mob. And the body of Edward Venn, their leader, this boy's father, sprawled across the threshold, bloodstained fingers spread in a vain attempt to hold back the tide of ignorance and superstition that had engulfed them.

"Are we there yet?" the boy said. "Is it over?"

"Come to me, Kory," Miranda said, leaning toward the child and putting her arm around his shoulders. "Something wonderful is about to begin. Your father's dream will become reality. And you'll have the most marvelous playthings any boy has ever had! Wait and see."

CHAPTER TWO

(ILIAN DATE: 528)

"Seek, Sivell," the jil tree called. "Seek. You can't find me!"

A gale of laughter seized the slender, crescent-shaped leaves, whirling them in the spring sunshine. Sivell passed by on the other side of the castle courtyard, shutting out the taunting voice.

"Sivell!" The jil tree grew taller, thinned out, its top branches faded. The trunk became transparent, the transparency spread upward to the boughs. The contours of the tree now blurred and slipped, and in its place a waterfall splashed over the low wall of an ornamental pool and onto the creamstone of the courtyard.

"Who am I, Sivell?" the waterfall tinkled.

Sivell felt the slight prickle of the shiftfield like bubbles on her skin. Shifting made a subtle difference in the air, hardly noticeable when one was otherwise occupied, but it was by such clues that the game of Seek was played.

A fountain rose up at the base of the waterfall, mingled with the downfalling water, grew taller. The tingling Sivell felt increased. The fountain became a pillar in which two liquid columns swayed together.

"*I* found you, Kela!" Zil's deep voice announced.

A slight metallic tang laced the air, another clue, evading all but the most sensitive noses. The image itself deflected scrutiny, concealing itself in myriad points of brightness like miniature suns. Sivell squinted her eyes

5

against light like tiny knives. Now she could almost see
the players whose real shapes swam up momentarily
against the background of the castle wall, then merged
again with the false image. Two laughing faces wavered
in the misty shiftshape, one male, one female. There was
a brief sunburst, and waterfall and fountain subsided. In
their place, two human figures glided together underwater, silver rippling away from them in a widening arc.
On the surface of the pool, a rosy jil blossom floated.

Sivell left the young couple to their shiftgame and
went out through the low stone arch. The castle stood on
the highest point of land, where Ilia met the sea. To the
east was Sorway Cliff and a straight drop. But to the
south and west, sloping down from the castle in a jumble
of roofs, towers, spires, and turrets, was the city of Tia-
ta-pel, home of the Lianis. In the late afternoon, the city
was filled with the music of songbirds in hundreds of
wicker cages under the eaves, and the voices of bells and
silver arils.

Sivell walked over the high-arched bridges toward the
center of the city, her sandals clicking on the dark wood.
Tia-ta-pel was beautiful—she always thought that—but
today, its springtime charm failed to chase away shadows
the mockery had raised. Others might think it, but only
her cousin Kela was brazen enough to taunt her publicly.

She stood aside in a narrow alley to let a group of
children run past. Bright eyes glanced curiously at her
from the shapes of bird and beast they'd chosen in their
game, as if they wondered why anybody would keep
their own body when they had so many marvelous
shapes to choose from. A flash of color, a clatter of hooves
and they rounded a corner and were gone.

Shiftgames, she thought, the whole city was a shiftgame. She looked back up at the towers of the castle
shimmering above the housetops. Just visible above a
blue tiled roof was the east tower, where she'd slept
since her birth, nineteen summers ago. The castle might
almost have been an illusion itself, a shiftgame made of
stone and wood—a fitting home for the Liani royal family
that played with such illusions so well.

Except me! she thought. Her cousin had a right to mock.

In a quiet street opening off a small square was a shop belonging to a Ganu jeweler. It was cool and dark inside, and smelled faintly of the tree bark the jeweler used to polish his gems. The bark was oily and aromatic as incense, and left the carved gemstones smooth and silky.

The jeweler was polishing a stone as she entered. She waited, but he didn't look up. The Ganus were shorter than the Lianis by a head on the average, and pale-skinned, pale-haired, as if the Great Shaper had made an outline sketch of the race but hadn't yet filled in the details. But the biggest difference was that the Ganus couldn't shift their shapes. Even Sivell could feel superior.

"Good evening."

He raised his eyes to see who spoke, but didn't stop polishing the gemstone with the bark.

"Are the stones I ordered ready?"

"Perhaps," he replied in the harsh Ganu accent. "It depends how easy satisfied you be."

The Lianis never demanded and never received respect from the Ganus, but honest work well done was a Ganu hallmark. She waited patiently. Presently, the man laid aside the work he was doing and turned to a wooden box on a shelf at the back of the store. He set it before her and removed the lid.

"See for youself if the gauds be done!"

Two stones glittered a hard, bright blue.

"Beautiful!" Sivell said. "They're just the way I designed them."

"There be no wires on the gauds. You didn't order any."

"They're not earrings. They're pendants, each to hang from a silver chain." She examined the finely engraved symbols. A jalu stretched its wings on one, a four-petaled jil blossom unfurled on the other.

"You've done very well."

Since the weather was warm, she'd worn no jacket over her short tunic; instead, she carried a small

shoulder purse, which she opened and withdrew two
gold coins.

"Ganu toil paid with Ganu gold!" the jeweler said
suddenly.

Startled, Sivell dropped the coins on the counter
where they rang and bounced, coming to rest behind the
box. Immediately, he covered her dark hand with his
milk-colored one, closing thin fingers over her wrist. She
stifled a cry.

"That sticks in the gull of many in this metros,
Princess."

She was too shocked to reply.

"Someday, the Lianis will wake and see how life in this
jarden be real made!"

His words made no sense. "We've done nothing to
hurt you—"

"Nay," he said, "that you haven't. But you be not of
help, either!"

Then he removed his hand and opened a drawer,
taking out two silver chains.

"You paid extra." He dropped the chains carelessly
into the box on top of the smoldering fires.

Before she could answer, he'd returned to his polishing and didn't look up again. She was still shaking as she
left the jeweler's shop and hurried toward the castle.

Then she was aware of ripples spreading slowly
through the darkening air and lapping softly about her.
She let them touch her, opening her senses to them.
From the darkness a current flowed up the narrow street
toward her, gathered itself together, crested, and broke,
revealing a tall woman wrapped in a cloak as misty as the
winter sea, her hair piled above her brow like a crown of
silver spray.

"Granddaughter," the Queen-Regent said. "Both
moons have risen. Canela some fifty minutes ago, and
Terel just now. It's as bright as day!"

That was an exaggeration, but Sivell saw that the city
was indeed filling with the light of the moons which hung
like curving jil petals against the indigo sky.

"I'm coming at once, Madam!"

The old woman turned regally, her silver hair sparkling. Sivell followed, conscious of her own movements compared to the liquid motion ahead. It seemed her grandmother's bones were rivers that flowed her from place to place, while Sivell's own had to be awkwardly extended and drawn up and extended again by sheer force of her will.

Grandmother and granddaughter passed silently through the courtyard where the jil tree had played with Sivell in the afternoon. No trees disturbed the even slabs of creamstone now, and no fountains splashed in the shadows. Ahead, a door leading into the palace stood ajar, letting amber light wash out. Somewhere high above the dark towers a nightbird began to spill its melody. Grandmother entered, and the light sent flashes of fire from her high-piled hair and her jeweled necklaces to dance ahead down the corridor. As usual, Sivell felt childish and grubby behind her grandmother's magnificence.

But on entering her grandmother's private chamber, Sivell's mood changed instantly.

"Parvey!"

Her brother stood with his back to the fireplace. He was taller than most Lianis, dark and angular, with a face like carved, smoked glass. He wasn't wearing even the most informal shiftemblem tonight, she saw, being for her benefit all Parvey.

"I thought you'd gone away. I couldn't find you," she chided.

"Would I desert you, little sister?" Parvey tipped her face up and gazed down at her with dark eyes.

How beautiful he was, she thought. Throughout her childhood and adolescence this perfect being had been her protector, rescuing her from the mockery of playmates and the watchful eyes of adults whose business was to monitor her progress toward the throne. She'd never felt awkward or inferior when he was with her. At such times, not even Kela dared to suggest there was anything wrong with Sivell's ability to shift. Alone, Sivell had difficulty shifting so much as the color of her eyes.

But Parvey had taken her with him when he shifted, so that she'd tasted the wild wine of shiftdancing and knew better than anyone how much she lacked.

"Look," she said. "I have a gift for you." She opened the box and drew out the pendant with the jalu carved on it. "I hope you like the design."

"Perfect," he said, smiling.

"You seem like a jalu to me," she said. "Strong and beautiful."

He bent over and kissed her on the forehead. "Thank you."

He slipped the pendant around his neck, and the blue stone gleamed against his sun-colored tunic. Sivell put the box with the remaining pendant back into her pocket. That one was for her dearest friend.

Behind them, the Queen-Regent cleared her throat. Sivell turned from Parvey with reluctance but kept hold of his hand. She was suddenly trembling. Parvey led her to a cushioned bench by the fire and sat with her. The Queen-Regent seated herself in a tall chair across from them.

Sivell gripped Parvey's hand and stared at the familiar scrolls and flourishes of the fireplace, the emblems and symbols of the Twelve Oldest Families of the Lianis, the royal crest in the center: a winged being robed in white, arms upraised, one holding a slender glass vial, the other holding a peculiar device, a double spiral twisting back on itself. She had often wondered what this odd thing could be used for, but since some said this winged being represented the Great Shaper itself—or at the very least, the Venn—it was presumptuous to think she should understand. On the mantel ledge, candles burned in golden holders.

"We will speak tonight of the fact that the Proving of Sivell is only half a year away," the Queen-Regent said. "We can't postpone it any longer."

In the silence that followed, Sivell was sure the Queen-Regent would hear how loudly her heart was beating. She had known she would eventually have to face this ultimate test—most queens were Proved at a much younger age than Sivell was already—but her grandmother had seemed in no hurry to relinquish the throne. Sivell had avoided thinking about it.

"Our people don't trouble themselves too much with custom, and form matters little to a folk who can change theirs at will. This you know already," the old queen said. "There's one custom, however, that's never been broken from generation to generation down all the years of Ilia's history since Kirili left the Great Shaper's Garden. I refer to the ceremony of Proving a Queen in Tia-ta-pel."

The old woman was about to embark on one of her favorite stories. Sivell knew them all by heart. Her attention wandered to the silver mist Grandmother wore as her hair. It was an elegant shiftemblem, finely detailed and regal. She herself had never quite had the courage to adopt the wearing of a shiftemblem at times when the natural shape of the wearer was required. Almost all the Lianis did this as soon as they were out of childhood. It would never do, for instance, for the royal council chambers to be filled with jil trees, jalus, or whatever. Even a Liani child understood that such shapes were more than merely playful; they had a bemusing effect on those that viewed them. At such times the Lianis wore shiftemblems—subtle suggestions of the shiftskill of the wearers—transforming hair or hands instead of the whole body, or carrying a living picture of some chosen bird or plant on their breasts. But Sivell had never been confident she could maintain one if she started it.

"This ceremony mustn't be taken lightly, Granddaughter. Before any princess may take the throne she must prove to the assembled Lianis that she's worthier than they to be queen. You are aware of this, of course?"

"Yes, Madam."

"And each queen in turn then selects a mate of superior power to father her daughter, so that the skill of the queens shall be strengthened, and peace and good fortune remain with our people. The skill of the queens is the luck of the Lianis. The Proving is a most important

ceremony, for it celebrates the time when the Great
Shaper shaped Kirili, mother of us all."

"No, Madam. I don't take the Proving lightly."

Grandmother continued. "My mother did this before
me, and I did it in my time, and your mother in her turn
after me. And now we come to the matter that brings us
here tonight."

Her grandmother had the ability to make Sivell feel as
if she were still a child. She stared at the floor, avoiding
her grandmother's eyes.

"Until now," the Queen-Regent said, "each princess
has passed the Proving. There's never been a dispute to
trouble the peaceful transition of the throne. There must
be none this time, either."

"Surely, Madam," Parvey began, "you don't anticipate—"

Grandmother cut him off with a gesture from her slim,
dark hand. "I anticipate nothing. But I know what all
three in this room know. Sivell has shown little ability to
shift. Any Liani child can do as well as she, and some can
do considerably better!"

For a moment, Sivell found herself wishing the floor
would open, so that she might slide down into the cool
depths of the castle cellars, away from the burning eyes
in the old woman's accusing face. But there was no
rescue from the truth that her grandmother spoke. She
felt the heat creeping into her cheeks.

Parvey spoke in her defense again. "My sister's just
more thoughtful than most. She's not amused by playing
as others are. But don't our queens breed for such
uncommon characteristics, Madam?"

The Queen-Regent gazed at Parvey a long time before
she replied. "I intend no evil when I speak of your
mother, Grandson. In the matter of your own ancestry, I
believe she did indeed select a mate with most uncommon and valuable gifts. But you can't inherit the throne.
I have misgivings about this other breeding!"

"Still, Madam," Parvey said, his eyes steadily holding
the Queen-Regent's. "What my mother did once, she
must have done again. Perhaps we should ask what

Sivell might have inherited as well as what she might not."

"Do you argue with me, Grandson?"

"No, Madam." He bowed his head courteously, but his dark eyes glittered in the firelight. "I say only that we may not know what this father had to offer, but I won't believe my royal mother chose unwisely."

The Queen-Regent was silent for a while. Then she said, "Not to know the father of a Liani child, even a royal child, is nothing. For a queen to leave her throne after giving a daughter to her people, as your mother did, is a small matter. But for a royal child to grow up clumsy-footed at shifting, that's cause for concern!" She leaned toward Parvey. "Make no mistake here, Grandson. I've learned who helped Sivell more than once when her playmates trapped her into a game of Seek!"

Parvey made no reply. Sivell slumped beside him, wondering who'd known her secrets and revealed them to her grandmother. The likeliest candidate was her cousin Kela. It scarcely mattered; the truth was out and she was disgraced.

And then came a stunning announcement. The Queen-Regent sat back in her chair, sighed deeply, and said, "I don't think Sivell's father was Liani."

"You surely don't imply that my royal mother coupled with a Ganu?" Parvey half rose, his voice heavy with anger.

The old woman shrugged, her dark face somber.

The floor opened up anyway, dropping Sivell into darkness. The enormity of this accusation stunned her. *I don't think Sivell's father was Liani—not Liani—*

She was aware they were both looking at her, as if she held the answer, as if she knew who her father had been and was willfully keeping it a secret.

"I could leave Tia-ta-pel," she said hesitantly. "I could let somebody else be queen."

In a soft, singing voice the old woman began to chant:

When Ilia's queen shall run away
The somber ones will have their day.

If she not shift to save her folk
Both dark and light shall feel the yoke.
Yet if she dare
The throne to share
Strong feet shall walk in Ilia.

"You don't believe that piece of nonsense, surely?" Parvey asked, his tone scathing. "Come, Madam! What use is it to scare Sivell?"

"That's an old prophecy, some say as old as Tia-ta-pel itself, in whose foundation stone it's carved."

Parvey said, "Words, only words!"

Then the Queen-Regent's eyes softened. "We'll not let the somber ones, the Ganus, rule in Tia-ta-pel, will we, Granddaughter?"

Sivell shook her head silently, unable to trust herself to speak.

"You believe the Ganus pose a threat to us, Madam?" Parvey asked.

"I see ominous signs, Grandson. We've been uneasy neighbors for generations. They envy our shiftskill, naturally enough! Until recently they gladly worked for us, or gave gold to have the pleasure of watching what they could never hope to do. But now . . ."

"Now?" Parvey prompted when the old woman fell silent.

"I see the difference in the tradesmen's eyes when they look at us, how they hesitate before doing our bidding. I hear a growing resentment in their answers."

"What do you propose to do?" Parvey asked.

"Obvious! We must prepare Sivell to pass the Proving."

Parvey frowned. "But how will that—"

She didn't let him finish. "We need the wizard Askar from the Islands of the Dawn. He was a good friend to the royal house of Ilia in the days when your mother was queen. He'll help."

Puzzled, Sivell asked, "How will a wizard know there's need for help in Tia-ta-pel?"

"Wizards know everything. The inner sight is theirs,

and the inner hearing, and the power to foretell the future—some say, to *make* the future!"

"But they live so far away—"

Exasperated, the Queen-Regent snapped, "Very well, I'll call. '*Askar! We need your help!*' There. Will that satisfy the child?"

Sivell lowered her eyes from her grandmother's angry face. "I still don't understand how a wizard will help me."

"Askar can teach you to use every drop of the shiftskill you have—you must have inherited *something* from your royal mother! Wizards have helped the Lianis before— Askar, of course, and Mirandil, and— Well, it doesn't matter! Alone, Granddaughter, I doubt if you can do it. But with Askar's help you'll pass the test and save Ilia from the prophecy. Grave problems require unorthodox solutions."

"Such help from a wizard will have its price, I think," Sivell said, hesitating to offend her grandmother, but full of misgiving.

The Queen-Regent stared at her. "Wizards are friends of the Lianis! They're descended from the Venn, who cared for Kirili after she left the Great Shaper's garden."

"But I've heard it said that wizard gifts have thorns, like wildflowers, and can draw blood."

Parvey too was staring at her now, turning the jalu pendant she'd given him between the slim fingers of his left hand. "Didn't I say, Madam, we're judging her too soon? There may be gifts here we don't suspect!"

The Queen-Regent snorted. "Of what use to the Lianis are such gifts of logic and argument, unless the throne be secured first?"

"Ah, but afterward?" Parvey said. "If you're right about this growing rebellion among the Ganus, then we may need more than shiftskill to counter it!"

The old woman dismissed this idea. "The fact remains that a queen of the Lianis must first be proved. Without that step, the greatest gifts have no value."

"What are they like, these wizards?" Sivell asked. "I've never seen one."

"Like you or like me! Will you never be satisfied? Enough of this idle chatter. Mark my words—Askar will be here tomorrow! And tomorrow we begin Sivell's schooling."

There were many more things Sivell didn't dare ask. Questions jostled in her head like a flock of startled corlis on the pond in the castle garden. Who was her father? If her blood was not all bad, as Parvey suggested, then why had her mother run away? But she knew how unlike a Liani it would be to ask so many personal questions.

"We have no alternative," the Queen-Regent told Parvey. "You yourself are highly qualified for the throne, and may even want it— No, don't interrupt," she said as he started to protest. "I read you very well, Grandson. Never think I don't know what lies in your deepest heart! But that's out of the question."

Parvey turned away impatiently, not bothering to answer.

"It *will* work," the old woman said, "because it has to. And besides, I'm tired of being queen in Tia-ta-pel."

Startled, Sivell glanced at her grandmother and found the planes of that old Liani face were splintered by a rare smile.

CHAPTER THREE

Where fog blurred the distant horizon, a remote archipelago rode the dark water, its colors muted and softened. Above it, like fish caught in a net, a few still-bright stars poked through the clouds.

A tall figure appeared, in a white robe draped over one shoulder and girdled with a fine gold chain. Mirandil walked along the shore of the smallest island as she had done every morning for the past five hundred years. Nothing disturbed the silence. Mirandil leaned down and stirred the streamers of mist about her feet with the tips of the least fingers of her left hand and of her right hand. At once, a shining quicksilver pulse ran over the silver-white air. The ripples spread slowly, and a land appeared like a reflection in a mirror. The rising sun tinted the sky gold and rose above her head, but Mirandil stared at the hologram she had summoned up. To the north, the sea coast of this land wavered and great mountains pointed fuzzy fingers at the sky as if through a terrible blizzard.

Mirandil narrowed her eyes and the image sharpened.

Now she could see hunters going out to hunt in the dark forests on the slopes of the mountains, fishermen setting out on the calm sea, and miners going down into caves in the mountains to fetch out gold and the peculiar fiery stone of the region that resembled an Earth opal more than anything else. All the tiny images moved about as cunningly as if by enchantment, and Mirandil herself was charmed by it. To the south, the hills of this land were gentler; the fields were full of fruit trees where birds nested and rivers where golden fish flamed in the

17

sunshine. Towns clustered along the southern coastline like pearls in the bright arms of the ocean.

Every morning Mirandil summoned up a hologram of this part of the planet called Ilia, and every morning she heard music in the city of Tia-ta-pel: birds in the treetops, bells in the steeples, songs on the lips of the people. It was a happy city, and its people were her children playing under her watchful eye in a pleasant garden.

But this morning she frowned and turned away. Behind her the mist ran black, lilac and rose like a bruise where her fingers had touched and withdrawn.

Now Mirandil heard the call of the Venn in her mind. She drew her gauzy robe up in one hand and walked over the rich green turf of the little island to meet them. By a small waterfall, she took care to put her feet on a path made of microthin layers of shell, a dazzle of light shimmering under the translucent surface. As she did so the land beneath her feet dissolved and reformed.

Koril was sitting on a scarlet carpet of blossom that spilled over a flight of white steps at the heart of the largest island. Behind him, the sun flamed on white columns, and birds with radiant, color-enhanced plumage sat on his shoulders. Mirandil lowered her lashes against their vibrant assault. His hair shone like spun gold, and today his eyes were green as the sea. The perfume of the scarlet blooms was as heavy as sweet wine. She bowed her head courteously and waited for him to speak. The coming together of the remaining Venn was like a breeze passing over the strings of an instrument. Mirandil felt the arrival of the other two before she saw them.

Koril extended his arms and the birds flew up. His thoughts flashed clearly into Mirandil's mind.

Something new arises in Ilia, something disharmonious, Koril began.

We have all heard it, Mirandil acknowledged, *to our sorrow!*

It was their purpose to know the meaning of every new thing in the lands they watched, for they were the last of the Venn. But sometimes, Mirandil thought, it was hard to remember why it mattered—it had all been so long ago.

Koril continued. *Ilia's children have grown and prospered. They're as different one from another as summer and winter, but they're all precious to us. Now, however, something we didn't plan is happening.*

Tagak, daughter of the Venn, stood before them, tall and dressed in leather hunting garb with a full-moon pendant on her brow. *The time has come for other things to happen, not just the events we planned. Fiercer things of battle and conquest. Surely we expected this? And some of those we shaped will perish. You, Koril, true child of the Father, must know this is inevitable.*

But Mirandil did not agree with Tagak's answer, for of all the children of the shaping, the dark-eyed metamorphs of Tia-ta-pel had been her special project. She asked, *Is there no way to avert this discord?*

We agreed from the first to watch only, Tagak replied. *Not to interfere, but to watch what they'd do alone. We took the risk not to become entangled in the results.*

The way to change a song is to change the singer!

Mirandil turned to see the thinker. Askar too was a son of the Venn, a watcher of the shaped of Ilia, though he had chosen to watch the ones that in her opinion were the least interesting, the pale ones who lived at the foot of the great mountains.

That would be interfering, Koril answered. *We're watchers. We don't do.*

However, Tagak put in, *we've been "doing" from the beginning! Or have the passing centuries caused us to truly forget who and what we are?*

These gaudy butterflies of yours, Mirandil, have become parasites, Askar told her. *They suck the lifeblood of my farmers and fishers!*

Mirandil stared at him, unsure how to answer but stirred by deep and disturbing memories of another time. *The Father-Shaper*— she began, but could not go on for she was not sure what it was she was about to say. It had been too long ago.

Now they want me to help them. But they should've

summoned you, Lady. You've a gentler heart than the rest of us.

And you've wrought enough mischief already! Mirandil replied stiffly, anger quickly replacing the confusion of a moment before. *Like the cuckoo bird that builds no nest of its own but deposits its young for others to raise!*

What I've done is my business only. Askar stretched his body languidly in the sunlight.

Mirandil's correct, Koril added. *We agreed after the beginning to watch only, not interfere.*

Oh, yes! The scientific method, Tagak put in acidly. *Only as we're about to learn once again, there exists no such thing as an impartial observer.*

Mirandil, you're jealous that I could do something you couldn't. Askar smiled at her, slowly turning so that she had ample opportunity to observe the ripple of finely toned muscle under his bronzed skin. *Ova that were present in your body from birth, my poor Mirandil, can't survive the long centuries of immortality, but spermatozoa are created fresh in me day by day, and are viable.*

You're very cruel! Mirandil's cheeks paled at the taunt.

Isn't it the truth, Lady?

Tagak touched Mirandil lightly on the arm, but said nothing.

Enough arguing, Koril told them both. *We must consider the destiny of these people.*

Why not choose? Tagak proposed. *Let the talismen decide what shall be done or not done, and who shall do it.*

A word out of the past floated up in Mirandil's mind, and she shook her head. *No! We pledged to let the—the experiment run its course.*

I for one grew bored with this experiment several generations ago! Askar interrupted. *I'll throw the talismen with you, Mirandil, or I'll act alone.*

This is too important to allow the talismen to decide! Mirandil protested.

Exactly because it's important is a reason to consider the effects of the quantum possibilities, Tagak explained impatiently. *Surely you haven't forgotten everything,*

Mirandil? We've known for a long time that we can't bind everything by human logic. A path must be open to the metalogical multidimensionality of the universe. The talismen do this for us.

Mirandil looked to Koril, youngest of them but first in wisdom for he spoke to them with the voice of the Father-Shaper himself.

Lord Koril, surely you have counsel to offer?

But this time Koril chose not to communicate his thoughts to the others.

She turned away. *Then you must take my place, Tagak, for I can't do it. And in truth this destiny will involve your people, too.*

Agreed.

So be it, Askar concurred.

Koril stood, and the towers and the white steps with which he had decorated the meeting place fell away. The red blossoms vanished, leaving a faint echo of their perfume behind. The bright plumed birds disappeared, and the sun was engulfed by dark clouds—though whether he had projected them, or they were heralds of one of this hemisphere's rare spring storms she could not be certain. Koril stood alone against darkness, arms outstretched. The four watchers waited, sitting on the grass, their robes arranged carefully about them. Then a crystal chalice appeared glowing in Koril's hand, carved with a single, four-petaled blossom, and in it were the talismen.

Stern-faced, Askar deferred to Tagak. She took the image of the chalice from Koril's hand, caressing it gently with her long fingers, then she overturned it in her lap, spilling the talismen on the air where they hung shimmering. Mirandil leaned forward to see. There were seven talismen: a cunning model of an atom in whose heart electrons spun in dizzying orbit about the golden nucleus; a double helix fashioned in silver; a dark-veined stone; a flowering branch; a bone from a small bird's wing; a drop of water caught in crystal; and a lock of human hair.

Mirandil drew in her breath, and Tagak bit her lip. Koril surveyed the pattern of the talismen's falling, then swept the holograms back into the chalice and handed it to Askar. Again they were spilled, and again spelled out their counsel on the air, and again Koril considered the pattern. Then he gave the chalice once more to Tagak.

On the third falling, Askar smiled. *My plan's favored!*

Doing, Koril agreed. *Three moves to the doer.*

Askar's taken one move already, Mirandil insisted.

That was earlier. It doesn't enter the count!

All things enter the count, Koril explained, *in ways even we can't foresee. Mirandil's right. Two moves remain to Askar.*

Askar glowered at Koril as if he were about to argue. Then he smiled. *But what they want me to do—what they themselves have summoned me to do—that doesn't enter the tally, surely? Even you, Koril, must see the logic of this reasoning. I shall do that as well!*

Before Koril could answer, Askar stepped on the shimmering path and was gone from the company.

Mirandil swept the talismen back into the chalice. The darkness grew light again and Koril sat once more on the scarlet-carpeted steps. Mirandil sat beside him and turned the chalice over. Now a haze like water ran out, forming a small pool in her lap. She touched the pool with the tips of the least fingers of the left and right hands, and a spark leaped from them into the haze. In its wake, the image of spires and steeples arose, and a steep cliff falling away to the sea.

Askar's move will do more harm than good. Mirandil's thought was somber. *I don't like this new precedent.*

Koril answered calmly, *Many things are possible.*

And Forever is a long sentence! Tagak stared at the hologram shimmering in Mirandil's lap. *The work is all we have. We four are the last. How much longer can we survive without going mad, knowing what price we've paid for this? I think I speak for us all when I say the Father-Shaper's gift has also been a curse.*

The path has been so long, Mirandil began. *And lonely . . .*

Tagak stood up. *Think about what's happened to us. We've come to believe the very myths we created and the despair is killing us. Askar's right!*

What do you mean, my Lady Sister? Mirandil asked uneasily. *We're the Watchers, the Venn—charged by the Father-Shaper with watching his creations—*

Our creations, Mirandil! Tagak interrupted. *You mustn't forget that!*

So—then a new path opens. Mirandil swept her hand across the surface of the little pool, disrupting the images. *Who can say where it leads?*

She stood too, leaving the holograms to slowly fade in her absence, and followed Tagak, who was striding long-legged toward a cluster of low buildings strewn across the foot of a hill. Tagak hesitated by a door partly overgrown by crimson vines and the webs and traps of predatory insects. Slowly, as if she too were having difficulty remembering this morning, she touched her fingers to a key pad and a door slid silently open.

*This—*Tagak waved a hand—*explains us. We mustn't forget this!*

Tagak hesitated on the threshold as stale, dry air sighed out. Sunlight pushed past her through the open door, dispelling the gloom of neglect; dust motes rose, shining like incomplete holograms in the shaft of golden light. Dials winked sleepily, glass caught the rays and reflected them back, banks of gauges and monitors, tanks, generators, taps and hoses, coiled wire—

Here's where it happened. Don't you remember? Here's where you created a race of metamorphs—an alteration governed by whimsy not utility—and set them on a path of pleasure-seeking. You did this, Mirandil! You shaped them.

Mirandil could no longer remember how all that equipment had worked once upon a time, and somehow she didn't believe Tagak that it was important to remember.

Tagak turned to Koril, her expression twisted by some kind of inner turmoil. *What have we done, Koril? What are we to do?*

We must wait, Koril counseled.

Silence flowed out from the abandoned laboratory. Having nothing else to do, they waited.

CHAPTER FOUR

In the days that followed the conversation in the Queen-Regent's chambers, Sivell learned there was no disguise that eluded the wizard Askar, no trick of shifting or maintaining shape that he didn't know and expect her to perform. Unlike the Lianis, however, who passed the hours pleasantly with shiftgames, Askar approached shifting rather grimly. He was short, like the Ganus, but dark like the Lianis. Yet where the Liani darkness suggested summer night, Askar's darkness was cold like a stone buried in the earth. Standing close to him, Sivell felt the hairs on her arms rising—such was the coiled power of the old wizard.

He had arrived the very next day as her grandmother had predicted, and knew already what was wanted of him. Though she was curious, Sivell never dared ask him how he'd known about such an intimate problem that few in Tia-ta-pel even suspected it. Her lessons began with the first rays of the sun and continued till late in the evening. By the time she'd finished firstmeal—a light array of honey cakes and fruit—the wizard was waiting for her. For the next eight or nine hours she was virtually his prisoner, expected to change any and all parts of her at any time into anything and everything he commanded. For the first time in her life, Sivell was expected to work at shifting and nobody came to her rescue, not even Parvey.

Askar was never pleased with her efforts.

"See the jil tree, blossoming there by the castle wall? Become like it!" he ordered. "No! No! One foot peeps forth yet. Does the princess jest? A jil tree that would

24

walk? Shifting is done by letting go. You are too full of thoughts."

She tried not to think, and found not-thinking harder than thinking. But after a time she found her thoughts settling, and then an image of herself as a jil tree floated up in their place. She held on to it for two heartbeats before thinking returned—and with it her everyday Sivell-shape.

"Again!" the old man shouted. "It was not well done."

Exhausted by the unaccustomed strain, she begged him to let her rest.

He wouldn't hear of it. "The least Liani child can hold such shapes for hours. Should a princess of the blood do less? Begin again!"

But it wasn't easy for Sivell and he scolded and grumbled at each bungled attempt. Finally she collapsed breathless and close to tears on the grass, and he let her recover.

Then the wizard pointed out a small gray-green waterfowl, floating in the rushes at the edge of the castle lawn. "See the corli, how it drifts effortlessly on the currents of the lake? See how difficult it is for the eye to follow the corli when it blends with reeds and ripples? Shifting is both a matter of shaping and reordering the contours of your body, and projecting the desired image to those who watch as well. You must manage both with skill."

"Perhaps, Sir," she began timidly, "perhaps if I could understand *how* this is to be done, I would be able to do it better."

"Does the baby have to understand breathing to breathe when it leaves the womb? Does the bird understand the aerodynamics of flying?"

"No, Sir. But I am no baby. And as for the bird, surely knowing how the task is to be done helps the musician who would sing like one."

Askar pursed his thin lips and stared at her for a moment. "You may be right. What these others do naturally may require a diagram for you! Very well. Pay attention."

He was silent for a long time after that, his eyes closed, drawn back into himself as if he were searching for something long unused. Sivell watched him curiously. She didn't doubt that he knew far more than the Lianis about shifting. The wizards were descended from the Venn. And legend told that the Venn had been present when the Great Shaper shaped its people. Surely the Venn had shared the Shaper's secrets—if not its power.

It was not like her people to try to puzzle out such matters. But Sivell already knew she was not like her people.

"The effect called shifting comes in equal portions from the body and the mind," Askar said after a while. "In order to know you *are*, you must first know you *are not*. The Ganus, who are far wiser in such things than the Lianis, have a saying: 'First was the void, now be the void, last will be the void.' Such is the wisdom of shifting. You are air. There are vast empty spaces within you. You are composed of nothing! And when you let go of thinking, and know that you are nothing, then you can be something. Then, and only then, you can use your altered DNA, rearrange the molecules—"

"Mol—?"

"Magic formulas!" he snapped. "Why do you foolishly insist on making the easy difficult?"

"If it's so easy, Sir," she replied, stung by his criticism, "why can't the Ganus shift as the Lianis do?"

He narrowed his eyes and glared at her. "You ask too many questions! Shifting is fluid but you are stubborn and wooden. First let the contours of the flesh glide, one to another. Let the angles melt and flow."

He stroked her cheeks with a gnarled finger. "Draw the flesh in."

She did as he said, using a sucking motion that did not involve the breath, feeling the cheeks sinking inward like one who was older than her grandmother. This was easy, something she might do if she were to act a part in an evening's entertainment.

Now his fingers traced down her neck to her shoulders, then down her arm. "Follow. I wish to see the path my fingers take."

She allowed his thumb to slide lightly down her arm, leaving a wake as if her skin had become liquid. He traced a curling line, and she followed it, her skin swelling and flowing, whitening along the path he marked. Any child could do this! It was a nursery game: *Close your eyes and say what I have written?* And the word would be there, raised above the skin, for all to see. What did he intend to gain by demonstrating what she already knew?

He turned her arm so the letters of her name were visible. "Can you tell how you do this?" he demanded.

"Of course! I—" She broke off in confusion. She'd never thought about how it was done. She only knew that whenever she wanted this result it happened. "Well, I suppose I think about how I want the skin to look—"

"Think?" he queried. "You give orders to your arm: *Ho, you six square centimeters there! Pull in a fraction! And you, circular area diameter three-point-five just two degrees south of my elbow, puff out!* Is this what you mean?"

Obviously not. But what did she mean? She let the altered contours of her arm and face return to normal while she thought about this.

"I *see* in my mind . . . without thinking . . ." she said slowly. "And then it happens."

"Yes." The old man nodded. "Visualization is a key. I could speak to you of chromosomes and ribosomes, of instructions coded in the genes to mold or flow, maintain or shift. I could explain the process whereby you make the change at the deepest level of the cells, bidding the whirling electrons alter their paths, create new images to project, like architects drawing blueprints for cathedrals and stables, ballrooms and storage sheds. But you wouldn't understand a word of it! Skin, bones, muscles— the Lianis find it hard enough to think about their bodies in even this elementary way. But it doesn't matter. The larva that becomes a beetle doesn't understand how he does it either."

Askar reached out suddenly and gripped her hand, making her jump. He rotated her wrist slowly until she felt the bones resist. She caught her breath.

"Let go!" he commanded.

Startled, she did as she was told, allowing the bones to unhinge and move across each other's path till the hand came full circle.

"Better," he said. "To start with, you must see that inside you are a river not a rock. And after that, you must convince me to see the change! Like the plant the Ganus call Sweet Deceiver whose scent attracts the bee but repels the beast that would eat it, you must hide yourself in olfactory deception. And lastly, you must alter the way your body reflects light to the eye of the beholder. Remember the corli, disguised against the reeds so that the sharp eye of the hunting jalu is deceived."

A prickle of something—knowledge that came without words—ran lightly over her skin. Her body *knew* what he was talking about, even if her mind doubted. It had always known, just as it had known to grow tall, narrow her waist and swell her breasts, when the time came to leave childhood and her childish form behind. Joy surged through her at the certainty of this power she contained.

"Now," he said. "Convince me you have become a rock like this one."

She glanced at the gray boulder streaked with mauve lichen and tried to blend with it.

"I am not convinced!" he said impatiently.

An image of rocks—*hard, cold, silent*—darkness welled inside.

"Come now!" he yelled. "You are shifting, but I see you still—a woman-shaped rock? You must change the way I see. The chromatophores—the cells you need to use—lie between the dermis and the epidermis—the *skin*! Idiot! Let your skin do it!"

Frustrated, she let go of thinking altogether.

"Better! But the sea is full of humble fish whose

photophores produce light to obliterate their outlines and confuse their predators. You have these cells, too. Use them!"

And then, with a swift change of mood, he wouldn't say any more. The lessons were over for the day.

When she could perform the basic patterns of shifting to his grudging satisfaction, he began to coach her in the more complex designs. Now she learned to assume the flowing shapes of water and flame. These were harder to do, but easier to maintain once done, for the forms slipped and glided together naturally, and the movement was less strain on her still feeble control.

Sometimes Parvey came to see the lessons, and then it went better. Together they moved through a shiftdance of shapes that were breathtaking in their beauty and power. Even old Askar seemed in a better mood then.

"Yes, yes," he said, as the brother and sister stood before him again on the lawn. "The royal blood will out, and the brother has skill enough for two. But at the Proving she must do all this and more alone."

"With your power, Askar," Parvey said, his arm resting lightly about Sivell's shoulders, "she can accomplish this."

"Wizard power is what it'll take, that's certain! But such power can only be contained by one who's born a wizard."

"Is this a riddle?" Parvey asked.

"No riddle," Askar said. "But a danger. The brother must stand ready to help the sister."

"Of course," Parvey said, frowning. "What's your meaning?"

"Walk with me a while by the river," Askar replied.

To Sivell's surprise, Askar led Parvey away, walking close beside him and speaking in low tones she couldn't overhear. She sat on the creamstone steps by the castle entrance, waiting for them to return, annoyed that they'd left her out of a discussion that obviously concerned her and her future. But the sun sank behind the jil trees and shadows stretched their dark lace across the lawn, and still they didn't return.

She rose to go inside when the shadows climbed to the top of the castle walls, and found the path blocked by a Ganu gardener, his pale arms full of rakes and hoes. She waited for him to step aside so she could go on, but he stood, glowering, holding his gardening tools like weapons. For a moment, both stood, staring at each other. Then Sivell broke the silence.

"Excuse me—I need—that is—"

The Ganu raised his arm slowly, a hoe gripped in his fist.

He was going to strike. His hatred crashed against her senses. Horrified, Sivell stepped back. A Ganu would never harm a Liani princess!

Or would he?

"Perhaps there be not room for tween in this jarden," he said.

"I don't understand . . ." This was madness.

The man glanced swiftly at something beyond her. Then he grinned, exposing broken teeth. "Excusing be what you need all right, Princess!"

He lowered the hoe and made a mock bow, then moved away around an angle of the wall.

Heart pounding wildly, she turned to see what it was that had rescued her from this frightening encounter. Parvey was coming back alone.

"Parvey!" She forgot everything and forgave everything in the pleasure she always felt on seeing him.

But he walked past her, his eyes fixed on some point only he could see, saying nothing.

One day, at the end of a particularly difficult session, when her shifting had at least partially satisfied him, Askar demonstrated for her what could be accomplished by a master. She sat on the lawn at his feet and watched him conjure shapes on the empty air. He spread his hands, palms upward, and a thin, gray mist arose, shot through with streaks of light. Then the light gathered itself and shapes formed in the air before her, images of silver mountains, and racing streams, and miniature castles with brightly colored pennants flying from their turrets. Though she knew they were formed from the mist—she could pass a hand right through them—they seemed as real as if they were carved out of rock. After them came the living shapes, processions of minstrels and dancers, proud courtiers carrying rainbow-hued banners.

Then all the shapes vanished, the castle garden was empty again, and the old man smiled down at her.

"So. That's how it's done."

His smile disturbed her more than his sharp words that she'd become used to. She knew that not even a queen had ever done what Askar the wizard could do, for the Liani power was to shift only one's own shape, not to create something new from nothingness.

"I don't call that shifting, Sir," she said, pulling all her courage together to disagree with him.

"And what do you call it?" He was still smiling, but his eyes flashed a warning at her.

She held her ground. "Magic."

Askar looked steadily at her for a moment longer; then he laughed soundlessly. "Isn't shifting itself magic to a Ganu who can't shift? But you're right. What I've shown you isn't shifting. It's a greater power called science."

"Shall I learn this *science* also?" She got up quickly from the grass and followed him as he strode on short legs toward the castle.

"No," the wizard said. "The power of science is dangerous and corrupts the user who isn't strong enough to control it."

"Then I'll do without it!"

"A wise decision," he agreed, nodding as he stopped to rest before going in.

Seeing that the old man was in a friendly mood, Sivell sat beside him on the broad steps, her arms clasped about her knees.

"Tell me, are you satisfied with your lessons, little Princess?"

She hesitated. "I have a question, Sir."

"Ask."

"If I learn my lessons well, can I become whatever I wish?"

Askar chuckled. "Not if you choose unwisely. The equations governing the translation of mass rule out your metamorphosis into a fledgling in its nest, you see! Nest and eggs and all would come crashing down! But things more your own size and weight are possible."

"Then of what use is this skill? Is shifting no more than a game?"

"A game?" he said softly as if he had forgotten her presence and were talking to himself. "A hypothesis, a dream. A strategy to pass the time. No *use* at all!"

"The wizards know so many things that are hidden from us," she said. "I think they must indeed be descendants of the Venn."

For a moment she thought she'd angered him. Then he shrugged at her. "The Lianis don't understand themselves or the Ganus, yet they would try to know the Venn!"

"Is that so wrong, Sir?"

"Whatever gifts your father gave you," Askar commented, "you don't think like a Liani!"

"But are wizards descended from the Venn?" she persisted. "The Venn who accompanied Kirili when she left the Great Shaper's garden?"

"That's one way to tell a truth. But enough!" he grumbled. "Tomorrow you must work even harder. You've much left to learn and you're a poor scholar."

The days until the Proving grew faster as the sun moved higher. Now the shapes Sivell held would have satisfied any of the Lianis. But were they good enough for a queen? One evening they returned to the castle after long hours of tedious practice. Tired as she was, Sivell still maintained the shiftshape she had assumed at Askar's command. He hadn't yet given her permission to resume her own shape, and she knew enough of the wizard's unpredictable temper not to ask. She slipped home behind him, light and shadow flickering over her as she moved against the stones of the castle's wall, splashed bright and dark by the setting sun.

They entered the castle courtyard where a small group of youths with whom she'd grown up stood talking idly before lastmeal, their rainbow-hued silks and velvets luminous in twilight beside the white columns that framed the door. There'd been a time before Askar had taken the matter of her instruction in hand when she could never have hoped to slip by her companions in shiftshape. She'd never outwitted them in the game of Seek, unless Parvey had chosen to help. A tremor of excitement ran through her.

The first ones knew nothing as Sivell passed them. But at the door a girl about Sivell's age leaned arrogantly against the wall, the center of her companions' attention. The golden birds that darted in and out of her shifted hair identified her as Kela. Askar had already entered the castle, passing through the open door; warmth and light streamed out, welcoming her home. Sivell focused her mind on following Askar, afraid that her shiftshape trembled a little about the edged in telltale fashion. Kela stood so close to the door that Sivell felt her breath as she slipped past.

Sivell was almost inside when her cousin started, and looked intently in her direction. Then she smiled, an inward, sharp folding of the narrow mouth that didn't reach to her eyes.

"A beautiful evening, Sivell," Kela said.

Control gone in a second, Sivell's own shape returned in the doorway.

Kela's laughter chimed. She turned to a companion. "See, Zil? Sivell plays Seek with us. But I found her!"

The young man's eyes were full of admiration. "Clever Kela!"

Sivell felt the hot flush of anger and embarrassment rise to her cheeks, but she stood unable to move as if her feet had taken root.

"Sivell." The Queen-Regent called from the now open door. "Come inside. Askar says you've done well today."

"Why do you look so glum, Sivell?" Kela asked. "An

ordinary person wouldn't have known you." She
laughed again.

"Hush!" the Queen-Regent warned. "Sivell does well
enough."

"My mother was only your second daughter, Madam,"
Kela retorted. "But I've needed no instruction!"

Kela raised her slim arms above her head. Her body
shimmered as if someone stirred the surface of a clear
pool, shattering it into a thousand points of refracted
brilliance. In her place now stood a living representation
of the figure on the Liani coat of arms.

"If Tuell's daughter can do this, how much more
should Falina's daughter be able to accomplish?"

"Leave the matter alone, now," the old woman
advised.

"The luck of Tia-ta-pel depends on it. A queen must
shift well to keep us safe." Kela resumed her own shape.
"We cannot allow the Ganus to rule in Ilia!"

It seemed unthinkable to answer her grandmother
back like that. But when Sivell looked, she saw the old
lady was smiling.

"I see it'll be no good thing for me in the end that I
allowed myself two daughters, and wasn't content with
one as all wiser queens are!" The Queen-Regent put her
arm around Kela's shoulder. "Join us at lastmeal, Granddaughter."

"It's not the number that matters, Madam," Kela said,
her eyes on Sivell. "It's the excellence."

The Queen-Regent laughed. "Sharp-tongued little
serpent! You'd best be quiet before you prove that
excellence lies in not creating a second to trouble the
first."

"The prize goes to whichever rival can outshine the
other. And secondborn is sometimes first."

"Enough!" The Queen-Regent's tone was sharp. "I'll
listen to no more nonsense."

She turned and flowed back into the castle, her
movements like an impatient mountain brook. Kela
glanced at Sivell, then flowed indoors after their grandmother in a perfect imitation of her angry current.

Sivell found her appetite for lastmeal gone. She left the castle and walked through the river meadow where the Lianis shiftdanced under the summer moons, crossing the bridge to the edge of the forest. Mist was rising about the gray trunks of the jil trees. A nightbird called out, and somewhere a flute answered it.

"Sool?" she called. "Please, I need you!"

The music stopped abruptly. A shadow detached itself from the trees and stepped forward, revealing a young man with light brown hair. On his leather tunic a pendant caught the moonlight, emitting a blue spark.

"I'm here."

She rushed headlong into his arms and hugged him.

"Ho, now!" he laughed. "Leave me some bones!"

She no longer remembered when she'd first learned that she couldn't shift as well as her playmates. But in all the years that had followed the discovery, there'd been only two she'd been close to: Parvey, who'd been her protector, and Sool, who'd understood and been her friend. The pendants had been her way of acknowledging this bond.

"I can't do it! I've tried, but I can never shift the way I should. And if the queen fails—"

"You won't fail, Sivell. You can shift well enough."

"You don't understand! It's Parvey's skill that takes me with it. Alone, I can't do it."

Sool held her by the shoulders and looked steadily at her. "Your brother's skill isn't unusual, Sivell. I've watched him dance. He's good—but that's all. The rest is in your mind."

She shook her head, brushing away his certainty. "The prophecy warns that the Ganus will take Tia-ta-pel away from us." She thought of the gardener who had menaced her right on her own doorstep. Was the prophecy beginning to come true already? "They hate us because they're different."

"I'm part Ganu," he said gently. "They're much like me."

"You're not a true Ganu. You don't speak in that outlandish way they do. Sometimes it seems to me they have a different word for everything just to make it hard for Lianis to understand them!"

In answer, he drew her down to lie in his arms on a bed of last year's jil leaves. The moons glowed overhead, both almost full, and the stars twinkled with a hard, cool light. Their stories filled Liani legends; they were the shining field where the Great Shaper had its garden. Slowly again she felt the warmth of sharing a shiftshape with someone who cared, the easy flow of body into body, passing through the boundaries of skin, the blending together of two to form one until all heartache ceased, all pain emptied into the night that swallowed it and shifted it to a shape more like love.

Then abruptly he kissed her and stood up.

"There's not much time for us any more." A faintly bitter line had appeared at his mouth. "You'll be a queen, and I'll be your faithful, half-Ganu friend, watching the stars and writing my songs!"

"Sool . . ." she began, distressed by his tone.

He relented. "But I'll be here if you need me."

"I'll *always* need you," she promised, taking the hand he offered and rising from the damp leaves. "Even when I'm queen."

CHAPTER FIVE

The morning of the Proving, Sivell was awake before daybreak. Pulling the corli coverlet about her shoulders, she went barefoot to the casement window and opened it.

From the tower she could see over the misty courtyard, far over the rooftops of Tia-ta-pel to the still-dark sea rolling in at the foot of Sorway Cliff. A few seabirds wheeled over the city, passing below her window, their thin cries echoing after them. Somewhere in the city a bell chimed the hour before sunup. She loved the bells of her city; she thought of them as Tia-ta-pel's voice. She breathed in the odor of sea salt and the gray-green things that grew secretly under the waves. Thin wreathes of mist curled about the turrets and spires of the city, giving the stones an air of unreality as if they, like their sleeping inhabitants, could change their shape and drift away.

She'd slept in this high chamber all her life, and many times she'd leaned out like this, gazing at the city. Strange, to think the Ganus had helped to build it. She'd never seen Goron, city of the Ganus, nor even a picture of it, but its very name was ugly. She couldn't let them "have their day," as the prophecy warned. She had to be good enough today to save her people, and their beautiful city of Tia-ta-pel.

While she leaned on the ledge, the sky changed color. The deep indigo of night was suffused with pink as the sun rose out of the sea. More bells began to ring in the city, heralding the dawn of Sivell's day of Proving. In the streets below her window, doors opened and people emerged; voices rose to her ear, snatches of laughter, a note or two of song, and to this the caged songbird in her window added its own song. The sounds drifted over the rooftops with the fast-vanishing mist. Sivell left the window and began to dress.

Her grandmother and brother were waiting for her when she came out of her chamber. The Queen-Regent wore a gown of gold velvet sprinkled with flamestones, the glorious gem the Ganus mined in the mountains to the north. Her hair that always carried her shiftemblem was a cresting ocean wave. She was magnificent. By contrast, Sivell wore a plain white gown, bare feet, and unbound hair. She might be the only one who attended the Proving today so simply dressed; she must demonstrate her right to the arrogance of such simplicity.

Parvey took her hands in his and kissed her lightly on the forehead. "You're beautiful."

He was dressed in a crimson tunic, and on his breast he wore his shiftemblem, a jalu crowned in gold. The wings were a trembling emerald display as the bird slowly folded and unfolded them.

The Queen-Regent finished her inspection. "Askar tells me you've been an apt pupil. You know how much depends on you today, for the Lianis and for Tia-ta-pel and our way of life."

"I'll do my best, Madam."

"Sivell," her brother said in a low voice as the old queen stopped to exchange words with an old man at the top of the spiral stairs.

Parvey stood by the narrow window through which a shaft of sunlight fell at his feet. How tall he was, she thought, wearing his height and darkness like an aura about his brows, needing no crown to proclaim his royal blood. He'd been her strong protector all her life, but today she must leave his protection behind.

"You've done well, little sister," Parvey said. "Very well. But the Proving is strenuous even for the most gifted. There may come a moment when you're tired, when you feel you can't go on."

Her attention was caught and held by his dark eyes.

"You must do this Proving alone, without Askar, for a queen can't be helped to become queen. But—if there's a moment when your strength fails, Sivell, in that moment there's no harm in thinking of lighter times when you and I played together at shifting. There's no blame, Sivell, if you can't go on alone, in thinking of me and drawing on my strength—as it exists already in your mind."

She leaned against the stair rail as he spoke, feeling strangely sleepy. She wondered what he meant, not understanding what he was telling her. Her eyelids drooped heavily, but his eyes commanded hers to stay open.

"If that moment comes, Sivell, you must think of me and of my emblem, and let it give you strength."

The crowned jalu on his breast seemed to grow, lines of sapphire and aquamarine running across the wings like summer lightning. Its eyes deepened into purple, then into black, and somehow the jalu became Parvey, until she couldn't distinguish the eyes of the bird from those of her brother which held her gaze steadily.

"Think of my emblem, Sivell."

"Come, Granddaughter!" the Queen-Regent said.

Sivell blinked, and found Parvey smiling at her.

"She'll do well, Madam," he said. "She'll make a fine queen!"

"Parvey . . ." Sivell began, and promptly forgot what she'd been about to say.

He took her arm and led her down the stairs. "Don't worry. Today you'll be invincible."

Descending the stairs, she felt the excitement rising up from the crowded great hall. Chandeliers suspended from the high roof sent light dancing over the walls and polished wood floors, finding an answering sparkle in the jewels on necks and fingers; the flash of intricate shiftemblems lit the dark corners.

She glanced around as she passed through the throng on Parvey's arm, glimpsing childhood companions who at this day's end would no longer claim to be her equals. She recognized aunts and cousins in the chattering crowd; some of them dangled infants of their own on their arms, reminding her mutely of the duty she bore toward her people once she'd been proven. Catching her eye boldly, a young man in scarlet and silver silks edged forward, his own eyes a matching silver. Others pressed behind him; she caught sight of eager faces, reaching hands. Soon they would be vying to please her, entertaining her with music and dancing, waiting for her to select one of them to be the first mate she took as queen.

The thought made her nervous, and she put it out of her mind.

Now she saw Kela, one hand resting on Zil's arm, watching her progress from the side of the room. Her cousin was dressed in a golden gown; she'd shifted her dark hair to a bright gold to match. Whether this was boldness or unspoken taunt, Sivell couldn't tell. But few Lianis ever chose shiftforms that resembled the Ganus, not even their gold-colored hair.

Parvey caught the direction of her gaze and whispered, "Kela dares a little too much. But after today she'll know who's queen in Tia-ta-pel."

They went through the doors to the little courtyard. Nobles from the Twelve Oldest Families followed them. Outside, a row of Ganus leaned against the wall, staring at her, blank-faced, straw-colored hair slanting across their brows. Like statues, they had all adopted the same stance; their hands were conspicuously thrust deep in their pockets. Ahead of Sivell, the Queen-Regent hesitated as if she were about to say something to them, then changed her mind and went on without speaking.

In the courtyard, a circular dais had been erected, paved with smooth tiles carved by Ganu artisans from the tusks of wild ferentis that roamed the northern forests. Two old figures waited for her, the Witnesses whose job it was to watch her shiftdance and pass judgment on its effectiveness. They were dressed identically in ceremonial robes in black with silver embroidery. Neither wore a shiftemblem, for the occasion was so solemn they honored it in their own shape. Parvey led her through the crowd to the dais, then stood back as she

ascended the steps alone. From now on, she must rely
on her own shiftskill and could ask for no one's help.

A hush came over the crowd as she stood there, one
white-robed figure between the two black-robed Witnesses. She looked out over her people, for whom shifting
was a game, something they did without thinking, and
saw beyond them the dull-clad figures of the Ganus
standing about in sullen clumps, come to marvel at what
they could never do. When she became queen, she
promised herself, she would remember those who were
not shaped in the likeness of the Great Shaper, and she
would be kind to them. She lifted her gaze beyond both
Lianis and Ganus, over the walls to Tia-ta-pel waiting in
the sunlight, and beyond it again to the whole country of
Ilia, a landscape of golden cornfields, lush river pastures,
and orchards heavy with fruit that she would inherit in
turn as every queen before her had inherited it, back to
Kirili, who was the first queen in Ilia.

The old woman Witness had finished chanting the
invocation, and now her partner struck a gong. Sivell
stepped forward, her hair lifting slightly in the breeze.
The white robe emphasized the darkness of her skin and
hair. Whatever her father might have been, her mother
and grandmother were royal Lianis, and that was
enough.

Unhurriedly she began. On Askar's advice, she did the
simple exercises first, letting her shape flow gently from
one form to another, patterns a child might play with, yet
performed with a simple grace. She'd learned well from
the wizard. She moved on to forms more complex and
varied, making a shiftdance of light and shadow. She
flowed easily, playing with her power as the Great
Shaper might have played in its garden, long ago at the
beginning of the world. Shifting was play, the poetry of
creation.

She felt her people's approval, but it wasn't yet
enough. The best of them could do what she'd done; a
queen must do more. She controlled her power now,
tightening it, narrowing down its focus.

Images welled up from deep within her, their echoes

rippling over her skin, exciting the organs Askar had named so oddly, "chromatophores" and "photophores." She felt herself become as bright as lightning; she caught the rays of the sun and refracted them, blinding her audience into seeing what she wanted them to see, as Askar had taught. *Convince me*, he'd ordered. She forgot the ugly words he'd used to explain what shifting was; she would remember only that she could do it. She *would* do it! She heard the indrawn breath of her people as she performed a particularly complex shift, the sigh of admiration as she transmuted the one shape into another even more subtle.

But was it enough?

Then she saw Kela and the outrageous hair.

Sivell tried again—molding the shapes of hand and thigh, cloaking herself in illusion—and read her failure in the smile that played around her cousin's lips. It would never be enough to outdo Kela!

She was tiring fast. If only she could find a little more strength. Not for her own sake—she didn't have to be queen!—but for Ilia's sake.

Strength—Parvey's strength. She called to mind what he'd said outside her chamber, and remembered how his shiftemblem had glowed as he spoke. The moment she thought of it, she knew it, as the mind knows its own body without looking. She felt herself at the center of something— What? Confused, she hesitated, her shape trembling on the verge of collapsing.

Parvey's voice seemed to speak to her, *Don't worry, little sister. Let go*.

Gratefully, she obeyed.

Others might make shiftshapes that were bigger, more daring, but the effects that now filled the courtyard were charged with a deeper meaning. The dance began with a pattern borrowed from the ruby eye marking on Parvey's jalu, and spread outward, layering color on color, design inside of design, the pattern of power creating shape. It was the shiftdance the Great Shaper itself might have performed in its garden at the beginning of time.

It seemed to last for hours, but it was over in a few

minutes. The circle drew in upon itself, falling inward till all that was left was the eye of a jalu.

When it was over, and Sivell stood once again in her natural shape on the ferenti tiles, the Witnesses took the gold crown of Ilia and placed it on her head.

The glorious, sonorous music of the bells shattered the air. Small children in bright garments sprinkled flowers in her path. At the head of the procession of nobles again, but this time not on Parvey's arm, she led her people back to the castle. Around her, young men from the Twelve Oldest Families formed a guard of honor, stepping proudly on the tips of their toes. Beyond them, she was aware of Kela's stormy face as Zil joined them. She would never have to worry about her cousin again.

The throng entered the great door of the castle, which had been flung wide in welcome to the new queen. Through the great hall they went, where those servants who were Liani bobbed and curtseyed, down the corridor to the throne room. Nobles and Liani servants alike crowded into this room, but the Ganu servants stayed outside.

Here, the glittering company gathered around a huge sea-green stone, with white flecks like foam running through it, and a shallow depression on top where she would sit. Some said it had been the Great Shaper's parting gift to Kirili, but others said it had been a tribute from a Ganu king who'd fallen in love with a Liani queen. Whatever its history, the throne stood polished but uncarved except for the rows of names around its base. Here were the throne names of all the queens of Ilia. Sivell saw the name of her great-grandmother, "Yna-Itilsdaughter," then her grandmother's name, "No-la-Ynasdaughter." After that came her mother's name, "Falina-Nolasdaughter," and then the space prepared to receive her throne name.

The stone carver took up his tools. A hush fell on the room, the silence broken only by the thud of the carver's hammer on the chisel and the squeak of stone chips breaking away. Soon all could see what he had carved: "Sivell-Falinasdaughter," the latest in a long line of

queens who had proved themselves in Tia-ta-pel. A sigh
ran through the assembly. It was done!

Later, in the evening when the dishes that had served
the ten courses of the Proving feast were empty, and the
Ganu servants had withdrawn, musicians began to play,
and clowns entertained the guests. Sivell hadn't eaten
much, being content to taste a forkful of each dish. Now
she sipped a pale spring wine and watched the clowns
who were performing a shiftdance, Ganu-style. Painted
white faces, hair shifted to the dullness of wet sand, two
clowns swelled their bodies and shrank their legs,
swaying ludicrously, while the third produced a shrill,
unmusical accompaniment on a wooden pipe. The
audience applauded the jest.

For a moment, Sivell felt uneasy. Something about
this clowns' dance was not as funny as her guests
supposed. But the Ganus *were* clumsy, and dull—
everybody knew that. They had not been made in the
Great Shaper's image. They were a natural subject for
comedy. Yet the quick answer didn't satisfy her this time.

A memory of a pipe's melancholy tune in a twilit
meadow filled her mind. Glancing round the table,
Sivell saw it lacked three faces. Askar, demonstrating
confidence in his teaching, hadn't stayed to see her
Proved. Kela had not attended the banquet; Sivell wasn't
too surprised at that. Where was Sool? Somehow, she'd
forgotten him in all the excitement of her triumph, but
she'd expected him to be there.

"Well, Granddaughter." The Queen-Regent's voice
broke into her thoughts. "Now that you're safely on your
throne, I intend to retire! Long ago while your mother
was still in Tia-ta-pel, I prepared my house on Donil's
Bay. Now, I think I'll go to it."

"What will I do if I need you?" Sivell asked. It was
unthinkable that this lady who had been queen and
mother both to her should leave her alone.

Her grandmother laughed. "A queen doesn't need
anybody, Sivell. Except perhaps a worthy mate when
she's ready to give Ilia a daughter. And I judge that will
present no difficulties! You'll find plenty of willing young

men to choose from! No, Granddaughter. I've been queen long enough. It's time for a new day in Ilia."

"Tia-ta-pel won't be the same without your presence, Madam," Sivell said courteously.

"I see change coming to Ilia, Granddaughter, great change. And not all of it good. It's just as well the city has a young queen to deal with it!"

Sivell felt cold rising in her veins. "What change do you mean? What do you see?"

"I don't think peace will hold with the Ganus for very much longer," the old woman replied. "Didn't you notice at the Proving? In other times, the Ganus brought gifts to the new queen—flamestones to adorn her neck and fingers, gold coins for her purse! And what did they bring today? Empty hands, sullen eyes, and insolent speech, that's what."

Unease prickled along her spine. Surely her grandmother was making too much of it, the way old people always complained things were not as they once were? Sivell turned to Parvey, who sat on her other side, for confirmation that there was no cause to worry. He'd been quiet all through the banquet, the colors of his shift-emblem muted and still.

"Parvey, what do you think of this?"

Instead of answering, her brother shrugged. He lifted his crystal wine goblet, studying it, as if the future were displayed within.

Sivell's unease grew. "You'll help me face whatever it is, surely?"

"I plan a short journey," he said, his eyes refusing to meet hers.

Surprised, she asked, "But you'll come back soon?"

"Of course. As soon as I'm needed."

"Where will you go?"

"To stay a while with my father," he said.

Stunned, she set her goblet down. "You know who your father is?"

"Yes," he said. "Did you never guess?"

She shook her head, bewildered. "How should I?"

"It's better so."

"Parvey!" His words upset her, dispelling the happiness of the day. "Parvey, don't go. I need you here."

"You'll be wiser not to ask me to stay! Remember, you're queen now, Sivell, and strong."

"I'll remember that I'm deeply in your debt," she said. "If it hadn't been for your . . . if it hadn't been for you . . ."

She found herself unable to complete what she'd been about to say, as if a door had shut on the words. "If you ever need me, Parvey," she said instead, "I shall count it an honor to repay."

Parvey pushed his chair back and rose from the table. "Promises are light to make. Let's hope that neither of us has occasion to break them."

The coldness of his tone froze the reply on her lips. Then he broke the mood and smiled at her.

"Don't worry. I won't stay away long."

He turned quickly and left the room.

She was still troubled by Parvey's words, when she was at last able to slip away from the castle. What did he mean?

She heard the sadness of the tune Sool was blowing on his silver pipe long before she saw him. The notes drifted across the river as she hurried over the bridge. She ran to him and hugged him. But he set her aside gently.

"You are queen now, Sivell," he said. "You won't be needing me anymore."

The weariness the day had produced in her crested at that and she answered him angrily. "Everybody's telling me what I won't need anymore! But I'm still the same. I need you."

"No, dear one. You are *not* the same as you were. Now you are queen. There's no place in the life of a queen of Ilia for a half-breed such as I. You owe it to Ilia to find a true mate."

"And what do I owe to me? Don't my wishes count?"

"Today, Sivell, our small friendship must be over."

"Nothing needs to change between us!"

"It's changing already," he said. "Go back to your people."

"There's a bond between you and me that can't be so easily broken. Even if I were never to see you again, I would never forget you."

He didn't answer. His silence hurt more than a rebuke would have done. She stared at him for a moment, so many things on the tip of her tongue to say to him. But she closed her mouth against them.

The new queen of Ilia walked back to her castle alone. But though tears pushed at her eyelids she was a queen now, and she was too proud to look back. Overhead the starry sky created a shiftemblem of its own.

CHAPTER SIX

Now the pleasantest summer Sivell had ever known began. There were picnics and boating expeditions on the calm sea, and moonlit festivals of shiftdancing which groups of solemn-faced Ganus paid their gold to watch. If there were fewer of them than before, at least they were respectful and caused no trouble. She was aware of their envy, these people Askar had told her knew so much. It clung to them the way the smell of long disuse clung to garments seldom worn.

Being queen was not so very different from being princess, for there were few royal duties in Tia-ta-pel. The difference was that now there was no lack of admiring companions for anything Sivell wished to do. In the past, the young people had seemed to prefer her cousin Kela's company, but now they had nothing else in mind but pleasing Sivell. She'd never had so many friends. Everywhere she went, about the city, out to the meadows, down to the seashore, she was followed by five or six young men and women, all gaily chattering and planning wonderful entertainments to fill Sivell's day.

She was glad the old wizard was no longer around to drive her. There was no word from Parvey either, but his absence didn't trouble her the way it once would have. For now if anybody thought her shifting was still less than absolutely perfect, nobody would dare say so of a proven queen. And indeed, Askar's teaching worked; she did well enough.

The first months of her reign, the months of high summer, passed in a merry round of feasting and dancing. The young men of Tia-ta-pel competed for

Sivell's favor, vying extravagantly with each other for the honor of being the new queen's shiftpartner or escorting her to some feast or celebration. Some brought her flowers, some wrote poems or composed music for her. All of them flattered her until she thought she was going to believe them when they said everyone had always known—even when she was a little child!—what a great queen Sivell was going to be. But luckily, she was able to laugh at just the right moment in these recitals of her praises, and the Lianis were never serious for very long in any case.

Of the many young men who thronged about her, there were two whom she'd known since childhood. They were brothers, both excellent choices for a new queen's first mate, graceful partners in the shiftdances, and both as dark as the eyes of night. The older brother was called Tey; the younger brother's name was Zil. On nights when Canela and Terel rode high in the night sky, Sivell danced in the meadow by the river with the brothers, or strolled through the streets of Tia-ta-pel. The old people whispered in the city that Sivell would choose a first mate from one of these two, though no one could guess which one it would be. Some thought it would be Tey, for he was quieter than his brother, and they pointed out that Sivell herself had been a quiet child. Those who thought she favored Zil were careful not to say this when Kela might hear it.

Only Sivell knew that she would choose neither.

For all their beauty, there was something lacking in these two young men. They seemed like highly polished mirrors in which she saw herself reflected. Whatever she did, they copied it. Whatever she said, they agreed. They were charming but utterly predictable and boring. There were moments when she shiftdanced with Tey and Zil, the meadow shimmering with shiftshapes in the moonlight, when her eyes turned to the other bank of the river. The forest rose up from the water's edge, and the nightbirds sang in the trees. She'd look hard at each shadow—but the meadow was always empty. Then she reminded herself that Sool had said a queen needed nobody. She returned with even more energy to the dance.

But one day she came upon Sool on the wide stone steps that led down from the streets of the city to the little harbor. Here, where the sea lapped gently and the corlis drifted by, she was about to enter a boat for a picnic on the water. Zil and his brother had already packed the little craft with baskets of fruit, honey cake, and berry wine, and waited for Sivell to join them. She came running down the steps that were striped by alternating bars of sun blaze and tree shade. Stepping on a patch of damp moss that low tide had uncovered, her foot slipped from under her. She would've gone straight into the water if an arm hadn't emerged from the shadows and fingers gripped her elbow, steadying her.

She looked at Sool, golden in the sunlight. He was wearing the jil pendant she'd given him once—so long ago, it might have been in a dream—and saw how it matched the color of his eyes. Beyond Sool, at the foot of the steps, the brothers waited, a contrast in darkness. There were so many things she wanted to say to Sool, but she hesitated, waiting for some sign from him, some token that there was still a bond between them. He looked at her for a long moment without speaking— perhaps because she was queen now, he thought she should speak first?

What could she tell him? Feasting and shiftdancing meant little to Sool. So she said nothing and silence grew between them like a wall. Then he let go of her elbow and she went on down the steps alone, giving her hand to the younger brother who helped her into the boat. But a dull pain had come to roost in her heart, and she took no pleasure in the picnic.

The memory of that meeting stayed in her mind. It wasn't like the Lianis to take anything seriously for very long, not even friendship as deep as she'd shared with Sool. It shouldn't have mattered to her that they could no longer be friends. But it did. It was another sign her grandmother might be right; Sivell's father might not be a Liani, for no Liani would grieve over a partner left behind. To a Liani, the partners changed and still the dance went on.

She tried to put Sool out of her mind, but she often came upon him in her dreams. Sometimes, she saw him standing on the other side of the river, watching as she fished with a net such as the Ganus used. Once he held the blue pendant out to her, but it turned into a black stone and she was afraid to touch it. And his melodies drifted in the spaces between her waking and sleeping.

Summer gave way to autumn when the leaves of the jil trees turned scarlet and purple, drifting down in the cool wind blowing in from the sea.

Time passed, and the dreams slowly faded. In the mornings now, when she looked out her window, frost sparked the rooftops of Tia-ta-pel, and the sea at the foot of Sorway Cliff rolled gray as glass. One night, a storm rattled the castle windows and loosened tiles on the roof, scattering the bells of the city like a chime of ice crystals over the darkness. Next morning, the great hall was cold when Sivell came down for firstmeal.

"Light the fire," she commanded, when the servant brought her meal.

"The chimney's blocked, Madam. The wind tore a great stone loose and it lies in the chimney," the servant said.

"Then have it removed."

"Who knows how to do this, Madam?"

She stared at him.

"The Lianis aren't stonemasons," the servant said.

She'd never wasted much thought on the builders of the castle, or Tia-ta-pel itself for that matter. Both had stood in place for so many generations they seemed to have grown there.

But she knew how unlikely it was for the Lianis to quarry stone, hew wood, or lay tile. The plan was Liani, but the labor was obviously Ganu.

"Then summon a Ganu stonemason and have him repair this chimney that forces the queen of Ilia to be cold!"

The servant hesitated before he answered. "They

don't seem so willing lately to work for us. There've
been . . . incidents."

"What incidents?"

The servant clutched the serving tray to his breast as
he spoke. "A woman complained of the price of fish a
Ganu fisherman sold her at the wharf. So the man
packed his catch back up and sailed away with it unsold."

"Was that all?"

"No, Madam. A man went to buy an aril and found the
instrument builders making a fire out of the heaped
instruments. All that music gone into smoke!"

"Well," she said reasonably, "what the Ganus make,
the Ganus have a right to destroy—though it does seem
madness! Is there more?"

The tray jerked round and round in his hands. "Two
children played at Seek in a meadow, near the road that
leads to Goron. A passing Ganu threw stones at them,
striking one in the foot."

"Why wasn't I told about this before?"

"What could you do, Madam? What could any of us do
against the Ganus?"

Sivell was to hear that fear expressed in different ways
many times in the next few days: "What could we do if
the Ganus made up their minds to attack us?"

"Surely they'd never do that?" she asked the old man
who'd been her grandmother's advisor.

"They never have," he replied. "But there's a growing
coldness between us, these days."

The next day, she visited the street of the Ganu
weavers to buy a new cloak for the winter. Though
several of the shops were closed, she managed to find
what she wanted. On her way home, Sivell met a distant
cousin of her mother who delighted in knowing all the
gossip in Tia-ta-pel. They strolled together, their new
cloaks bright against the gray stone.

"What do you hear about the Ganu king?" Sivell
asked, when the stories of friends and relatives, feasting
and dancing, had been exchanged.

"Mordun is known as a scholar-king," the woman said.
"And they say he's still no enemy of the Lianis. But the

word is that one of his sons has gone outlaw—fled to the hills—disobeying his father!" Her voice dropped dramatically. "They say a band of discontented Ganus followed him."

"Whatever for?" Sivell asked. "What could they be discontented about?"

"Does 'what for' matter?" The woman shrugged. "Each person you talk to guesses differently, in any case. But it can't mean well for us!"

"I must find the reason."

"I hope you're lucky!" her relative replied. She tossed a fold of her cloak over her shoulder and was gone like a bright green bird around the next corner.

In the castle there was a small room that housed the books and musical instruments collected by Sivell's ancestors. She went there after lastmeal, to which Zil had invited himself. He followed her, hoping they'd make some music together. But she was looking for a book.

She took them down one by one from their shelves and scanned their contents—books of poems, books of former queens, stories of the Great Shaper and of the wizards, pleasant books with which to while away an evening. She didn't know which book she was searching for, but she needed one that would explain the roots of this growing dislike of the Ganus for her people. She looked at small volumes edged in gold and fat ones bound with metal clasps, but none gave her the clue she was seeking. It seemed that no one had ever found the subject worth writing about before, or if they had then no queen had ever found it interesting enough to keep.

"Why would you want a dull book like that, Sivell?" Zil said, when she told him what she was looking for.

He threw himself into a low chair and picked up an aril, exquisitely carved in silver. The instrument chimed like a peal of bells when he stroked it.

"Because I want to understand," she replied, leafing through a book of pictures of both Tia-ta-pel and Goron.

Zil struck a flight of notes in quick succession. "What for?"

"I want to know what we've done that might cause the Ganus to be so angry. If I know that, maybe I can do something about it."

"Why should you do anything?"

"They built Tia-ta-pel for us, did you know that?"

"What does it matter?"

His lack of interest irritated her, although she realized it was her own behavior that was unusual.

"Have you never wondered what their own city must be like?" She stared at the pictures, but the ones of the Ganu capital were lacking in detail, as if the Liani painter hadn't been able to bring herself to actually go there. "They're such clever builders, and their mountains are full of gold, so the stories say. I wonder what they might build for themselves."

Zil shrugged and sent a melody flying from the aril. "Put away the dull books. I'll play and you can shift-dance."

Her patience with him ended. "No! I must find the answer."

"How tiresome that would be, Sivell!" he said.

Sivell gazed at him. It wasn't his fault that he couldn't understand her sudden interest in history. Until a few days ago, she too had found the subject dull. Liani children were taught the stories of Kirili's shaping and how she left the Great Shaper's Garden, and of Donil the Venn who went with her into Ilia. But more than that was a bore to think about.

Zil unfolded his slender body from the low chair and stretched his arms high above his head, deliberately drawing her attention to the dark gracefulness of his movements. She knew he was expecting her to be impressed, to react to his beauty. When she turned her back on him, he left, sulky as a child. She turned her attention back to the books, turning the pages in hopes of answers to questions she didn't know how to ask.

For the next week or two, everything seemed as it always had been in Tia-ta-pel. There were fewer Ganu shops open than usual, but there were enough that the Lianis felt little hardship. And if some Ganu servants did not show up for work, at least they had done the harder, outside work anyway, and there was less of that to do with the approach of winter. After a while, people learned to ignore the heaped leaves and untrimmed flowerbeds; they turned their minds to pleasanter things as they stepped over rubbish that began to blow unchecked through the streets.

Sivell forgot about the Ganu problem and busied herself with her friends, planning feasts and celebrations for the coming winter.

One evening after lastmeal, feeling restless and wanting to get away from the young men who followed her everywhere, Sivell left the castle by a back door to walk alone along the path at the top of Sorway Cliff. The nights were cold already, and the sea glittered icily under Canela's solitary light. The grass underfoot was stiff with frost, so that it splintered noisily as she walked over it. In summer there'd been fishing boats on the water, summoning the fish into Ganu nets by means of bell-shaped lamps, their light jumping and sparking over the waves. But now it was deserted as far as she could see. She gazed over the water, thinking of the Ganu folk, pale as the moon of winter, until the cold rose up from her feet, chilling her bones, reminding her of the warm haven of the castle. It would be safe to go back now, she thought, smiling at the thought that too many friends should be more of a problem than too few.

As she returned along the winding footpath, she saw lights blazing in every room of the castle except her bedchamber in the east tower. She quickened her pace. Coming through the small inner courtyard, she heard a babble of anxious voices. She hurried into the great hall and found a group of servants and nobles all talking at once, nobody listening to the others.

"What is this?" she demanded. "What's happened?"

They were silent for a moment, staring at her. Then they all began again.

"I can't hear you all at once! Zil, you speak for everyone."

"It seems your worries were well-founded," he said.

"An hour ago a messenger brought a report of a Liani being attacked by a Ganu."

"*Attacked?*" The word shocked her. She stared at him.

"An artist—unable to obtain supplies, because there've been so few Ganu suppliers in the city in the past few weeks," Zil explained, his arms making unhappy gestures on the cold air. "Finally, he decided to go to Goron to get them for himself. On the road, he was overtaken by a band of Ganus who knocked him to the ground and beat him. He was found an hour later by children picking berries along the way."

Hearing the tale retold, the little gathering began to chatter again, and a few shifted nervously, outlandish and incomplete shiftshapes telling of their anxiety.

Sivell took a deep breath, holding in her own fear which threatened to become as great as theirs. She was a queen and queens didn't give way. "Do we know which of the Ganus are to blame for this?"

"The artist said they spoke the name of Bor several times."

"Bor? Does this name mean anything to anyone?"

The old man who'd been her grandmother's advisor answered. "Bor's the son of King Mordun—the oldest son, who's gone outlaw."

"But why? There's never been a quarrel between our royal houses. What's changed this?"

"Strange things have happened in Ilia these last few years," the old man said. "When I was a child it was said the star spirits walked on Sorway Cliff. Now some say they've been seen again, and this is a bad thing for the Lianis!"

"Since when have the Lianis believed in star spirits?" Sivell asked scornfully. "Enough of this tiresome talk! Zil, summon the full council of the Twelve Oldest Families. We'll discuss what has to be done about this threat to our peace."

Sivell left them quickly before they noticed she was as disturbed as they by the news. She turned the corner of the corridor, deep in thought, intending to go to the room that had been her grandmother's study to await the gathering of the council. A flash of movement caught her eye at the last minute, and she was almost knocked to the ground by the galloping hooves of a small hati. Its horns grazed narrowly by her arm.

"Let me pass!" the hati cried as she put out her hand to detain it. "I have news for the queen!"

She gazed at the child winking excitedly in and out of its imperfect shiftshape. The shiftfield he projected flickered wildly; she felt its effects on her perception like a feather's tickle on her bare arms. A boy's eager face came and went between the horns.

"So, give the news to me."

The human face frowned at her. "You're not the queen! You wear no royal shiftemblem!" Hati hooves struck the ground impatiently.

Sivell thought about that. It was true enough. Now that she felt she'd earned the right to wear a shiftemblem by her Proving, she'd never been able to decide what it should be. But this was the first of her subjects to object. She thought for a moment, remembering Askar's lessons.

"How about this?" She smoothed her hands over her skirt, filling the hems with singing birds in jewel colors. "Will this do?"

"No," the hati replied. "Even my *sister* can make an emblem like that!"

Sivell tried again. This time tongues of flame licked over her gown, making the shadows jump and dance on the walls. "What do you think of this?"

The hati shook its horns stubbornly. "A real queen wouldn't wear such a big emblem. She wouldn't need to."

"You're right," Sivell agreed. The flames vanished. "Watch this."

She loosened her hair that had been caught up in a knot at her neck, allowing it to tumble freely over her shoulders. Then she sprinkled it with pinpoints of light, like distant stars. There was something of her grandmother's oceanic hair in it, but understated and more delicate. "How will this do for a queen?"

The hati nodded.

"Do you recognize your queen now?"

"Yes, Madam," the hati said meekly. The horns and hooves disappeared; the hati stood upright, lost its thick pelt, and revealed itself as a small boy.

"Now give me your message."

"There's a man—I met him outside Tia-ta-pel—who wanted to be taken to the castle. So I brought him."

"You trouble the queen with this?" Sivell frowned.

But the child didn't give ground. "Yes! The man's not a Liani, though dark of skin and hair—"

She caught her breath. *Sool . . . ?*

"But he isn't Ganu either," the boy went on.

Sivell sighed, relief and disappointment mingled.

"I don't know what he is. I thought the queen might know."

She gazed at his earnest expression. "Where is this wonderful man, who's neither Ganu nor Liani?"

"I made him wait outside in the inner courtyard," he replied proudly. "I didn't think I should bring him in just yet!"

"You've done well. I'll speak with him later. You may tell him this."

The child bobbed his head, resumed his shiftshape, and galloped lightly away. Sivell went past her grandmother's study to the throne room and mounted the steps to the green stone. She waited, facing the empty chamber, for the gathering of the council.

CHAPTER SEVEN

Sivell had often attended council meetings when her grandmother was Queen-Regent, but this time she'd be presiding over the first meeting held since she'd become queen herself. The council made policy for the people on the rare occasion that some kind of decision had to be made. The Lianis much preferred feasting and dancing to affairs of state, so meetings were infrequent and informal. All the members of the Twelve Oldest Families who wished to do so came and gave their opinion. It was an informal system that worked well in a city where little happened that disturbed the inhabitants' well-being for very long.

She didn't have long to wait. The council members made their way in twos and threes into the room, talking earnestly together. She watched her cousin Kela enter, deep in conversation with Zil. Catching Sivell's eye, Zil raised his fingertips to his lips and blew her a kiss. Kela arranged her green gown to its best advantage on the bench and motioned Zil to a place by her side. She hadn't worn the shocking yellow hair again since the Proving, nor had she spoken anything but pleasantries to Sivell. Tonight she wore her shiftemblem, the golden birds singing in her dark hair. Was that a good sign, Sivell wondered, or would her cousin use her sharp tongue instead to embarrass her?

Several older nobles entered together, the old advisor amongst them, and made their way to the front tier of benches. Observing their shiftemblems, Sivell realized how the fashion in shift signatures had changed. The older nobles wore imposing creations. Females used glittering rainbows as coronets, or turned their eyes to kaleidoscopes of jewels. Males chose for their symbols tremendous flashes of lightning and dazzling sunbursts out of which their worried faces peered intermittently. But the younger members of the court, such as Zil and Kela, chose subtler statements of flowers and birds, confining them to their hands and hair, or else they wore discreet, abstract designs of light.

Somehow, she found herself thinking now, what Askar had taught her about shifting—although she understood it incompletely—drained the act of importance. It was just something the Lianis did. A more serious question she'd have to answer someday to her own satisfaction was *why*.

It must be the stress of the occasion that caused such strange ideas to enter her head, she thought. She made an effort to dismiss them.

Young and old, the Lianis waited for her to speak.

Sivell's mouth went dry. Before, when she'd sat in this room as her grandmother presided, her mind had been free to wander at will. The business Grandmother conducted hadn't seemed very important to little Sivell. But now she was the queen in Tia-ta-pel, and it was her turn to preside. Not even her grandmother, queen twice as long as most, had faced a problem like this. Somehow, she'd have to find the right words.

"My ladies, my lords, " she said, opening the meeting.

They all stood and raised both arms in answer to her, like the winged figure on the royal crest. She gave them a second to settle down in their seats again.

"Who wishes to bring this matter before the council?"

It wasn't etiquette for a queen to broach the matter herself, for that would suggest its gravity was something that should compel the Lianis' attention away from their normal concerns of pleasure seeking and the creation of beauty. Her grandmother's advisor rose, his shift emblem a great mountain tree through whose branches the old man's face appeared.

"We won't waste words. Bor, son of King Mordun, has gone outlaw. He rejects his father's rule."

"Yes! But why?" Sivell broke in.

"Madam, it seems that some of the Ganus have no liking for us."

"Perhaps they're jealous?" Kela said. "After all, not being able to shift must be painful to them." She glanced sideways at Sivell as she said this.

Sivell held back her angry reply. "Go on, my Lord."

"With him is a company of Ganus, of what size we don't know." The old man sighed. "They've already committed hostile acts against several Liani individuals. We don't know if they plan to attack Tia-ta-pel, but we fear it. We must decide if anything can be done about this threat."

"Does anyone have anything to suggest?" Sivell asked.

Several old nobles rose at once and began to make speeches full of legends and anecdotes from history. There was much arguing between them on the order and importance of the various points in these accounts.

Sivell listened to them in disbelief. Surely they didn't think this would help? But the longer she listened the more they retreated into fantasy.

"Silence!" she ordered at last, cutting off an old woman rambling on about the exact order of appearance of several star spirits, and the meaning to be read in this. "If someone knows from her own experience something that will help unlock this puzzle, let her speak. Otherwise, be silent."

The noise died down; everyone waited to see who would speak up.

Kela rose slowly from her seat. "There is, of course, the old prophecy."

All eyes, natural and shifted, turned to her.

Kela began to quote the old rhyme in a singsong voice:

When Ilia's queen shall run away
The somber ones shall have their day.

Absolute silence fell on the chamber. The only sound Sivell heard was the pounding of her own heart.

Kela brushed her gown carelessly with her fingertips as if removing some invisible dust she'd picked up from

Sivell's castle. "It's well-known that Sivell's mother, Falina, ran away."

There was an explosion of voices at that. Every member of the council wanted to speak at once, some rising formally and others not. Sivell herself sat thinking long-forgotten thoughts. There'd been no shame in her mother's leaving. Liani mothers often grew tired of raising their offspring and left them to others, with no harm to the child nor blame to the mother. Even a queen might tire of her castle and leave. Her grandmother had told her many times: a queen's only duty was to provide a daughter. Falina had done that. Was there a deeper reason for Falina's disappearance?

The uproar subsided a little; most of the nobles seated themselves again. Kela remained on her feet.

"Perhaps I do an injustice to Falina," she said. "Perhaps the fault doesn't lie with the mother. As I remember, the prophecy goes on to say, 'If she not shift to save her folk, / Both dark and light shall feel the yoke.'"

This time there was no outcry. Instead, the council members stared at Kela, puzzled.

The old advisor spoke. "The prophecy refers to a queen who can't shift. Sivell passed her Proving. It can't refer to her."

"Perhaps she had help?" Kela suggested sweetly.

A hot, churning tightness seized Sivell's stomach and pressed against her ribs. "If you have proof of that claim, Cousin, we'll hear it now. If not, then it's treason you speak against your queen."

A buzz of horror filled the chamber at Sivell's angry words. Treason wasn't a word heard very often anywhere in Tia-ta-pel, and especially not here in the castle. A very old nobleman lost control and shifted completely in a great chaos of shapes that assaulted the senses of the gathering in a most uncivil fashion, then floundered down from his bench to the floor and flowed away under the door. But this breach of manners was hardly noticed, the quarrel had made so great a stir.

Zil spoke soothingly. "Both Sivell and Kela are disturbed by the Ganu threat. Let's be careful not to do the Ganus's work for them. Let's not fight each other."

Sivell hardly heard the rest of the council's discussion, but it didn't matter greatly for little was accomplished. The council members couldn't bring themselves to agree on a course of action. The debate swung back and forth between those who didn't recognize the seriousness of the Ganu threat, and those who felt shifting would take care of it. Not once did she hear a practical suggestion. When Sivell left the chamber she wasn't missed.

At the end of the corridor a small door opened onto a narrow balcony facing north. The cool night air soothed her, allowing her to recover from the shock of Kela's accusation. What could she have meant? The only help Sivell had received had been the wizard Askar's instruction, and while being taught to shift was unusual, it wasn't forbidden. She closed her eyes in frustration. The immediate problem was more serious: her people's inability to deal with the threat that had arisen.

She gripped the balcony rail and stared out into darkness. Few ever stood here, even in summer, for the view opened over the vegetable fields where Ganus toiled in mild weather and in harsh. Beyond the fields, a dark silhouette spoke of the low hills that lay between Tia-ta-pel and Goron. In these hills, Bor the outlaw was hidden in one of the many caves with which they were riddled. Did he look out at Tia-ta-pel, she wondered, thinking how he would capture her city? What had driven him to this? So many unanswered questions.

She turned away from the bleak view and found Sool standing behind her.

"You need me now," he said.

By the right of his mother's heritage, Sool should have sat in council with the Twelve Oldest Families, for his mother's family was as noble as any. But although nothing had ever been said to exclude her or her son, it was understood that the taint of Ganu blood wasn't welcome in the highest councils of the Lianis, and so they never came. Now his eyes held hers without wavering. Memories of evenings with him along the river or in the forest overcame her, so that for a moment she was aware of the thoughts of a much younger Sivell inside her, a Sivell who'd found those alien-blue eyes a source of comfort. With a rush of longing to hold him, she realized how much she'd missed him since she'd passed the Proving, how much she'd yearned for the comfort of his presence. Her arms rose to embrace him.

Then she let them drop to her sides.

She was older and stronger now. And he himself had said she needed nobody.

"I think I've heard enough advice tonight."

"I've no advice to give you. I'm making you an offer. Will you hear it?"

A cold draft blew between them, scouring the shared memories of summers under the jil leaves. That was all a long time ago, when she was a child. Now she was a queen.

At the same time she knew that to say no immediately would send him away.

"What is it?"

He caught the door to prevent it banging in the draft. In the starlight, his bare arm seemed made of silver. Her eyes were drawn to it against her will.

"Mordun's still king. Perhaps he doesn't know what his son's doing. That seems most likely. The Ganus are hunters but not warriors! Something's gone wrong. Let me go to Mordun in your name. With his help you can prevent this war that threatens."

"By all accounts it's too perilous a journey right now," she said. She found the fingers of her right hand coming close to his moon-silvered left arm.

"The Ganus will not see Liani when they look at me. They'll see Ganu. I'll be safe enough."

"Can you be sure?" He was wearing the jil pendant she'd given him—in some other lifetime, it seemed. Pain began to gather in a knot in her throat.

He took the fingers that were straying beyond her control and raised them to his lips. "I'll take care, Sivell."

"Oh, Sool!" The cry was out before she could suppress it.

"It's our only chance," he said, drawing her into the circle of his arms.

She laid her cheek in most unqueenly fashion on his rough jacket, smelling the tang of sea spray and meadow herbs that clung to it. He held her tightly, soothing her.

"I've missed you so much," she murmured. "I don't want to lose you again!"

"It's not a very long journey. I'll be back before Canela's next quarter."

"We could be friends, Sool, as we were before. Things don't have to be different between us."

He lifted a lock of dark hair in which the stars of her shiftemblem glittered. He smiled, a suggestion of irony in his expression, but he said nothing. She realized he'd never seen her wear a shiftemblem before.

"Let me go to Goron, Sivell. I'm probably the only person in Tia-ta-pel who could get through."

"How can I let you go? You're my dearest friend."

"And you are also my queen," he pointed out. "Give me permission."

She felt as if winter had entered her body and flowed through her veins like an ice-clogged river; she shivered. "I do so very reluctantly."

"Come away from the door." He drew her inside. "See, it's starting to snow."

Light flakes drifted past the balcony; some settled on the stone rail, shining with a pale, ghostly luminescence. It was the first snowfall of the year and might stop soon or go on for hours, filling the streets with white silence, making the path across the hills more dangerous.

"I must leave before the weather turns too bad for traveling."

She clung to him and he kissed her brow.

"I have this very bad feeling—"

He stopped her mouth with his before she could say more. Then he gently disengaged her arms and left.

She watched his back retreating from her as if it were the last thing of him she'd ever see. Leaving the snow to drift in the open door, she walked away from the balcony. Long ago, when she'd been a child, she'd come across a corli dead on the castle lawn and had felt this same sense of loss. Grown Lianis coupled and parted many times with no sense of bond made or bond broken. Sool's leaving shouldn't have bothered her. She couldn't explain where this heavy knot of pain had come from, nor what it was.

The throne room was buzzing like a swarm of frightened insects when she returned, but she saw they'd progressed no further in their planning. One face was missing: Kela had left the room. Sivell gave the council members the news of Sool's mission and saw their immediate relief.

"That settles the matter!" the old advisor smiled, summing up what all of them seemed to be thinking: *As long as somebody's doing something, we can put it out of our minds!* "We must wait and see the outcome of this before we make any more plans."

The Twelve Oldest Families of Tia-ta-pel filed out of the throne room, their chatter turning again to plans for feasts and dancing.

She sat on one of the benches facing the green throne, staring up at the high windows. The snow came down faster now, fat flakes already settling into a blanket of white on the window ledge. It would be a hard, cold journey for Sool. But he wasn't soft like these nobles, and he knew the hill country better than most Lianis. She let her mind follow him a little way, imagining the way the snow would feel crisp underfoot, the way breath would smoke and curl behind them as they spoke.

"You offer poor hospitality to a traveler, making him stand outside in the snow!"

She whirled to face a stranger in the doorway, brushing snow off his shoulders. His hair was touched with gray, though his carriage was still upright and lithe as a young man's. When his eyes met hers she saw that they were tilted at the corners. He was no Liani. Tall, dark-hued, lean as any of them, yet he was distinctly different. The hati had been right.

"Who are you? What's your business in Tia-ta-pel?"

"My family name's Chetek. The other's not important here," he said. "And for now my business is to seek shelter from the weather!"

He had an odd way of speaking, she thought. It lacked the music of the Liani manner, but wasn't as harsh as when a Ganu spoke. The name was odd too, one she'd never heard before.

"You asked to speak to the queen?"

He looked at her for a moment before replying. "I've told you who I am, but you haven't told me to whom I'm speaking."

"I'm Sivell, queen of the Lianis."

"Pardon me, Majesty!" He bowed his head, but she thought his eyes were laughing. "I meant no offense. But that animal—or whatever it was that met me at the gate—made me wait outside. My blood is about to freeze solid in my veins! Perhaps when I was a young man I could've taken it, but now—" He spread his hands in a gesture of surrender. "You must forgive a poor traveler for forgetting his manners in such a condition."

"We've forgotten our manners, too," Sivell said. "We don't always treat travelers so harshly. Come in and be welcome."

"Thanks. I'm not a lover of cold weather."

"Are you hungry, Chetek?"

"Now that you remind me of it," he said.

His smile revealed even white teeth in a nut-brown face. The coloring was not Ganu, either. What was he then, another half-breed like Sool? But she'd never known mixed blood to affect the tongue. She led him to the small room that had been Grandmother's study. There, she summoned servants to bring food and tend the fire.

"Now, Chetek," she said as he settled himself in a chair in front of a low table on which the servant set his food. "Tell me what brings you to Tia-ta-pel."

Before he answered, he took a spoonful of the steaming broth and broke off a hunk of bread. To fill the silence between her question and his answer, he nodded at her while he chewed. Then he swallowed and peered into the bowl.

"That's very good. What is it?"

She realized he was more used to asking the questions than to answering them. Though not at ease with her as one of her own people would've been, he was neither servile nor hostile. This was an interesting thought! But she too could avoid giving answers.

"A traveler like yourself must have tasted better, surely?"

She waited while he finished the soup, turning her wine goblet by the stem, watching the colors swirl ruby and amber. At last he made an end to the soup and took the last piece of bread to wipe the bowl clean.

"I'm on my way north, through the Ganu lands," he said. "But I hoped to find a woman I once knew who lived in Tia-ta-pel."

"Why do you come to the queen for this?"

"I thought she might've been a member of the queen's family," he replied simply. "Not from what she said—she didn't even tell me her name! But from something in her bearing."

"If you don't know her name, she'll be hard to find."

"It was a long time ago. Even if I found her, she probably wouldn't remember me."

"Tell me of her shiftemblem."

His eyes were on Sivell's hair. "I don't think she was wearing one."

"That makes a search difficult. As the old saying goes, we must find the right pebble on the pebbly beach!"

"It was just a passing whim," he said. "But she was kind to me when I much needed kindness."

A young servant tapped on the door then entered and stood staring openmouthed at the stranger.

"This is a bad time for me to bother you," Chetek said, rising. "I'll be on my way."

"It would need to be far worse before we forgot our duty to the stranger at our door. You're welcome to stay tonight. The girl will take you to a room. In the morning, I'll see that you're provided with food for the rest of your journey."

Chetek stood up and made as if to follow the servant. Then he hesitated. "I haven't been totally honest with you . . ."

She dismissed his words. "I don't wish to know who you are or where you're from. That's your concern."

She had enough problems of her own, after all.

He bowed and followed the servant out of the room.

CHAPTER EIGHT

Tagak floated on a cloudsoft bed in a sheltered bay on her favorite island. Her long red hair streamed out over water that was as clear as glass. The air was fresh with the scents of seafern and fish and the clean smell of the water itself. She held her closed hand in front of her, then opened her fingers and gazed at the mirror in her palm, inlaid with blue shells. She looked into her own eyes a moment, then blinked. Abruptly her image was replaced with a tiny drama about the land called Ilia. In the mirror, hours went by, then days. Tagak watched although she knew all the events unfolding in this drama for they had already happened. Silver fish rose to the surface of the water and nibbled at the thick red tresses. She ignored them. The warm sunlight of mid-morning sparkled on the sea.

Then Tagak touched one of the blue shells, and the image shifted from what had been to the channel of quantum probabilities of what might be, a representation of one of the possible future paths the inhabitants of Ilia might follow. Tagak considered these images carefully. She saw sunrise and sunset, plants growing up and snow falling down, the living and dying of children not yet born in Ilia, and the births of those children's children.

When she was dissatisfied with what she saw, Tagak blinked her eyes and it was all changed. Now the sunsets and the snow and the lives of the children made new patterns. Twice more Tagak blinked, and then she flicked her fingers and all the images disappeared. She set the mirror aside.

Tagak rose from her floating couch and found Koril looking at her. He was sitting on the back of a servo'd sea dragon with iridescent scales. The creature opened and folded its wings like a parasol in a translucent shimmer of green and gold glass; an obvious intelligence regarded her calmly from the glowing eyes. Seeing the dragon, Tagak was filled with a sudden regret; it had been one of Koril's most successful creations, in that extended childhood immortality had bestowed on him. It reminded her how long it had been since any of them had used their skills in this way with the native life on Ilia. There had been such an exhilarating sense of play to their lives at first. Like tempest-tossed wizards, they had created their own Ariels and Calibans to do their bidding on this island world.

There had been more of them then too, and a sense of infinite potential in their hands. But unlike Prospero, these wizard-princes would never be rescued, never return home. Now those few that were left had learned first boredom, then despair.

I don't like Askar's doing, she told Koril.

Koril smiled. *It's going where Askar hadn't planned.*

Tagak gathered up her damp hair and braided it, then coiled the braids on her head where they gleamed in the sunlight. She stuck in a long silver pin decorated with gaudy flamestones to hold them in place. Of all the Venn, Koril was her favorite. She'd watched over his growing up, but now he was wiser than they were, and somehow untouched by this creeping despair that choked the life out of the others.

Mirandil's folk are like dependent children still. But they'll grow.

A Mill colony of enlightened egoists! Tagak replied sharply.

An experiment, he reminded her, *about whose parameters we tried not to make value judgments.*

Still, she demurred. *Askar's path is dangerous.*

For Askar, too.

She glanced at Koril in surprise, but he didn't elaborate.

I see the danger in becoming too fond of any one of them, she explained. *No sooner do we notice their brief lives than they're over! But we endure.*

That's a real difficulty, he agreed. He reached down and gave her his hand, and she mounted the sea dragon behind him. He touched a control behind one tufted ear. They flew soundlessly through the bright air.

Tagak sighed. *I'm afraid of the consequences of starting to believe our own mythology.*

He glanced back at her face.

"Kory Venn," she said aloud, challenging.

"Elena Tagak," he replied easily, his expression not changing.

"Yes. We'd do well to remember that, once every century or so!" But she was smiling now.

"Perhaps you're worrying needlessly. Shaper, Watcher, Venn, wizard, scientist—these're only ways to express a truth, Elena."

"You left out God!" she said sarcastically. "The word we choose makes a difference to our thinking. Our creations may confuse the terms. We dare not."

They were flying over the lesser islands of the archipelago, scattered like bright mosaics of jade and topaz on the burnished glass of the sea. The air flowing past them was cool and salt-laden.

"Do you think we're confused?" he asked.

"The danger is that in successfully creating new theologies, we run the risk of believing our own lies."

"Because we're immortal, we believe we must be gods?" he said. "You may be right. But you're regarding the situation as static and external. Everything's connected with everything else; everything changes. You know better than to discount flux and connection, the twin laws of the quantum universe!"

"You see something that we don't, Kory. What is it?"

He smiled at that but didn't reply.

The servo'd dragon came to rest on the boulder-strewn top of a high mountain on one of the islands. They stepped down onto thick turf; far below them the sea rocked, dappled and veined like fine, dark marble.

They turned toward the peak where Askar sat cross-legged, his hair and skin golden today, golden wings spreading skyward behind him. He looked like a huge carving of an ancient tribal deity, Tagak thought, and her unease grew. Askar was going to be a problem.

Askar pointed to the sea where a tiny speck moved toward the islands. *I sent for him.*

Tagak enhanced her vision to see what he pointed at. A small dot now resolved itself into a fishing boat with a solitary occupant.

You presume too much! she answered angrily.

It's the way I've chosen in my doing, Askar replied. *I shall make him my heir.*

You'll shatter him with a truth he can't possibly handle!

Perhaps, Askar agreed. *Perhaps not.*

Koril took no part in this exchange. He watched the progress of the dot over the water as if the beauty of the pattern it created were all that mattered. The sea was calm, the air clear, and the boat came straight as an arrow to its destination. Once it reached the shore, a tiny figure stepped out at the foot of the mountain on which they stood. Askar spread the fingers of one hand out and immediately a circle lit up in the pebbles at the little figure's feet far below. They watched as the visitor hesitated, then stepped onto the glowing ring of the teleport. Tagak and Koril withdrew a little way off. Askar raised his arm and the ring of light detached itself from the beach and rose up into the air, bearing its living cargo.

Now a man stood on the grass before Askar, shading his eyes against the sun's dazzle reflected off clouds and rocks and Askar's golden wings. He stood without speaking, half eager, half amazed.

Askar nodded approval at this. "Welcome, my son."

Parvey met his gaze without flinching. Askar took an infosphere that lay among the many pebbles strewn over the mountainside and held it out. Parvey hesitated.

"Take it. You made the journey here to learn the

secrets of the Venn. I'm offering them to you. Or are you now afraid to learn the truth?"

Parvey seemed to make up his mind that if he were there at all he might as well take whatever he was offered. He seized the sphere from Askar's palm and closed his fingers over it.

At once a cry escaped his lips, and he threw it to the ground as if it had burned him.

Askar didn't move. The infosphere lay at the man's feet, pulsing with faint radiance. Parvey glanced wildly from the stone to Askar, but Askar offered no advice. Then he stooped and reached for it, his fingers trembling. This time he didn't cry but closed his eyes and clenched his teeth as if against a great pain as he held the sphere. He began to shake like a man in the throes of a terrible fever. Light seeped between his fingers, and his fingers began to glow, then his hand, his arm, and soon his whole body seemed to have caught fire as the osmotically transmitted information progressed up his neural pathways. His lips parted in a silent cry.

Enough! Tagak couldn't hold back her thought. *This is too much.*

It's not your move, Koril reminded her.

But this knowledge will destroy him!

And if it does? Koril asked.

Even in their brief lives, they feel pain, Tagak replied. *I wouldn't do this to one of them.*

Askar touched Parvey's clenched fingers and loosened their hold on the infosphere and took it away from him. The light faded from his body. He stood blank-eyed and disoriented.

"Now you have the truth, my son," Askar said. "Your courage is rewarded with powers not given to the others."

Parvey's mouth worked soundlessly.

Askar smiled. "To those who dare are given the greatest gifts."

On the mountain the sun was still shining, but stormclouds were gathering over the sea far below. Askar spread both his palms before him and the circle of light descended, bearing Parvey away. After a while, they enhanced their vision and could see a small boat battling the cold waves.

You act as if you were a god! Tagak stood angrily before Askar.

No god, but a wizard perhaps, even as they call us! he replied. *Oh, Tagak! Like Mirandil, you're jealous because you have no child.*

Tagak stalked back and forth, scowling. There was a certain amount of truth to Askar's accusation. Although she didn't pine quite as much as Mirandil, she wouldn't deny she thought about it, too. The child she'd once given birth to had been dead five hundred years. There was no more pain in that thought, only a lingering curiosity about what might have been. But if she'd been male, wouldn't she have done what Askar did, to have a child? Without children, what was the point of such an extended life?

Over the years Edward Venn's followers had fallen victim to despair; some, like Donald, had left the labs on the archipelago soon after their initial success shaping a metamorph—what had they named this specimen? Oh, yes: Kirili. A name pulled from the computer to have no previous associations, no resonances, a new beginning. (Miranda, Tagak remembered suddenly, had wanted something from Shakespeare, but had been overruled.) Others had killed themselves. Things might have been very different if they'd been able to form a normal human colony on Ilia, having babies, raising children— the work might have fallen into place then. But the women had outlived their childbearing years; though their bodies had renewed themselves, their ova had not. Barren as they were, their thinking was warped. She could understand the passions driving Askar. Yet there was always a risk in telling the child its origins, more so with this one. Well—at least its anguish wouldn't last long.

But Askar's would endure centuries.

You've had two moves, she reminded him.

The talismen promised three.

Askar's correct, Koril acknowledged. *You must wait and watch, Tagak.*

In fury, Tagak turned on Askar. But he didn't move when her eyes locked with his, and in a little while she turned calmly and walked down from the mountaintop, following the old, overgrown paths, disused for centuries.

The servo'd sea dragon stirred restlessly. Koril mounted and it sprang lightly off the rock and flew away, the precision machinery of its translucent wings beating the air softly.

CHAPTER NINE

The following day, a hard wind blew and snow swirled down from a ragged gray sky. Sivell tried not to think of Sool alone on the frozen hills.

After the noon meal, a servant told her the stranger hadn't left on his journey yet, but that Parvey had returned from his. She waited for Parvey in the small study.

He strode in as if he were in a hurry to depart instead of having just arrived. She felt a mixture of relief and unease when she saw him. Something seemed different about him.

Parvey leaned over Sivell's chair to embrace her—not the warm hug she was used to from her brother, but a quick tightening of his hands on her shoulders. His eyes avoided meeting hers. "I came as fast as I could. It looks very bad."

She watched his face as he sat down, reading strain in the lines that had appeared about the outer corners of his eyes and mouth. Sivell's sense of unease grew; he was changed somehow, but she couldn't quite say what the difference was.

"Haven't you been well, Parvey?" she asked.

He glanced away. "It's nothing."

"I shouldn't have let you leave Tia-ta-pel. Visiting this father of yours hasn't been good for you."

"There are more serious matters at stake now!" he replied sharply.

Shaken by his angry tone, Sivell recoiled. But before she could think what this meant, there was a stir at the door.

"May Nola's third grandchild be a party to these plans?"

Kela stood in the doorway, ebony hair piled in a high coil on her head, a shift emblem of tiny birds in a coronet binding it.

Sivell met her cousin's gaze steadily. It wasn't unthinkable that close kin would confer on such important matters, but there'd never been real friendship between the cousins, and neither had ever looked to the other for advice or comfort before. She couldn't imagine what had brought Kela at this time. She didn't want Kela here—especially when she hadn't seen Parvey for so long. But to refuse her would mean continuing the quarrel begun earlier, and that would risk splitting the royal house of Ilia at a time when it desperately needed unity.

"In a time of trouble, Ilia needs the counsel of all its children," she said as graciously as she could manage.

Parvey, she noticed, didn't seem surprised by Kela's appearance. Kela seated herself beside him, facing Sivell. For a moment, she had the sharp sensation they'd allied themselves against her for some undisclosed purpose.

"The possibility of war between Ganu and Liani was foreseen," Parvey began, "though it wasn't expected so soon."

"Who foresaw this, Parvey?" she queried. He didn't answer. "And why has this happened at all? The Ganus for all their faults are not warlike!"

"What does 'why' matter?" Kela stroked the folds of her gown.

"Liani and Ganu together built Tia-ta-pel," Parvey said. "The Lianis knew how a city should be, and the Ganus knew how to build it. We share more in common than you would ever dream, Sivell. But the difference is crucial."

She stared thoughtfully at her brother, trying to hear what it was he wasn't saying. "There's something here beneath your words, Parvey. What is it you're afraid to say?"

"Not afraid!" he countered roughly. "I haven't found the right words yet."

A servant entered quietly. They were silent while she went about lighting the fire. Dusk filled the room, but soon the fire flickered in the grate. The girl withdrew.

Kela stirred impatiently. "This isn't helping us know what to do now against the Ganus! Come, Parvey, make an end to the story."

He patted her hand. "The Ganus built their own city of Goron on the other side of the hills, because they knew what was concealed from us and they couldn't bear to face us."

"They're jealous of our shifting," Kela said, nodding. "Everybody knows how envious they are because we're shaped in the Great Shaper's image and they're stuck with their ugly bodies!"

"They envy the shiftskill itself, true enough, but not those who possess it," Parvey agreed. "We need them more than they need us. And that makes them dangerous. But that doesn't make an end to the truth."

Darkness had fallen outside the window. The firelit room was an oasis of warmth in a wintry world. Soon the long night would close the castle in its snowdrifts. But this year there'd be no comfort in winter's snowy embrace.

Sivell sighed. "They've forgotten, just as we have, that we're all kin, all children of the Great Shaper—"

Parvey's face twisted in an ugly mask. "How could we forget what we never knew? You don't understand, Sivell!"

"What is this knowledge that gives you pain, Parvey?" she asked. "Tell me what I should know."

But he shook his head.

"It's not important!" Kela tossed her head, setting the songbirds twittering anxiously. "The question is, what will you do?"

Annoying as Kela was, Sivell recognized the correctness of the question. Whatever the puzzle was of Parvey's strange new knowledge, the situation at present was too tense to take the time to solve it. "I've already sent an ambassador to ask Mordun to help me prevent war between our people. Because, surely, Mordun cannot know what these rebels are doing in the hills!"

"Who took this message?" Parvey asked.

"Sool."

"Oh, what a wonderful choice!" Kela exclaimed, her voice sharp with sarcasm. "A half-breed Ganu as ambassador for the Liani royal house!"

"Perhaps that was wiser than it seems," Parvey said. "Who better to seek peace between Liani and Ganu than one who's part of both?"

"It's not what *I* would have done, if I'd been queen!"

But you're not queen! Sivell didn't say it, though she was stung by Kela's words.

"It was a hard journey for me to get here in time," Parvey said. "I'm still weary. But before I sleep I'll look to some defense for Tia-ta-pel, in the event Sool's mission fails."

"It mustn't fail!" Sivell said. "We daren't consider war."

Kela jutted her chin. "I don't see why not."

"Neither of you knows what you're talking about!" Parvey said. "The Ganus do—and their mood is ugly. I need time to think this through before we react."

Sivell had never seen her brother looking so exhausted. There was a strangeness about him too that his tiredness was allowing to show through. It was almost as if he weren't the Parvey she knew, but someone else wearing Parvey's personality as another man might wear his gloves. Outwardly he looked the same, but inwardly he had changed.

He rose and she held out her hand. "Rest well, dearest brother."

Kela followed Parvey out of the room with barely a glance at Sivell.

She put her cousin's disrespect out of her mind and went up to her chamber alone. Snow was falling steadily now, like a soft gray-white curtain catching the light from her window; the songbird huddled miserably in a corner of its cage in the window nook. She moved the cage to a warmer spot in the room, then curled herself in a deep armchair. She pulled the corli feather coverlet over her, meaning only to rest for a few minutes and think about what Parvey had told her.

She didn't know how long she'd slept when a prolonged knocking at the door wakened her. The moon had risen and the chamber was full of stark, white light. She sat up, shivering with cold. The knocking at the door continued.

"What is it?" She pulled the coverlet around her neck sleepily, hugging its warmth to her.

The door opened, revealing the old advisor, the branches of his shiftemblem quivering. His face peering through the green needles was a picture of grief.

"What's happened?"

"Madam," the old man began. Tears streamed down his face. "Madam—"

He pointed back to the stairs with a shaking hand, unable to put his grief into words. Wide awake now, she leaped out of the chair and pushed past him, the corli quilt trailing behind her as she ran barefoot down the stairs to the great hall. Here she saw a small group of servants and nobles gathered about something in the center of the room. To one side, an elderly woman, shoulders hunched and hands clasped, was keening in a high voice. No one paid her any attention.

"Let me through!" Sivell tried to push through the group to its center. "What is it?"

Parvey's hand grasped her arm, restraining her. "Wait."

The group opened for her, and with Parvey holding her arm Sivell advanced to the center. A litter such as Ganu fishermen used to carry their catch to the marketplace in Tia-ta-pel lay on the ground. Something on it was covered with a gray Ganu shawl. Without her consciously willing it, Sivell's hand began to move toward the shawl—slowly, slowly, an hour seeming to pass between the beginning of the movement and its end.

But as soon as her fingers made contact with the cloth,

a cold shockwave of knowing spread back up her arm to her heart.

She drew the cloth back, revealing the silent body of Sool.

He might have been sleeping, she thought. Once, she'd come upon him asleep under a jil tree, dark lashes hooding his eyes, and she'd kissed him, feeling his warm breath meet hers at his lips. Remembering, she bent to him now on the litter, her hand seeking his. Her hand touched ice. When she drew back, the ice was spreading through her own veins.

"He can't be dead," she said. "I won't believe it. This is some trick—"

The old woman began to wail again.

Sivell turned to Parvey. "Tell me he isn't dead!"

Parvey shook his head. "Two Ganu fishermen brought him to Tia-ta-pel. They were bringing their catch of winter lengu to the castle when they came upon a band of armed Ganu hunters carrying something heavy. These men told the fishermen to take it out in their boat and dump it in the sea. But when they were gone the fishermen looked at what it contained. They brought it here instead."

Her heart felt as if it too were dead, with Sool. She wanted to collapse across Sool's body and wail as the old woman was doing. But a voice inside her head kept repeating, *You are queen. No time for grief! You are queen.*

"Where are they now? I must question them."

"They ran away as soon as they'd told their story. Scared, I suppose. Nobody likes a messenger of bad news."

Sivell looked down at Sool, lying so still where the first catch of winter lengu should have lain. She'd looked upon the faces of the dead before, but never on a man killed by other men. The phrase every Liani child learned from her mother filled her mind: *Great Shaper, let me never spill another's blood, nor she mine.* Even the Ganus—though they were hunters and meat eaters—weren't known as killers of men.

The old woman's voice grew louder, filling the great hall with her grief. Sivell turned from the litter. "Who's that?"

"Sool's mother," the old advisor said, his voice still shaking. "Somebody ran and fetched her when they brought the litter in."

Sivell looked at the old woman she'd met only rarely, and saw an echo in her face of Sool's fine features. She put her hands on the old woman's shoulders. "Mother, your son's embassy to Mordun was answered in brutal fashion. Now we must decide how to reply to the message he brought back."

She left the woman to the comforting hands of one of her relatives and went back to Parvey. Her mind seemed oddly calm and clear.

"The decision has been made for war," Parvey said. "Though I might have wished it otherwise—together we could've made the Venn pay a price for playing with our lives! But this way is better than no action at all."

"What are you talking about, Parvey? The Lianis don't know anything about war!"

"I'll teach them. All you have to do is give the word."

"How can you do that? What do you know of weapons and—"

"I know what I know!" he said.

She recoiled from the fury in his words. After a while she said, "Isn't there any other way than to answer bloodshed with more bloodshed?"

His face was distant and expressionless like a statue's. "I know of no other. Do you?"

She felt as if she were holding her fists clenched so tightly the blood had stopped. Her lip had begun to tremble and she could not control the tears gathering in her eyes. "Leave me alone with Sool for a little while. Let me mourn first." When she'd said good-bye to the past, maybe she'd be better able to speak of the future.

Parvey murmured to the group around the litter and they withdrew quietly, taking Sool's mother with them. Alone, she knelt down beside the litter and looked at Sool's bloodless face.

She'd been five years old when she'd first met Sool who was ten already. Her mind went willingly back to that happier time. She'd been lying in bed one morning, thinking about the birds and how she wished she could be like them. She stretched her arms experimentally, wondering how wings would feel, and was aware of an odd trembling in her body. The door opened, and her grandmother came in with another woman—perhaps it had been the last time she'd seen her mother?—and they looked at her. "See," Grandmother said. "The child progresses daily. It'll be all right." But she knew they were disappointed. She padded down the stairs and out of the castle by herself when they were gone. Somewhere in the castle, someone laughed; she was sure it was at her. She began to run, blinded by tears, straight through the courtyard and out to the river. She would have fallen into the water in her headlong rush if a young boy hadn't caught her in his arms. He let her bawl out her frustration, then hoisted her up onto his shoulders and carried her about the meadow until dusk. She thought he was the most beautiful person in the world.

Now, stroking the pale hair back from his cold brow, she still thought him beautiful. The years of childhood had forged a bond between them. He, whom few Liani females would consider as a mate because of his Ganu blood, had been a gentle, affectionate friend. And she, who could now have her pick of the Lianis, wanted only to be with him. She cared nothing for the throne. Sool was dead. How could Sivell be still alive?

She laid her cheek against the rough jacket that still smelled faintly of woodsmoke and meadow grass. Something hard met her, and she felt for it, locating the slim silver pipe he'd played for her. "Terel's minstrel," he'd called it. Terel, the moon of summer that shone in so many of her memories of Sool . . .

Now the tears overflowed and she made no more effort to hold them back.

Later—though she had no sense of time passing—she was aware of hands touching her bare shoulders, replacing the corli quilt that had slipped unnoticed to the floor.

She looked up. Chetek stood beside her, his brown angular face grim.

He gestured toward Sool's body. "How did it happen?"

"The Ganus."

"With what weapon?"

"What do you mean?"

"I don't see a wound, or any blood."

"The Ganus are skilled hunters."

"Even an animal bleeds. May I look?" Gently he withdrew the gray shawl, moving aside Sool's jacket and the tunic under it, and lifted the arm that lay stiffly across the cold body. "That's what I was looking for."

She saw a curious-looking mark on Sool's chest just under the rib cage, a thin curving red line like a crack in a fine porcelain cup. There had been no bleeding, although a few red drops show here and there along the line.

"What is it?"

"You don't know the weapon that made that cut, but I do. It's not a Ganu weapon—or one they should have! I don't know how they got it, but it's an evil thing to possess."

"Chetek, I don't understand."

"Perhaps I should be honest with you about myself," he said. "I should explain how I know these things."

"You're neither Liani nor Ganu, that much I know!" she said. "Who are you, Chetek-Stranger? Are you a wizard?"

"I'm no wizard. My people live north of Goron, on the other side of the Kai-weh mountains, in the land known as Kaimir-Rho."

"Then you're . . ." She hesitated. There had been other legends she'd found in the queens' collection, of another race shaped long ago in the garden—but like the Ganus, not in the Great Shaper's own image. The Ganus too had sometimes spoken of these mysterious people who moved at the edge of the known world. "*Rhodaru?*"

He nodded.

Thoughts whirled in her mind at this revelation. If this legendary third race really did exist—

But there were more immediate problems. "Tell me about the knife."

"It's a Rhodaru weapon, a knife made for an assassin's hand, a blade to kill a man secretly."

"This is astonishing," she said slowly. "The more so because when the Ganus spoke of the Rhodarus, we always believed it to be a hunter's tall tale."

"The Kai-weh mountains form a wall that has shut your people in since the beginning. And perhaps, as the Ganus say, that was wisely done by the wizards to keep the fiercer Rhodarus out!"

"Your words are very disturbing!" she said. "They answer some questions, but they raise more. But there isn't time for me to think about them now. One thing I see clearly. Someone gave the Ganus a weapon they shouldn't possess, and no good can come to the Lianis as a result."

"You're right to be worried," Chetek agreed gloomily.

She looked at him carefully, watching the changes of expression that might tell her if he was lying. "You tell me the weapon is Rhodaru, and that you are Rhodaru. Therefore it seems your purpose isn't the same as those who gave this weapon to the Ganus."

He gazed out the window without answering. Frost flowers had bloomed on the glass, covering it with delicate, icy arabesques. Something about this stranger persuaded her to believe him. She trusted this odd ability of hers to tell when someone spoke the truth, even though it wasn't a skill shared by other Lianis. And she really had no other choice. Parvey, harboring secrets he either would not or could not share with her, was planning war as the only solution. That was unacceptable.

"You had a mission when you came here, and I have a mission, too," she said. "I must prevent war between my people and the Ganus. And beyond that I want to find whoever killed Sool. Perhaps I can make a bargain with you."

"Propose it." He turned to face her.

"Take me with you to Goron. I'll personally deliver my

message to Mordun. I'll take the chance that he doesn't know what his son does in the hills with Rhodaru weapons. And if you do this for me, I'll help you find the woman you once knew in Tia-ta-pel."

He hesitated. "It's a dangerous journey."

"Will you accept my bargain?"

"And what if you're wrong about this? What if the Ganu king did indeed order this killing?"

"Sool never reached Goron. He didn't have time! I *must* do this, Chetek. If you won't go with me, I'll go alone."

"A perilous mission for a woman."

"A *queen*, Chetek."

"Then you leave me no choice."

"We'll tell my brother now," she said.

CHAPTER TEN

"This is madness, Sivell!"

Parvey paced back and forth in the small study. She'd never seen him so angry before. If he'd taken the shiftshape of a forest blazing, she couldn't have felt more scorched by his anger. But she held her ground.

"Look again at Sool's death wound. Could you name the knife that kills without drawing blood? It isn't a Ganu weapon."

"And if it isn't, what then? A Ganu used it to kill Sool. That's how Mordun answered the queen's ambassador. There's only one reply to such a message."

"Parvey! He never reached Mordun. Mordun has been a friend of the Lianis for many years. Why should we believe him capable of treachery now?"

They'd been over this ground several times since she'd told him of her plan. His view was always the same.

"Then perhaps Mordun no longer controls his people!"

"Sool went over the hill road. But we know Bor holds the hills."

"Yes! Mordun's kingdom falls apart. Don't you see, Sivell? His son leads the rebels against him. We must seize the opportunity to destroy all of them!"

She was suddenly calm in the midst of his tempest, as if she'd been standing on a wave-battered rock from which the sea had suddenly withdrawn. There was something else beneath his anger; she was sure of it. His fury was not for the Ganus at all. They were only the scapegoats for a far more terrible enemy. She knew, just as clearly, that he wasn't ready to tell her who that enemy was.

"We'll have to try a different route this time—the west road, around the places Bor holds."

"Far too dangerous!" Parvey snapped. "Even in shift-shape it would take too much time and be hazardous. And you, Sivell—"

He left the thought unfinished. She felt her cheeks flame at the criticism. But who knew better than Parvey how hard she'd had to work to pass her Proving.

"We could go by sea," Chetek suggested. "I can handle a boat, and Goron lies on a river. We could probably make it."

"Ridiculous!" Parvey turned his back on the Rhodaru in a display of disgust.

"Between Sorway Cliff and the mouth of that river lie the rocks called Kri's Necklace," Sivell explained. "They're named for a giant who used to collect skulls for jewels. The tide runs fast by those rocks, and the currents are dangerous. In winter, even experienced Ganu fishermen have been shipwrecked. We have no boat that could face the Necklace."

"Perhaps you are Rhodaru, as you say," Parvey told Chetek. "But that doesn't change my belief that we have to prepare for war with the Ganus. It's not wise for the queen to be gone from Tia-ta-pel at a time like this, especially on such a crazy errand!"

Sivell knew he was speaking the truth. She might have been wrong to send Sool—Parvey would've advised against it if he'd known in time. She winced, thinking of Kela's scornful words. Yet Sool's mixed blood wasn't the problem. And of course Parvey was right. It was certainly dangerous for her to go alone to Goron. But she was tired of playing at being queen; Sool's death had ended the time for play. And hadn't Parvey himself told her she didn't need him anymore? That day seemed so long ago now. She wasn't the same scared little Sivell she'd been before her Proving. To go in shiftshape might not be possible for her. The road was long and the weather fierce. She knew better than he how fragile her control might be under such poor conditions! And shifted or not, she'd have the same cold distance to cover.

But perhaps that was a strength, not the weakness it first seemed. The Ganus feared the shiftskill. It would be a gesture of peace to do without. She had a strong feeling that she was going to need Chetek who couldn't shift at all.

"We'll go by land," she said.

"Don't do it, Sivell," Parvey said, and she had the odd sensation he fought with himself to get the words out. "There're some in Tia-ta-pel who're jealous of you, some of your own kin who'd put your absence from the throne to good use."

Kela, she thought. Her cousin had always envied her because she was Falina's child, while Kela was Tuell's, Nola's second daughter who couldn't become queen. He was right again. But it made no difference anymore.

"I'm queen here. I'll decide."

Parvey caught her hands in his strong grasp. "Have I ever given you poor advice, Sivell? Haven't I always protected you?"

"Parvey—"

"Stay here, little sister," he said in a low, tortured voice. "Stay because I need you! Otherwise, I might—"

"What's wrong, Parvey? Tell me what it is that's driving you like this?"

"You can't possibly understand!" he said harshly. "Just give up your plan."

In her heart she felt as though two magnets had been wrenched apart. She might indeed be making a tremendous mistake for which she'd later be required to pay.

"I'm sorry, Parvey. But I must go to Goron."

He withdrew his hands from hers, his eyes blank as windows over which someone had pulled a curtain. "Very well. You've chosen your path."

He walked quickly from the room. She listened to his footsteps retreating, echoing down the corridor. The air that filled the room seemed suddenly to have grown heavy; she could feel its weight pressing her down. She covered her eyes with her hands, worn down by the argument with her brother.

So she'd won—a hollow victory at best! Her adult independence had been paid for with the loss of the two people she'd been closest to in childhood.

"We'll need warm clothing," Chetek said, rubbing his arms against the chill. "And food for two days."

She wrenched her thoughts away from Parvey. "Can you be ready to leave in the morning?"

"I travel light," Chetek said.

At dawn, everything was ready for their departure. They met at the castle's west door, dressed in Ganu-made winter clothing, long, bulky coats insulated with corli-down and heavy, fur-lined boots. Servants had wrapped parcels of food and tucked them onto a low sled such as children used to pull each other over the icy roads in the brief winter. It was the best they could find at such short notice, the Lianis being reluctant to undertake long journeys in bad weather. Two corli-feather sleeping bags went on top. Parvey was nowhere to be seen.

When the sled was ready, Chetek pulled the fur hood around his face, but Sivell allowed hers to hang down behind, her hair spilling over it. She had omitted her shiftemblem; if they met someone on the road, it might be better not to be identified immediately as a royal Liani. Chetek tested the small sled and found it ran smoothly on its waxed runners. The sun was already climbing the pink and gray sky.

They set off.

Sivell looked back once as they left the castle, feeling hollow inside where her heart should have been. "They'll have buried Sool before I return."

"We could've waited," Chetek said.

She shook her head. "It's better that we leave now before my brother thinks of a way of preventing me! And besides, among the Lianis death isn't made much of. The angel on our royal crest is sometimes called the Angel of Death, for what is death but a final shiftshape?"

Chetek considered this in silence as they walked. They followed the lane winding down to the western edge of the city and on to the plain that lay behind. For a time, they walked without speaking to each other, crossing narrow bridges over frozen streams where corlis squatted on the ice. The houses thinned out and were left behind as they approached the edge of Tia-ta-pel. The sled hissed behind Chetek, and the only other sound was the squeak of their boots in the new snow.

At the city gate they saw the central plain of Ilia lying white and shining before them, dappled with violet shadows in the hollows under the ice-hung jil trees. Here in summer the grapes grew, tended by Ganu workmen, that were made into the wine served in the Liani royal palace. Here too, the vegetables and fruits that made up the Liani diet were carefully tended by Ganus. The sight of these pale, silent figures stooped over the rows of little plants in these fields was forever bound up in her memory with the concept of summer itself. For the first time she wondered when they found the time to tend their own fields, since they always seemed so busy serving the Lianis. It was not a life she would have chosen, bent double, dirt under her fingernails, the sun blazing all day on her back. It was becoming obvious that the Ganus had many more reasons to despise the Lianis than just the lack of shiftskill.

The thought made her uneasy.

Though the snow was thick underfoot, it wasn't cold outside as she'd found it to be in the castle these last two days. The difference, she realized, was that now she was doing something about her problems, as a queen should.

"This is the first time I've been so far from the castle without a single attendant since my Proving," she commented. "I hadn't realized how a queen is never *free*. I think I'd find any world lovely right now! But the Great Shaper has indeed made Ilia beautiful."

Later Chetek asked, looking up at the sky, "How far do you want to go before sundown?"

"There's a small summer settlement in the foothills of the western range, about three hours' walk from here. No one lives there in winter, but we can use it for shelter. From there, I'm told, it'll be a long day's walk to Goron."

"I estimate we've got about four hours' more light," Chetek said. He hesitated for a moment. "A long walk for one not used to it. If—in the manner of your race— you should prefer to adopt a shape more comfortable for traveling . . ."

"Thank you. No."

He bent himself to the task of pulling the little sled, and they walked on in silence again. But before they reached the summer settlement, her feet had begun to protest the unusual activity she demanded of them. *Hati hooves or jalu wings, a shiftshape would've tired, too,* she comforted herself. Yet she couldn't deny she might have reached her destination much faster. Chetek would have been left behind, of course— Well, she'd made her decision to do without, and she was never one to fret over what might have been.

Except for Sool, her heart whispered.

"It puzzles me," Chetek said suddenly, "that a race that could dance its way to magic should ever bother to use feet!"

Amazed, she gaped at him. Then she realized he was teasing.

He smiled at her expression, then asked more seriously, "Why don't you use your power to shift shape more often?"

Sivell thought about it for the first time. It was a valid question. "I think we found that of all the beautiful shapes we could—and do!—assume in play, there is none so useful as the human shape."

Chetek nodded thoughtfully. "Shifting must be a pleasant game to play. But to those who don't have the power—"

He left the rest of his thought unsaid.

The long shadow of the hills had fallen across the settlement as they approached it. At this point the road forked, one half running to the mountains that formed the wall on Ilia's western side, and the other running north to Goron. These mountains weren't as forbiddingly high as the Kai-weh range to the north; nevertheless, no Liani had ever crossed them or seen the coast that was supposed to lie behind them. Chetek was right, she thought; mountains shut the Lianis in from harm. But somehow the danger had managed to slip inside the protective walls anyway.

The snow was stained a dark red with the rays of the setting sun. *The color of blood—* She put the thought quickly out of her mind. As she'd predicted, the small cabins weren't occupied, and they were weatherproof. They entered one at random for they all seemed about the same size. They pulled off gloves and boots, glad to stretch freely and rest from the long walk. Wood was stacked in a neat pile beside a clean fireplace; two sleeping benches ran along the walls on either side of the cabin. Apart from these, the cabin had no furniture. Chetek took the wood and kindled a fire; soon the cabin was warm and filled with a cheerful, flickering light.

They sat on a blanket on the floor by the fire and Sivell unwrapped the bread and cheese and corli eggs they'd brought. They ate slowly, watching the flames, feeling the weariness of the day catch up with them.

"I'd never thought before this day, how like walls the mountain ranges are," Sivell said. "Your people live to the north, but does anyone live in the west?"

"That land belongs to my people, too," Chetek said.

"How little we know of the world outside Ilia!"

"My father came from the west, several days' journey beyond these hills. Chetek is the great clan name of the west."

"You know who your father was? Parvey does, too. It's very strange."

"To my people it would be strange not to know! But I see that the Lianis don't value fatherhood."

She smiled. "Choosing the right father for a child is very important to us, especially for a queen. But once it's done, there's nothing for the father to do, is there?

Raising a child isn't such a big matter. But perhaps father and mother would be beautiful together?" She was silent then, thinking of Sool again.

"My people think so," he agreed.

"Tell me about your people." She took fruit from the pack and passed him some.

"My people like to rule," Chetek said. "Whatever they do, they give themselves wholly to it, and they don't like to acknowledge anyone greater than themselves. So they fight a great deal. The desert—which is much of our land—is a fierce place and breeds fierce people to live in it. We call ourselves the firstborn of He-Who-Rules, whose symbol is the great-maned karami, king of the desert. And if we knew about shifting, we'd probably hate it and those who practiced it!"

"Do you have a queen like us, or a king like the Ganus?" she asked. Thinking about these legendary figures in a land she'd never see served to take her mind off the coming confrontation with Mordun who was only too real.

"Neither. But we do have many leaders, and when there are too many at one time, we go to war to settle the matter."

"How terrible!" Startled out of her own reverie, she stared at him. This sounded far worse than the dreary life of the Ganus.

"It's the way of a hard land. By this method the strongest survive and become stronger."

"And killing solves the problems?" she asked incredulously.

He smiled bitterly. "Killing comes easier to people who can't be lied to."

"What do you mean?"

"He-Who-Rules chose to give his people few gifts to help them. The truth sense is one. We hear the truth beneath the most skillful lie. It encourages quick endings to arguments."

"Sometimes," she said, "I almost think I too know things people hesitate to put into words."

Chetek leaned back, fingers clasped behind his head, and stared at the flames in silence.

Perhaps shifting made a difference in people. When you could change your shape at will, ruling other people or taking their possessions didn't seem so important. Sometime, when the present crisis was over, she wanted to learn more about these fierce-sounding Rhodarus. The Lianis were uninterested in the world beyond their boundaries, but a queen should know as much as possible about her neighbors.

"How strange it is that the Great Shaper gave us playful gifts, while your He-Who-Rules gave you sterner ones," she said, watching the flicker of firelight playing over the roof beams.

"Tell me about your Great Shaper. Does he protect His people?"

"It," she replied. "Not He. The Great Shaper is a beautiful spirit! Once upon a time, being lonely in its garden where the sun is always rising, it began to dance the dance of shaping. And out of the mist that surrounded it as it danced, the mother of my people was shaped. For a long time Kirili was happy in the Great Shaper's garden with the Venn for her companions. But the day came when Kirili wanted to have children of her own, and to do this she had to leave the beautiful garden."

Chetek raised his eyebrows, but said nothing.

Sivell continued. "The Great Shaper was very sad at this, but it let her go. One of the Venn, Donil, chose to go with her into Ilia. And Donil too could never go back to the garden!"

"A pretty tale," Chetek said, noncommittally. "Did you know the Ganus acknowledge no god?"

"Yes. But what do you suppose that means?"

"Either they're jealous that they were left out of the gift-giving, or they're closer to the truth than the Rhodarus—who'd hear it if it were ever spoken!"

She sat up and stared at his face. "What do you mean?"

"I've heard rumors."

"Will you tell me?"

He shook his head. "Only rumors."

A memory of the strangeness she'd felt in Parvey—his odd words—surfaced. But Chetek wasn't about to say anything else, and whatever the answer might be, she didn't have it just yet.

She drew out Sool's pipe and set it to her lips. She blew a sweet, high song, speaking of dew on summer petals, woodsmoke at twilight, hatis in the jil shadows by the river, things she'd shared with Sool. But tonight the pipe also spoke of Kri waiting in the wintry sea for unwary fishermen, and of jalus circling silently above the hati young. Abruptly, she set the pipe down.

"It's always hardest for those left living." Chetek spoke softly out of the shadow by the fireside. "They have to carry the pain."

"Death shouldn't trouble a Liani!" she said stubbornly.

"Even a Rhodaru mourns the loss of loved ones."

"Among my people, love is reckoned as lightly as any other pleasure." But she was different; she didn't believe that.

"I wouldn't apologize," he said.

After a while she said, not looking at him because even if he wasn't Liani it felt somehow shameful to admit such feelings, "It feels as if a hole had been cut in my breast. As if some part of me had been cut away." She thought of Sool's death wound which he wore like an evil jewel in place of the pendant she'd given him.

"That's how love feels when you've lost it," Chetek said.

She gazed at his face in the firelight, seeing the deep lines that loss had etched there. "You've lost much in your time, I think."

"My wife and infant son, many years ago. I was a leader of my people, like the ones I described to you. But my rival led a rebellion against me, and killed my wife and the boy. I had to flee for my life."

She laid the pipe carefully away in her pack, respecting his pain. "What did you do then?"

"Defeated leaders aren't welcome anywhere in my

country, and I'd been higher than most. I went into exile in Goron. Then I came farther south, passing through Tia-ta-pel, and on to the seacoast at Donil's Bay. Liani and Ganu live side by side there, and strangers aren't so obvious. One day, the wizard Tagak told me my enemy was dead. So I'm going back to my people."

The fire had fallen away to embers; the cabin was growing cool again.

"I'm sorry, Chetek . . ." she began.

He set aside the wine flask he'd been drinking from. "Let's sleep. We'll start out at first light. It'll be a long walk tomorrow."

When they'd settled in the corli-feather bags on the sleeping benches, she said, "You're a good man. May you return to your homeland in safety."

She lay in the warm sleeping bag, thinking of Chetek and his lost loved ones. In all the years since their deaths, he'd found no one to replace them. Once there'd been a woman in Tia-ta-pel who was kind to him, but even she was probably lost now. Wasn't it better that the Lianis took love and death so lightly? Yet her heart was heavy with her own loss, and in that she was different from her people.

There was no answer to this. So many ways in which she was different! So many questions. When she was a little girl she'd supposed that if she passed her Proving she'd have all the answers. Now she knew that wasn't so at all.

CHAPTER ELEVEN

Sool had on a scarlet coat trimmed with sapphire. He held out his hands to her, with the jil pendant on his palm. She could see his honey-colored hair glistening. His lips moved, but no words came to her. Then the men in the black hoods began to draw him away. She could hear the thud of their heavy boots against the cream-stone of the courtyard.

"Sool!" she screamed.

She woke up, her cheeks wet with tears. The noise of the hooded men's boots still echoed in her ears. In the instant that she realized it was a dream, relief flooded over her. In the next she remembered Sool was dead and the tears flowed again.

But the noise continued.

Alarmed, she sat up in the corli bag. The cabin was filled with the gray light of early dawn. Across from her, Chetek huddled in his bag, snoring slightly. From outside came the sound of men's voices. She reached for the fur jacket she'd laid beside her bag. Before she made contact, strong fingers closed around her wrist, imprisoning her hand.

"Be not so fast!" a voice hissed in her ear.

She twisted in the iron grasp to see the face of the owner, but succeeded only in wrenching her wrist.

"I said be not so fast!"

Chetek rolled over, muttering. A second hand clapped across her mouth, silencing her warning cry. Sivell jerked back and forth, loosening the man's hold on her mouth. She sank her teeth into his thumb. Cursing, he let go of her wrist and she rolled quickly away.

"Chetek!" she yelled. "Wake up!"

The door of the cabin opened and three more Ganus stood silhouetted against the milky sky.

"Get that she-ferenti!" The man she'd bitten sucked his injured thumb, his round face flushed with anger. "She has fangs!"

The other three strode across the cabin. Two seized Chetek as he struggled up out of sleep, and one locked Sivell's arms behind her back.

One quick shift and she'd be free.

And her mission to Mordun would be compromised. She held her own shape against the urge to slip away.

"What have we here?" one of the Ganus said, tilting her head back in the thin light. "Liani, by the look of it."

"Tween of them," said the one who had hold of Chetek.

The first man removed his injured hand from his mouth and slapped Sivell hard across the jaw.

"No woman does that to Hathor!" he snarled.

Her face burned, but as much with anger as with pain.

"What'll we do with them?" one of the men asked.

"Kill the tween! The woman first!" Hathor replied. He drew a knife from his belt.

"Nay," the man holding Sivell said. "We do better taking them to Lord Treng."

"Take the man," Hathor said. "The woman goes when she be dead!"

"Put away the knife." A new speaker loomed as a black shadow in the doorway. "Bring them outside."

Sivell's captor pushed forward. Outside she saw a group of Ganus wearing leather jackets and boots that reached to their knees. Their blond hair lay on their shoulders where fur hoods had been pushed back. At each man's belt hung a long, bone-handled hunting knife. Beyond them in the snow, several thick-maned beasts she'd never seen before pawed the ground impatiently, their breath steaming above them.

Sivell was pushed forward till she stood in front of a tall Ganu, Sivell's own height, with eyes as cold as ice in sunlight. His shoulders were broad, his jaw angular but not heavy. There was an air about him, a hard, pale brightness hinting of the storms he could unleash if provoked.

"A she-ferenti, Lord," Hathor said. "A worthless Liani witch."

"If you're this man's lord," Sivell said, "order him to take his hands off me. What have you to fear from one unarmed woman?"

"The Lianis be known as enchanters," Hathor's lord replied. "What hunter can prevail against sorcery?"

"We use no sorcery," Sivell said, glad she'd resisted the urge to shift.

The Ganus she'd seen in Tia-ta-pel had been sullen in manner, both craftsmen and fishermen avoiding her eyes. She'd never met a Ganu hunter before. But it was his speech that puzzled her most, for though he spoke his words the Ganu way he lacked the harsh tone of his fellows.

"But I give you my word I won't shift. Your underling's bruising my arm!"

The man behind her growled. But the tall Ganu nodded at him and he withdrew his hands from her arm. She rubbed them vigorously, erasing the marks of his fingers. The leader turned his attention to Chetek.

"This one be not Liani." His hand moved to rest on his hunting knife. "Be you not one of the Rhodarus who come and go in our metros?"

"I'm Rhodaru," Chetek acknowledged. "My name's Chetek."

The wintry eyes flashed from Chetek to Sivell. "The Rhodarus call themselves friends of the Ganus. What be a Ganu friend doing in the company of a Liani witch?"

Chetek fastened his tunic, and smoothed down his hair, rumpled from sleep. His tone was deceptively casual, but Sivell found herself understanding what lay underneath the words. "I wasn't aware the Lianis were your enemies. I was on my way back to Goron. This woman was my guide."

The Ganu leader's hand left his knife. "You be well

found, friend. We too be returning to Goron and will escort you."

The other hunters turned away to the huge restless beasts, tightening saddles and adjusting bridles. Sivell was aware of Hathor's eyes on her across the intervening bulk of one of the creatures.

"I've been away too long. I don't know the situation," Chetek said to the Ganu leader. They walked away from her, back into the cabin.

Sivell waited, uncertain what was expected of her, till one of the men pushed her after them.

"Get your bundles, girl! Don't keep Lord Treng waiting."

She followed them inside, her thoughts racing. So this was Treng, Mordun's second son? She'd heard very little told in Tia-ta-pel about him. Yet he spoke as though he too, like his brother Bor, had no friendship for the Lianis. It was good that Chetek hadn't indentified her. The Liani queen mightn't have met with much civility from these rough hunters.

She realized that Treng was speaking of his brother. She dressed quietly and listened. Treng had apparently dismissed her from his attention, and Chetek, pulling on his fur jacket, carefully avoided meeting her eyes.

"He makes camp in the hills above Kri's Necklace. From there he guards the pass between Goron and Tia-ta-pel. There be many hunters with him who urge him to attack the Lianis now, before they've a chance to arm."

"What caused this enmity?" Chetek pulled on his boots.

"For generations the Lianis have lived off our toil," Treng replied. "We build their castles. We supply their food. We mine the very gold they pay us for our labors! And what've they given us in return? Nothing. They play while we toil. But the time for play be at an end."

"Does the king approve this action?" Chetek stuffed his corli bag back into its carrying case. The billowing folds seemed to occupy his full attention.

"My father be too old," Treng said. "He doesn't see

the need to break this stranglehold the Lianis have over us."

He paced the floor restlessly as he spoke. "Old men worship what they cannot do."

Sivell packed her bag silently, thankful she'd followed her cautious instinct.

"The Ganus are free," Chetek said, straightening up from his battle with the corli bag. "What power can the Lianis have over free men?"

Treng inspected the blade of his knife, running a finger down its edge. "The old men hang on Liani shifting. They think the Lianis be more worthy than themselves. They worship the sight of a Liani shift-dancing!"

"Is there any harm in this foolishness?"

Treng extended the hunting knife at arm's length till the tip reached almost to Chetek's throat. The two men stared down the length of the blade at each other for a long moment. Sivell, remembering the bloodless wound Sool bore, held her breath. Her heart pounded painfully under her ribs. But Chetek, his eyes still on Treng, buckled his belt apparently unconcerned.

Treng laughed and put the knife away.

"Now we'll free ourselves. And for this we've the Rhodarus to thank. You taught us to dream of hunting men as well as ferentis. Ferentis are ferocious, but their meat be sweet. We shall see if all Lianis be as ferocious as the one you chose for a guide, but we'll taste the sweetness of their defeat."

He spun on his heel and strode to the door. "We've a long morning's ride ahead of us before we reach Goron."

Chetek glanced at Sivell, then followed, his bag slung over his shoulder.

The heavy beasts stood in the clearing between two cabins, saddled, anxious to depart. One pawed the ground restlessly; another lifted its great head and bellowed angrily. The hunter who stood by its head smacked the beast between the horns, and it silenced. A Ganu took Chetek's bag and slung it over his mount's back; then he did the same with Sivell's.

"There be an extra medwi," Treng said to Chetek. "Will you ride?"

Chetek nodded. Sivell stood by the group, conscious of Hathor making his way toward her.

"I'll carry the witch," Hathor said.

She knew she'd have to break her promise and shift before she'd let that happen. Hathor raised his arms to reach her. She pulled back.

"She rides with me," Treng said.

He lifted her as if she were no more than a leaf and swung her onto his mount's saddle. She seized the long curling horns to steady herself, feeling the powerful muscles beneath her thighs. Treng swung up behind her. As soon as all the Ganu were mounted, the huge beasts uttered a horrible roaring noise and lurched forward.

After a while she was used to the rolling motion, learning how to rise above the moving muscles, and fall without bumping against the surprisingly bony shoulders of the great beast.

"Do you like the medwi, girl?" Treng asked.

Sivell nodded, but was unable to relax enough to speak.

"They be the fastest way to travel when snow lies deep on the plain," he said.

Bouncing on the back of the medwi was exciting. It wasn't efficient—a Liani child could have traveled faster in shiftshape—and it was too bumpy to be comfortable. But there was something compelling about it. Sivell considered this effect; she'd never ridden any creature before, and the sensation of moving in unity with the medwi was extraordinary. She decided to enjoy the ride for its duration, and not think about the danger she was in.

The hunters rode silently through unmarked snow, skirting the low hills to the east. There was none of the conversation or laughter that would have accompanied a Liani procession. In the absence of voices, she heard the clatter of medwi hooves on the frozen earth, their puffing breath, the yips and moans they uttered constantly. She was aware of the rise and fall of Treng's hips in the saddle behind her, the rub of his leather jacket against her back, his warm breath against her neck where her hair flew back.

Once a shadow passed overhead. Looking up, she saw a jalu drifting on a high current of air from the hills, its head turning slowly, seeking prey.

They were skirting snow-buried fields on both sides, their boundaries marked by low hedges and lines of windbreak trees, their interiors often broken by jagged boulders that poked up through the snow. Once they passed beneath the bare branches of an orchard. There were Ganu fields, smaller and stonier than the fields Ganus worked for the Lianis, but somehow neater, the trees more lovingly tended.

They were traveling toward the distant range of the Kai-weh mountains, spread like a gray-white smudge on the northern horizon. She'd only seen them on clear days in summer, shimmering in the haze at the edge of the plain on the other side of the hills outside Tia-ta-pel. The Lianis usually avoided the hill country, preferring the lush river meadows and the calm sea for their summer picnics. But Sool had taken her walking in the hills and pointed out the distant Kai-weh range. Now she could see the range was much wilder than she'd imagined.

Hour by hour, the mountains rose higher, their peaks and troughs became clearer to the eye, dark gashes scoring their sides where the snow melted. Toward noon, the group came in sight of buildings huddled at the foot of the mountains. She narrowed her eyes against the snow glare, and gradually was able to make out details. The buildings seemed to be one-story, dull brown against the shining snow, with steeply pitched roofs of dark tiles, but no spires or towers to break the monotony of the skyline.

Treng spurred his medwi faster. "There lies our metros. That be Goron!"

She stared at the houses crouching like a cluster of drab domestic fowl, miserable in the cold, and didn't know what to answer. Could this be the city of a king richer than any queen in Tia-ta-pel?

Finally she said, "I thought Goron lay on a river. At least—I saw that in a book."

"You be an unusual Liani, to know anything of Goron!"

She was afraid she'd offended him in some way.

But he continued. "The river flows underground through the metros, and emerges just before Goronway where it joins the marne."

They came to an arched gate in a mud-colored wall and, passing through this, entered the main street of Goron. At least, she supposed it must be the main street, for it seemed to lead straight ahead from the gate, and lesser streets joined it on both sides. It was lined with rows of identical brown houses, built of creamstone darker than that used in the building of Tia-ta-pel. Each house had its low door and one square window. The only distinguishing feature she could see was that some houses had the window at the left of the door, and some to the right, while an occasional larger house had two windows, one on either side. There were few trees along the street, and they were bare now and powdered with snow.

She felt the hopeful mood of the morning slipping away. How could the people who lived in such a city not dislike those who lived in Tia-ta-pel? The procession went single file up the almost empty street; the few Ganus who passed by ignored them. She stared at them curiously. For the most part, they seemed paler in the face and more solemn in their demeanor than the Ganus who worked in Tia-ta-pel—if that was possible. Apart from the clatter of medwi hooves on the cobblestones and the jingle of harness, the street was quiet. How good it would've been to hear the voices of bells! But there were no towers where bells could swing in this flat city. Sivell tightened her grip on the medwi's heavy mane, aware how out of place her dark hands seemed in this drab world.

Their medwi, which was at the head of the line, stopped by a door that looked exactly like any other on

the street. Behind her, all the other medwis were
coming to a halt and their riders were dismounting.
Treng slid down and strode forward, leaving Sivell to
manage by herself. Cautiously she worked one leg across
the beast's wide back, but it was a long way down to the
street.

Chetek held out a hand to help, and she reached the
ground safely.

"This city's very different from mine," she said in a low
voice meant only for Chetek's ears.

"The city isn't the only thing you're going to find
different," he said.

He seemed about to say more, but Treng returned.
"Welcome back to Goron, friend Chetek," Treng said.
Coming home seemed to have put him in good humor.

Chetek bowed his head courteously. "I'd like an
audience with the king when it's possible."

"The presence of the Rhodarus pleases my father. He
learns from their company. We'll go in to him now."

This was the king's palace? Sivell stared in disbelief at
the ordinary-looking doorway. Treng had entered the
house and Chetek followed, so it must be. But as Sivell
was about to cross the threshold, someone seized her
arm and held her outside.

"Liani witches don't enter the king's herth," Hathor
said.

"Let me go!"

"Order me, would you, witch? We be not in Tia-ta-pel
now. You'll learn who gives the orders here."

He jerked her toward him. Sivell screamed.

Luckily Chetek hadn't gone too far ahead to hear. He
came running back.

Hathor didn't release her arm. "Be this your woman,
Rhodaru? You should teach her manners."

The other Ganu hunters, wishing to enter, found their
way blocked by Hathor and Sivell. They crowded in the
doorway. Angry voices arose. Now the commotion
reached other ears.

"What be this delay?" Treng demanded.

"The Liani witch would follow you," Hathor explained.

Treng looked at her. "Wait outside, girl," he said not unkindly.

"If I might make a suggestion, Lord," Chetek said with elaborate politeness. "The king should hear what she has to say. Let her enter with us."

"As you wish," Treng said. "But hurry now. We be late enough already."

Hathor leaned toward Sivell's ear as he released her. "Later, witch!"

She followed Treng and Chetek into the dim interior of the Ganu king's palace.

CHAPTER TWELVE

When her eyes had adjusted to the gloomy interior, at first so dark after the blinding glare of the snowy landscape they'd been traveling through, Sivell saw that the house which served the Ganu royal family as palace was much larger than it appeared from the street. It stretched back a long way, rooms like square boxes opening off from each other in what seemed unplanned fashion. They gave Sivell the impression that, each time more space had been needed, a room was added at the exact spot the owner had been standing when he thought of it.

The rooms she passed through were high-ceilinged, clean, and plainly furnished. They lacked bright color and ornament, yet not comfort, for there were padded benches embroidered in simple designs and muted tones, books on well-polished, sturdy tables waiting to be read, and thick rugs in dark colors before the small, square fireplaces. The workmanship was simple, but possessed a clean elegance that was attractive. And even in rooms where the fires weren't lit, the air wasn't cold as it might have been. Sivell loosened the heavy coat. In some rooms, great lamps hung from the ceiling or stood about on the floor, giving a bright, steady light that couldn't have come from candles.

It was obvious the Ganus kept some secrets from their neighbors. Magic? she wondered. That seemed unlikely, given the Ganu distrust of anything they thought was sorcery. Comfort but not luxury seemed to be the Ganu way. Where a Liani room would have been a feast of statues, carvings, paintings, stained glass, the Ganu king's palace was as plain as a farmer's meal of bread and cheese. And there were no songbirds singing in sunny window nooks.

The little group halted in a room somewhat larger than the rest, with one plain window giving a view of an inner courtyard that seemed as if it too had just happened. In the center of the courtyard was the twisted shape of a solitary, winter-bare tree. A fire burned in the hearth, giving off rather more smoke than heat. Unlike the mantels in other rooms, this one did bear a carved decoration, a ferenti rampant which Sivell recognized as the arms of the royal house of the Ganus. It was said in Tia-ta-pel that the Ganu king owned a huge treasure house of gold and flamestones, taken from mines in the Kai-weh range. But she saw that he evidently didn't believe in displaying his wealth. The room was sparsely furnished like all the rest. A servant in Tia-ta-pel would have expected more variety.

An old man in a long brown robe sat by the fire. In his hand he had a round piece of polished glass, framed in silver and attached to a heavy silver chain; he held this up between his eyes and the book he was reading. Treng, who was leading, sank to one knee in front of this man.

The older man put down the book and allowed the glass to fall back onto his chest. He leaned forward and touched Treng on both shoulders.

"Welcome back to your herth, my son."

Treng remained kneeling. "Majesty, I've brought with me a Rhodaru, called Chetek."

The Ganu king looked from his son to Chetek, who also dropped to one knee before him.

"Welcome to our metros," the king said, and touched him on one shoulder.

Sivell watched this formality with interest. How different from the Liani royal home where all could come and go at will, and many forgot to call their queen "Madam" when they spoke. Then she saw the king's gaze was on her.

"Majesty," Chetek said, "I've brought a Liani who seeks an audience with you."

It was her turn to kneel. The thought struck her with horror. A Liani queen didn't pay homage to a Ganu king! Yet that was obviously expected of her now. She wouldn't do it. She'd rather go home than kneel to a Ganu.

Instantly, her mind showed her an image of Sool with his death wound. She'd traveled a long and dangerous way to prevent that happening again.

She overcame her pride and knelt.

"Welcome, daughter of my Liani friends," Mordun said.

She met his eyes steadily. He was a little younger than her grandmother, she guessed, but his white skin was wrinkled and mottled. He wore his hair only to his shoulders, and both hair and beard were iron colored. His eyes were an astonishing shade of deep blue, full of light and intelligence.

He gazed at her thoughtfully. "Do I know you, Youngling?"

"No, Majesty," Sivell said. "We've never spoken before."

"I thought for a moment—" the king said. "Well, arise!"

Treng and Chetek stood before the king. Sivell remained kneeling.

"Majesty, I've something to say to you in private."

The king glanced at his son. "My son remains."

She had no choice but to accept his words. "You and I have never spoken before, Majesty. But I know of you and you know of me. I am Sivell-Falinasdaughter, queen of the Lianis. I put myself into your hands, Mordun-Grynson, king of the Ganus, in the name of both our people."

She felt Treng's startled movement behind her at the revelation, but Mordun didn't move an eyelid.

"Welcome, daughter of the Liani Queens," Mordun said again. His voice was calm and without expression, his eyes unblinking. But he touched her this time on both shoulders as he had done his own son. "You've nothing to fear in my herth."

Treng turned angrily to Chetek. "Rhodaru—you betrayed my trust!"

"Patience," Mordun said. "We'll hear the message the queen brings us."

Sivell stood. His sons might be hot-tempered rebels, but there was an air of calm strength about this scholar-king that inspired her trust. She forced herself to speak clearly, without hesitation. "There are some among your people, Majesty, who plan war against my people. Do they do this with your consent?"

Mordun considered this abrupt statement carefully before answering. "Neither with my consent nor my knowledge, Queen of the Lianis."

"I'm glad to hear you say that!" Sivell exclaimed. "I've come to ask you to stop them before it's too late. There's never been war between Ganu and Liani. I believe there needn't be any in the future."

"What proof do you have that this be my people's intention?"

"A few days ago I sent my ambassador to you to seek your aid. He was returned to me, dead."

Mordun glanced at Treng who was staring out the window, apparently absorbed by the old tree.

Chetek said, "I saw the body, brought to Tia ta pel by Ganu fishermen. I heard their story of the Ganu hunters who told them to dispose of it."

"Who leads these hunters?" Mordun asked.

"Your son Bor," Sivell told him.

"Did you know what your brother does?" Mordun demanded of Treng.

"And if I did, what then?" Treng turned sullenly from the window. "There be many with no love for the Lianis. We've been servants in Tia-ta-pel too long. We should be masters!"

"A brave speech indeed," Mordun said. "And made by a fool! What be this masterhood you speak of, and how should we gain it? Have you forgotten the old saying,

Liani without Ganu be a herth without underpin, but Ganu without Liani be a herth without windows?"

"There's more you should know," Chetek said. "The Liani was killed with a weapon that came from my people."

Mordun rose and stood by the window looking out at the courtyard. His head rested against the window's edge, as though he'd suddenly grown tired of being king, Sivell thought, as her grandmother had once grown tired of being queen-regent.

After a while he said, "That tree was a sapling when I was a youngling. Now it and I be oldlings together."

She was conscious of Treng's tension, coiled tight as a spring. But no one spoke.

"What do you want of me, Queen of the Lianis?"

"Only that you prevent your son from attacking Tia-ta-pel," she said. "Let Ganu and Liani live peacefully together."

"As befits master and servant?"

"No, Majesty. As befits kin."

"I need time to think the matter through," he said. "When I've decided what can be done, I'll send for you. Until then, rest, enjoy whatever my house can offer you."

He left the room, his steps slow and careful as though he carried something heavy.

Then Sivell was aware of the soreness in her muscles from the long ride, the brief hours of sleep, the tension of the days before she'd left home. Her limbs were suddenly so weary she doubted they'd hold her up any longer. By the window was a small stone bench built into an angle of the wall. She sat down.

Treng was taking out his anger on Chetek. "I regret now I didn't let my men kill you this morning! Some of our people warned against the Rhodarus, fearing you'd turn on us. But I trusted you, taking you for honorable men!"

"I haven't betrayed you," Chetek said. "The king had to know. Where the Rhodarus go, war and killing spread like a sickness."

"It be inevitable we fight the Lianis someday." Treng paced the room, fists clenched at his side. "Granted, I be not as great an enemy of the Lianis as my brother. I was raised by a Liani who came to the palace shortly after the death of my mam. For her sake, I don't seek to rid Ilia of the dark race. But we must be free of them, and my father doesn't see that!"

He strode out of the room, slamming the door behind him.

"Why do they hate us?" she asked.

"You're shapeshifters. They aren't."

"It isn't magic. That lamp there—now *that* might be magic! Should I fear that?"

"You don't know what it is, but you know what it isn't," he said. "That makes a difference."

"We've never hurt them by our shifting."

"You've danced," Chetek said, "while they toiled to feed both races."

She stared at him.

A gray-robed Ganu woman stood in the doorway, her straw-colored hair lying in one thick braid down her back. She avoided Sivell's eyes, and led her away from the room without speaking.

The room she showed Sivell into was small with a high window. It contained a low table on which a light snack of bread and cheese had been laid for her, and a dark wine. When the servant left, Sivell threw her coat on the chair and drew off her boots; she stretched her toes in relief. The food was much like the room, plain but wholesome. She set the wine aside.

It was growing dark when she finished. She stood on tiptoe to look out the high window and saw the first moon rising over the black shoulder of the mountains.

The door creaked behind her and she turned.

"Who is it?"

A woman paused in the doorway, holding a lamp. Her rough-spun robe was Ganu, but the hair she wore knotted back on her neck was true Liani black, though touched with silver.

"Who're you?"

"I'm called Gera," the woman said. "I looked in to see if Ilia's queen needed anything."

"You're Liani—though you have a Ganu name. You must be the woman Treng spoke of, who raised him."

The older woman looked Sivell full in the eyes. "Yes."

"Sit down and talk to me," Sivell ordered.

The woman sat on the chair, hands loosely folded in her lap, the smoky Liani skin contrasting oddly with the coarse Ganu cloth. Sivell studied her. She had obviously been quite beautiful in her youth, for even now the lines of her face were still handsome, her bearing calm. There was an indescribable air of sadness about her, as if she'd been singing a sad song and couldn't shake off the mood.

"Tell me, Gera. Do the Ganus treat you well?"

"I've been lucky to gain Mordun's favor, but there've been others who lived well in Goron."

"But why would you leave your own people?"

"Some come because they tire of the pleasures of Tia-ta-pel, finding them empty. Some come to find answers."

"And can answers be found here?"

"Yes!" Fire flashed between them, leaving Sivell shaken by the intensity of the woman's glance. "I've raised the king's son as if he were my own. And any gentleness of heart, any kind thought he has of the Lianis, he owes to me."

"Who knows when the Lianis will be glad to receive kindness at the hands of a Ganu?" Sivell said. "Forgive me. My own problems have overshadowed my manners."

"Youths always challenge the policies of their elders," Gera said. "In Bor's case, I feared that would mean rebelling against Tia-ta-pel. I did what I could to forestall this with his younger brother. But I've failed. Bor's influence with Treng is greater than mine."

"Treng's still here in Goron," Sivell pointed out, "not in the hills with Bor."

"For how long?" Gera asked. "It's written, when Ilia's queen fails, war will come between Ganus and Lianis."

Sivell felt the blood rushing into her cheeks. "You insult your queen!"

"It's not written of you," the older woman said. "It's written of your mother."

"What do you know of this?" Sivell demanded, her heart pounding.

"Nothing," the woman replied, rising. "Nothing at all."

Sivell sprang up and clutched at her wrist. "Stay!"

Her fingers grasped air as the woman shifted, lightning-fast, slippery as a jellyfish in Sivell's hand. Caught off guard, Sivell stumbled to her own shifted shape in an effort to braid her essence to Gera's and so catch her as children did their opponents in Seek. The shiftfield crackled about them, and Sivell's nose tingled with the faint, acrid air that was generated. But Gera was no clumsy child, and try as hard as she might, Sivell could not pin her to a shape.

They struggled together in the doorway, flickering in and out of shiftshape, evading each other, like mist sliding through mist, neither gaining the advantage.

Then Treng strode through the door just as Sivell caught her breath in her own shape.

"What be happening here?" He seized Sivell's arm. "You be not queen in this herth!"

"There's no harm done," Gera said, returning to her own form.

Her arm still in Treng's grip, Sivell turned to Gera. "Who are you? I order you to tell me who you are!"

"Haven't you already guessed?" the woman replied.

"We'll take this matter to my father," Treng said firmly, cutting off further argument. His face was flushed and his eyes sparked angrily.

Gera touched him lightly on the cheek as she passed him in the doorway. He motioned Sivell forward. They went through the palace single file, the woman called Gera leading. Seeing the woman's liquid motion, Sivell felt a flood of memories tumbling at once through her mind.

Mordun was sitting at table when the group entered. Servants were bringing covered platters from which steam rose, and baskets of fruit and bread. At the far side

of the table she saw Chetek staring at them, his mouth
half open as if he'd forgotten to close it.

Mordun looked quickly from Gera to Sivell, then
gestured to the empty places at the table. "Sit down.
The food grows cold!"

Gera took the seat at Mordun's left hand, and Treng sat
at his right. A very old man sat by himself at one end of
the table, his thin hands shaking and twisting in his lap.
He paid no attention to them, lost in his own dreams.
Sivell sat opposite Mordun, next to Chetek. She was
trembling with anticipation, anxious to continue her
confrontation with Gera. But Ganu meals, she learned,
were eaten in silence, and she had to control her
impatience for its duration.

The servants carried food from one to another, always
beginning with Mordun and Treng. One servant stood
constantly beside the very old man, cutting his food into
small pieces and occasionally lifting it to his mouth.
Sivell found it hard not to look at him from time to time,
but eventually since nobody else paid any attention, she
forgot him also. Though most of the dishes contained
meat, the soft pink flesh of the ferenti that the Ganus ate
with relish, there were several platters of vegetables and
fish for the Liani guests at table. Although Sivell was
hungry, her excitement was so great she could hardly
manage more than a bite or two. Gera too spent more
time toying with her knife than eating. Chetek, who ate
meat with the Ganus, seemed unable to take his eyes off
Gera.

At last the plates were empty. A young woman came
and gently led the old man away. Now Treng took the
wine flask and filled his father's goblet. This was the
signal for conversation to begin.

"Something troubles you, Youngling, that you don't
eat?" Mordun asked.

Sivell spoke to the point. "Majesty, who is this woman
by your side?"

"Of what importance be that?" Treng demanded. "She
be a member of our herth."

Gera's hands twisted together on the table, her wine remained untasted.

"Why do you wish to know?" Mordun asked calmly.

Treng rose, pushing his chair back from the table so that it scraped loudly on the floor.

But Gera put her hand on his arm, restraining him. She turned the full brilliance of her jet eyes on Sivell. "I'm Falina, Nola's daughter and your mother."

Treng stood frozen in mid-action. Wide-eyed, Chetek stared from Falina to Sivell and back. Only Mordun appeared unshaken, drinking his wine peacefully.

"Why?" The single syllable was a cry Sivell felt she'd waited all her life to utter.

"Because I'd failed," Falina said quietly.

"Failed?" Sivell questioned. "How could you fail before you ran away? It was the running that fulfilled the prophecy!"

Falina looked to Mordun.

"The time be come for the tale to be told," he said. "I judge the youngling can stand the telling."

"I failed because I'd tried too much. Each queen tries to produce a child who'll be greater than she is. This is the Liani way. But I overstepped the boundaries in my search." Falina stopped and looked away from Sivell. Mordun laid his light hand on her dark one. "The first time, the child was all I could've hoped for, gifted with powers that would've been valuable. But Parvey was male and couldn't inherit the throne. And I knew by then the horror of the truth about our shaping."

Sivell's mind seethed with the remembered pain of her childhood so that she hardly heard the half of what was being said.

"How can I make you understand? I believed Ilia needed a queen with gifts never before seen among the Lianis if she was to save the people from the destiny that threatened us. So I took an unusual mate, with unusual powers, and in due time my daughter was born—"

Then Sivell couldn't hold back. "I know what happened next! You watched my growth as I lay in my cradle, and you saw that I wasn't like other Liani children. You'd been too clever in your choice of mate, and I couldn't shift! You couldn't bear to watch your deformed child grow up, so you left."

Hot tears welled up in her eyes, but she forced them down. She wouldn't cry in front of this woman who hadn't cared enough about her to stay with her.

"What was done was done," Falina said in a low voice. "I couldn't help you. And I couldn't take the mindless pleasures of Tia-ta-pel any longer, knowing what I knew. It seemed better to leave."

Mordun set his goblet down. "You don't have to speak of this if it be too painful."

"It must be told," Falina said. "I owe this much to my daughter. I made a grave mistake in your parentage, Sivell. Great gifts you have from your father, I see their presence already. But they're not gifts the Lianis find valuable just yet."

Sivell's heart contracted into one question. "Who is my father?"

"This pointless interrogation must stop!" Treng said. "I won't allow—"

"Believe me that I sought the good of Ilia—*all* Ilia," Falina said. "Don't you see who the real enemy is?"

"Are you saying that my father is a Ganu?" The shadow of this doubt had never left Sivell completely, even after the Proving. She'd always carried the secret thought that it would one day rise up to mock her.

"Ganu?" Falina turned sharply to her daughter. "Is that what you think? Will you hear the truth about your father?"

"No!" Sivell cried, anguished. "I don't want to know. I've come this far without knowing. Let him continue unknown!"

"By your own words you've survived this legacy," Falina said. "Why do you waste tears now on what's past and over with?"

"What good were those great gifts you spoke of?" Sivell countered. "First I had to pass the Proving, and for that I needed help."

"Help for the Proving?" Falina seemed startled. She

glanced at Mordun, but he shook his head. "I heard nothing of this."

"Askar taught me how to use the limited gift of shifting that you gave me. To Askar I owe the throne, not to my mother or my rare father."

Falina's face became a dark mask of shock.

"Askar's debt be not a comfortable herth to dwell in," Mordun observed presently, setting his goblet down.

"Excuse me," Falina said, rising from the table. She was gone before anyone could say another word.

Treng was the first to break the silence. He was still standing beside Falina's empty chair. "What should be done with this knowledge?"

"What be your advice?" Mordun asked Chetek, who'd sat through the whole discussion like one under an enchantment.

Chetek shook his head. "I've been away from my people too long. No one has the right to play such a role in the affairs of another."

"The past be the past!" Mordun spoke sharply for the first time. "There be more afoot here than petty rivalry between our races. You've lived long enough among the Ganus to have heard truths the Lianis still don't know. I command you to speak your mind."

"Then prevent war between your people," Chetek said. "Send word to your son Bor not to attack. Give Sivell safe passage home to carry the same message to her people. Punish any who break the peace. And lock your doors against the Rhodarus, for they are doers of dreadful deeds!"

"I like the advice," Mordun said, nodding. "Be not too harsh in judging yourself, Rhodaru. Few of us see the future clearly. Or understand the past."

"I've been an exile for twenty years." Chetek played with a knife as he spoke. "Long enough for old hatreds to have cooled, perhaps. I'll go home."

"As soon as it can be arranged, Youngling, you shall return to Tia-ta-pel," Mordun said to Sivell.

She sat with her head in her hands, unable to face any of them for a time. Then she took hold of her turbulent emotions, remembering that no matter what her parentage was, she was a queen.

"Bor controls the hills," Mordun said. "I may not get word to him in time. You'll be safer going by marne. Treng shall accompany you."

"Majesty," Treng said urgently. "Withdraw that command and send me to my brother instead!"

"She be Gera's daughter, after all," Mordun warned. "Remember that!"

Treng left the room abruptly, his footsteps echoing after him.

Mordun gazed at Sivell, the wrinkles around his eyes deepening. "You may yet be more than you think, Youngling. And we all need that!"

Sivell rose, inclining her head briefly to Mordun. She glanced at Chetek, but he was lost in some pain of his own again and didn't look up. She left the room.

CHAPTER THIRTEEN

Mirandil was dancing in a shower of rain when Tagak found her. Her hair floated green and shimmering like a waterfall about her shoulders, and her eyes, the color of emeralds, matched. Though water fell all about her dancing form, her long white gown did not get wet. For a moment, Tagak watched green birds darting in and out of the rain. The valley in which Mirandil danced echoed with the thousand-year-old music of violin and harpsichord.

Tagak waited for the dance to be ended.

Mirandil clapped her hands. The music stopped, the long-dead harpsichordist caught in the middle of executing an ornament. Birds and rain vanished, and the sun stood at its high point in a cloudless sky.

Mirandil sighed with pleasure. *After all these centuries, I still love Vivaldi! But I know you don't. Would you prefer to hear my newest reformulation of the Pachelbel Canon instead?*

Tagak shook her head.

What a work of genius the Canon was! As simple as DNA, and just as complex in its potential for variation. I often think, if I had only that little piece, I could recreate all of musical history.

"We need to consider the effects of Askar taking his second move," Tagak told her.

Mirandil put her hands over her ears at the sound of Tagak's words. *Why do you insist on this—this grossness?*

"Because I think we need to remember from time to

time," Tagak replied. "And our toys seem to get in the way."

Toys?

"Microchips—those little golden splinters in our frontal lobes that help us escape the limitations of the flesh."

Mirandil picked up a gossamer fine white shawl that lay on the grass and wrapped it around her shoulders. *Let's look together at what Askar does.*

She walked lightly across the grass until she reached a small pool. She bent down to the water and touched its surface with the tips of the little fingers of her left and right hands, stirring it in circles till ripples spread over it.

They studied the holograms that formed in the pool.

Then Mirandil looked up at Tagak. *All's well. Askar may not need his third move.*

Tagak was not comforted. "He's going to destroy them! Look again. Look at the future."

She drew the mirror of quantum possibilities from her pocket and held it out to Mirandil.

Mirandil looked. *If it were my choice—*

"But it isn't," Tagak said, taking back the mirror. "And Askar misjudges."

Tears sprang in Mirandil's eyes. *I have a memory of a time when we first were, and of a purpose that was set in us.*

"We all have that memory, certainly. But some of us choose to act as if the myths we implanted in our creations were real."

It's all a dance of the Father-Shaper, don't you see? A masque for a midsummer's entertainment, as it were.

"That's what I mean. *We* are the shapers!" Tagak said. Was it imagination, or was Mirandil's thinking becoming more muddled as the centuries progressed? They'd worried at first that the cells of the brain wouldn't replace themselves as they wore out, and that mental deterioration would slowly become evident. Was this an ominous sign? But then, she told herself, Mirandil had always been the most giddily romantic of them.

And even if we are, haven't we followed the path set for us by—by—

"Go ahead and say the name," Tagak invited her. "Edward Venn was a scientist, not a god."

Then what does it matter? If you're right, and these are our creations, why shouldn't we do as we wish with them, as Askar does?

"Because they're human," Tagak said, surprised at this unexpectedly shrewd comment. "We made them from the human pattern."

It isn't forbidden to change the pattern!

"We didn't think so once," Tagak agreed. "But we were angry then, anxious to avenge our own pain. Did we think clearly what burden the changes would impose on us?"

Mirandil looked at her blankly, the jewel-green eyes empty of understanding again.

Tagak sighed. "No, we hypothesized only in terms of 'subjects' and 'variables,' 'control groups' and 'predicted results,' forgetting that the experimenter becomes part of the experiment by the inexorable laws of the universe. Do try to remember, Mirandil!"

But they're beautiful, sister! Especially the ones I watch.

"The metamorphs, yes. Perhaps the most spectacularly successful part of the whole experiment! Ed would've been proud of us," Tagak said bitterly. "Ed died—so long ago, even I can hardly remember—to protect our right as humans to pursue knowledge. For what? So that we might treat other humans as if they were something growing in a petri dish?"

Were we so wrong then, Tagak?

"A century ago I would've answered: no, not where it concerned mine. I worked with changes that were beneficial rather than arbitrary. Practicality, not whimsy, guided my scalpel! But these others—how can we justify what we did to them?"

Mirandil leaned over the little blue pool again. Now it contained the images of a man and a woman riding on a great horned beast. Her tears fell into the water and the hologram wavered.

"Even God has certain responsibilities," Tagak said.

It won't work!

They both looked up to see Askar standing behind them, arms crossed over a bare chest. He had shaded his skin down to a dark, creamy amber; his irises were golden as a karami's.

"Shall the doer be touched by his doing?" Tagak wondered.

To act is to become entangled in the fruits of action, Askar replied. *To do is to accept the burden of that doing, for joy or pain. I won't be free again of this action. Like the bird that plucks its own feathers to line a nest for its babes, I shall not fly as high again.*

"What a mass of contradictions you are!" Tagak exclaimed. "One moment ruthlessly twisting lives, the next wailing at misery you yourself caused."

His thought came sharply. *I thought that was an idea we disposed of centuries ago, that humans were consistent or that their thinking made sense! You wouldn't expect that of a god.*

"Is that how you've come to think of yourself, John?"

Only the Father-Shaper remains free of the shaping, Mirandil interrupted. *For only the Shaper can act without will. That's why we're the watchers.*

"For once, Miranda Illing," Tagak cried impatiently, "face the truth about yourself—ourselves! We—not some saintly Edward Venn we misremember—*we* are responsible for the pain these people feel."

Askar looked at her for a moment, his expression grim. Then golden wings unfolded from his shoulders, emitting the slight hum of well-tuned machines. "No, Tagak," he said, choosing to bypass the link. "I don't deny our responsibility. But whatever we've developed into over the past five centuries, we're human still. And humans must always test the limits of their powers. If you'd grant freedom of action to them, how can you deny it to me?"

"They don't live long enough to suffer unduly from their actions. You, on the other hand, have all eternity!"

"In the endless cycles of the universe, everything works its way out," he commented cryptically. "Let it be the way of my choice. Watch and see."

When Askar was gone, Tagak and Mirandil leaned over the blue patch on the green grass.

The ones we used to measure by, the ones we didn't alter, Mirandil began, and then stopped.

"What about the control group, Miranda?"

They mustn't be allowed to harm my dancing ones! But I see there's a certain nobility about them, too.

"They can suffer," Tagak agreed. "Like us, they're human, too."

Oh, Tagak! What have we done?

Tagak squeezed Miranda's hand and they gazed at the hologram.

The sun-warmed scent of herbs arose where their hands crushed tiny leaves in the grass. From the hills, Vivaldi's trumpets cascaded down to them again. The images blurred and changed, and another day passed in Ilia.

CHAPTER FOURTEEN

The hours of waiting passed slowly. Allowed to roam Mordun's palace freely, Sivell found little to occupy her attention for long; favored colors were the muted earth tones of brown and tan, patterns seemed restricted to simple geometric designs. Nowhere could she see the riot of unfettered imagination that she was used to in her own city. These people were dull and grim!

Were they her people, too? She couldn't bring herself to accept the thought. It wasn't possible that any part of her could be Ganu.

Sometimes, though, she heard faintly and far away down some corridor a scrap of melody, as if a door had opened on a room where someone played, then shut again. There were secrets here, of that she was certain.

On the following day, she found one room in the palace that offered some hope. In the wing that housed Mordun's own quarters, Sivell found a large, bright room with a floor of polished slabs of black marble like mirrors in which she could see her own feet. The walls between high, narrow windows were lined with bookshelves. She'd never seen so many books. Nor were they the kind in the small book room in her own castle. The books collected by the Liani queens had been full of old tales, songs, and poems to fill a winter's evening. The Ganu books, by contrast, covered more serious subjects. Opening one at random, she found detailed observations on the lives of various animals, and drawings of the beasts with all their parts carefully labeled. The next contained maps of the sky, with names given to each star and star group. She stopped at a drawing of the sky as she saw it from her window in the east tower. The Ganus named the green star that she saw each night, "The Awakener." There were books on planting and harvesting, others on medicinal herbs. There was more information in this room than in the entire city of Tia-ta-pel.

Gold lettering embossed on a red leather cover caught her eye: *The Origin of the Various Races on Ilia*. She turned its densely printed pages curiously, frowning at the graphs and diagrams. Again she had the strong sense of hidden knowledge. The book was full of words she'd never seen before and she couldn't make much sense of it.

"That be a good subject for a queen to study," a voice said behind her.

She turned to find Mordun standing in the doorway, blue eyes bright in his wrinkled face.

"I hope you don't mind, Majesty . . . ?"

Mordun shook his head. "Read what you will."

"This seems important," she began hesitantly, reluctant to admit she couldn't understand very much of what it was about.

"It be *very* important," Mordun said, coming to stand beside her as she held the book. "And it pleases me the queen of the Lianis be interested."

Sivell decided on the truth. "It's very difficult for me to understand. There are so many new words here."

Mordun smiled. "Honesty be a great virtue in a monarch! The words be new to your understanding, but the subject be old as the Venn. Have you thought much about the Venn, Youngling?"

"Only what we all think, that the wizards are descended from the Venn, the Great Shaper's firstborn, who were companions to Kirili when she left the Garden. Do you mean this, Majesty?"

"This be what they want us to believe. The truth about our shaping be more ugly."

Shocked, she wanted to argue. "How can you say this? Surely, the Great Shaper who made us both—"

Then she remembered that the Ganus didn't seem to believe in the Great Shaper and she didn't know what they believed in, if it was anything. She said softly, "A Liani can't accept that our shaping was ugly when she offers witness to its beauty each time she shiftdances."

"Aye—and considers herself shaped in the image of that Shaper, be I not correct? And, further, whispers that the Ganus who be condemned to spend their lives always in the same shape be abominations, because they be not like this marvelous spirit—be that not so?"

Too late, she realized how she'd inadvertently insulted him. "Majesty . . ."

But rather than being angry at her, Mordun touched her gently on the arm. "I take no offense, for you meant none. But there be a truth here about the shaping of Liani and Ganu the tween, and it be not a tale to tell younglings."

"What do you mean?"

"I judge you be not yet ready to hear it. The wound you've suffered in your heart be not yet healed, and pain prevents clear thinking."

"Won't you explain *anything*?" she cried. "You hint that there is something not right about our love for the Great Shaper—surely you must go on? You can't leave the matter there!"

"Even the way you *think* about these things be shaped. It be hard for you and your race to come to truth through the very words you've been given to use!"

"I don't understand."

"Aye, it be difficult." He looked away for a moment, letting his gaze roam over the bookshelves as if he were searching for one that might make the difficult easier for her and not finding it. "But you must try, Youngling. You must come to this yourself. The answer to many puzzles be here."

"Won't you at least help me to solve this puzzle you say is so important?" she cried in frustration.

"Look beyond the tales you've been told," he advised. "Try not to think the way they taught you."

He took the book from her hands and set it back on the shelf.

Though she was unsure exactly what he meant about

the way to think, Sivell felt the weight of his words.
There were enigmas here, but he seemed to be saying
the key was not to be found within a library, but within
herself. She decided to try out his advice immediately.

"Why—since you gain so little from it—do the Ganus
bother with the Lianis at all? I see that without you we'd
be hard put to grow our food and build our castles! It
would seem you'd be happier without us."

"Good!" Mordun said heartily. "You be seeing clearly
for once. But happiness be not the only goal humans
should strive for."

"Then why?"

"Because the tween of our races have been wronged."

"But—"

"You saw the oldling at my table?"

She nodded, remembering how the servant had
gently wiped the drool off the old man's chin and lifted
his hand out of his soup bowl.

"A distant cousin, senile now. It would be a light thing
to send him away, put him out of mind. It be not easy to
enjoy the feast when he be present!" Mordun chuckled.
Then his expression changed. "But he be there to
prevent me forgetting a great truth: we have only each
other."

"It seems a very great kindness—" she began.

But he shook his head, dismissing this. "If you could
stay longer, I'd show you more of the way we live. We be
not so dull as you fear."

"Oh, but—"

"Aye!" Mordun smiled at her. "That be a common
Liani belief! Someday, Queen of the Lianis, perhaps we
shall sit down together as royal folk do, and listen to the
tale tellers. We be not much for painting and dancing,
but we appreciate a tale well told. And there be no lack
of tales, both dark and light, in Ilia."

Sivell went back to the room they'd given her, and lay
on the bed, staring up at the plain ceiling, thinking over
Mordun's words. Later, a serving girl brought a cold

supper, which Sivell couldn't finish. Still later, a message arrived from Mordun. She would leave at dawn.

The Ganu palace was full of strange sounds at night. Footsteps echoed; low voices conversed in monosyllables; machinery hummed far below in the cellars, powered by the river that flowed beneath Goron. She understood that the Ganus could do many marvelous things by some power that wasn't magic, but thinking about it didn't help her understand *how*. Instead of finding answers in this plain palace, she was finding ever more puzzles. There was some mystery here, she felt sure. What if it had to do with the mystery of the knowledge Parvey had gained from his unknown father—the knowledge that had made him so uneasy?

Questions, questions, questions, and no solutions. The strangeness of it all wouldn't allow her to sleep. She would be glad to leave this place!

Hour after hour she lay in the darkness, turning over the events of the day, sorting, arranging, patterning them until she could have cried in weariness, but still sleep didn't come. So many years to have gone without a mother, only to have found her in the palace of the Ganu king. So much doubt and secret fear over a father, only to learn her grandmother had been right.

But was that the truth, that her mother had mated with a Ganu? What else could it mean that Mordun was sheltering her mother?

A new thought occurred to her. Mordun himself might be her father.

Somehow, she doubted this although she couldn't say why. And in any case, would it make a difference whether the unknown Ganu father was royal or peasant?

Self-pity wouldn't do. She'd come to Goron to prevent a war, and that was still the only thing that was important. What did parentage matter, next to the horror of kin shedding the blood of kin—and they must be kin, all children of the Great Shaper, even if the Ganus chose not to recognize this. Even Chetek had understood. She thought of Mordun's words to his son: Ganu without Liani was a house without windows. The

Ganus lacked the things of the spirit that made up the very fabric of Liani life.

Yet that wasn't true. She remembered the old relative at the supper table, and Mordun's tenderness toward her mother, and Treng's concern for the woman he thought of as his nurse. What could the Ganus become, given the shiftvisions of the Lianis?

The other half of Mordun's words was harder to accept. Could the Liani house need a foundation? Sool had often spoken to her of his dreams of something greater than either Ganu or Liani. She tried to imagine what this could be. It was difficult to know the best course to take for the future—a future which looked increasingly grim. Falina had tried twice and been wrong.

And then there was the question of why the Great Shaper had shown such kindness to the Lianis, and at the same time denied its gifts to the Ganus. How could so potent and benevolent a spirit have made such an unfair decision? The Ganus had been disinherited by their Shaper. For them, the Great Shaper must seem little better than the Rhodarus' stern He-Who-Rules.

When Sivell judged several hours of the night had passed, she abandoned the attempt to sleep and sat up. In the darkness she reached for the fur jacket and slipped it on. Restless, but with no plan of what to do, she decided to walk for a while. She found the door and slid her hand along the edge to locate the latch. As she did so, she heard footsteps approaching the other side. She stopped, hand still raised against the latch, and felt it moving.

Someone was entering her room.

She pressed herself back against the wall behind the door as it cracked open. A shaft of yellow light cut across the bed on which she'd recently been lying, revealing the quilt mounded in the center as if it still covered the bed's occupant. The crack widened. A man entered. She could see only his back, but he wore the leather tunic of a hunter, with a sheath at his belt for a knife.

In the instant that she realized the sheath was empty,

she saw the glint of metal in his hand. Her blood turned to ice and her feet took root in the darkness behind the door. The man was bending over the bed, one hand reaching to pull back the quilt, the other holding the knife. Sivell's heart had lodged itself in her throat, and she could neither breathe nor cry out.

From outside came the sound of voices. The man spun on his heel and lunged toward the door. The knife flashed not an arm's length from her neck as he passed her. She had a fleeting impression of a round, fat face. Then he was gone, running heavily down the corridor as the voices approached.

One of the approaching figures shouted, and Sivell, still pressed behind the door, heard footsteps in pursuit. Two more figures crowded into her room. Someone reached for the lamp, flooding the room with light.

"Sivell?" Chetek said. "We thought we saw you running down the corridor. But—then who—?"

"Hathor," she replied quickly. "The man who took us in the cabin. He was going to kill me! But you disturbed him."

The Ganu with Chetek scowled at her. "No one would attack you here in the king's herth!"

"Nevertheless," she pointed out, "Hathor had a knife!"

The third man who'd run in pursuit returned alone now and shrugged at the group. "Nothing."

"It's time to leave," Chetek said. "But we'll see that Mordun hears about this."

She fastened the jacket and pulled on the Ganu boots. When they left the room, the Ganus walked on ahead, speaking in low voices. She knew they didn't believe her story. They'd be glad to have the Liani queen out of their king's palace; the air was heavy with their distrust. Well, that was all right—she'd be glad to leave, too.

The way led down a corridor she hadn't explored in her wanderings, past several closed doors. They descended a short flight of stairs—the sound of machinery growing in her ears like the growl of a mighty torrent—and came to a door. One of the men fitted a key into the

lock, and the door swung open, revealing another flight
of stairs descending again in semidarkness. The Ganu
motioned for Chetek and Sivell to go through.

"We're taking the direct route to the coast," Chetek
said. "There's a boat waiting on the underground river
that'll take us to Goronway Port. We'll transfer you there
to a fishing boat to go down the coast to Tia-ta-pel."

"And you?"

"Treng spoke of other Rhodarus in Goronway. I'll find
them."

They went on down into the gloom as the door swung
shut behind them, the clang echoing from the damp
walls. Small hanging lamps cast pools of yellow at each
turn of the stairs.

"I'll be sorry to part company with you," she said.

"You'll be safer with Treng than with me."

"He's not a friend to me."

"Maybe not. But he won't defy his father's command to
see you safely to Tia-ta-pel."

Dampness rose up the steps to meet them, carrying
with it the smell of the river flowing in the dark under
Goron. The last turn of the stairs revealed a low archway
of slick stone, lit by the swinging lanterns, and beyond it
a stretch of black water. There was a narrow ledge
between the foot of the steps and the water where a
small boat bobbed on the current. Two men tended it,
one on the ledge holding fast to a line tied to the bow,
and one bending over in the boat, making ready. A third
figure, cloaked and hooded, waited to one side on the
ledge.

At the sound of their feet, the hooded figure turned
toward them. The yellow light fell obliquely across the
dark face of Falina.

Sivell felt her heart miss a beat and her muscles
tighten. She hadn't thought she'd have to see her mother
again.

"Chetek," she whispered, not wanting to have to
speak to Falina.

But the Rhodaru had quickened his pace and was
already striding across the narrow ledge, leaving her to

fend for herself. He bounded into the boat, rocking it perilously so that water slapped up against the ledge. The lamp suspended from the boat's mast swung to and fro, making the shadows leap and jump. The startled Ganu looked up from his task and muttered at the Rhodaru.

Pulling her jacket close to her, Sivell prepared to pass Falina without speaking. But the older Liani put out her hand, detaining her daughter.

"There are some things you don't know."

"Enough was said last night, Madam," Sivell said, her voice tight.

Falina spoke with simple dignity. "I won't speak of *your* father since you choose not to hear. That's your own choice. But in the matter of Parvey's father you will listen, for it concerns the throne itself."

Sivell felt a ripple of fear pass over her. "I'll listen."

"Ilia is in danger. The time when Ilia's queens could pass the time feasting and dancing, never thinking about anything more serious than what new gown to wear, is over! No longer can we value our queens for shiftskill alone. We need a new kind of queen in Tia-ta-pel, a queen with unusual gifts," Falina said. "At the time, I believed I'd chosen the father well. I believed that the next queen of the Lianis would be without a match anywhere in shiftskill. And by your own admission, Parvey is so skilled he can make up for another's lack! Unfortunately, he is also male. But have you never wondered why Parvey had skill enough for two?"

The question took Sivell off guard. She'd been so glad of Parvey's presence that she'd never thought to ask. "What father could be powerful enough to give a child such a gift?" She wanted to go on trusting Parvey, not wanting to have to fear him. But she had to know the truth. "Who is Parvey's father?"

And as she said this, she knew. "Askar!"

Falina lowered her eyes.

So many things became clear, so many small, insignificant things that had bothered her about Parvey, especially since his return to Tia-ta-pel. How much of his father's wizard power had he inherited? The thought made her stomach lurch and her knees turned weak with a fear she couldn't explain.

"If Parvey had been female, the throne of Ilia would've been safe against all who tried to harm it."

"But a *wizard!*" Sivell said.

Her mother took her gaze steadily, without replying.

For generations, the queens had selected their mates for nothing more serious than beauty and shiftskill so that the luck of Tia-ta-pel would continue. Life in Tia-ta-pel was a game, a long dance. No one had ever troubled themselves about the future. No one had ever had to! No one had faced the threat from the north before. No one, that was, until Falina. She looked at this woman who'd planned so far ahead for her people, who'd dared so much for Ilia.

"One thing, Lady Mother . . ."

"Ask."

"Why did you leave?" She hadn't meant for it to come out like a cry of pain. A queen ought not to care.

"Because I was afraid to face what I'd done," Falina said in a low voice. "And every day that passed showed me the danger growing in Parvey—I had only thought to provide Ilia with a superior queen. Too late I learned something else came with my bargain!"

Sivell stared at her mother for a while, absorbing this. Falina's leaving had not been a desertion of her daughter, but of her son. After a while she said, "Thank you for this knowledge."

Falina's eyes misted in the lamplight, and she touched her daughter's face briefly. "Arm yourself with it, for the sake of our people. But try not to use it against Parvey."

Again, a cold wave of fear passed through her.

"There's more you should know about the beings we call wizards—" Falina began.

"Sivell," Chetek called to her from the boat. "The tide!"

Sivell glanced down the steps. "I should go—"

"Someday, Sivell, you must learn this!"

Not until much later, when the boat was gliding

without sails on the swift current of the dark waterway, did it occur to her that if her mother had taken such an unprecedented chance for the sake of the throne once, she might well have chosen so uniquely again. No wizard had been her own father, of that she had ample proof in her clumsiness at shifting. Perhaps he had been Ganu, but if so, there'd been good enough reason and she'd learn why someday.

The outgoing tide hastened the little boat toward daylight and the open sea. Chetek was seated in the stern, his hand resting on the tiller, exchanging words with the seaman who accompanied them. From time to time she felt his glance on her as she sat in the bow, staring forward toward where the light should appear.

"I'm anxious to see Tia-ta-pel again," she told him. "I didn't think being away so brief a time would make me long for my home, but it has."

"You never get over that longing for home, no matter how many years you're away."

"It must be worse for you," she said, remembering his long exile that put her brief absence to shame.

He didn't answer, but turned back to the Ganu seaman. "Is the tide always this strong on the ebb?"

"Aye. That be because we dam it on the flow," the man said. "On its downward rush to the marne it turns the wheels that give power to the metros. A pretty trick, be it not?"

"A pretty trick," Chetek concurred. "I sense that much in Goron comes from the application of such tricks."

The seaman chuckled. "Aye. And with every one we challenge the Venn on their own ground!"

Now she saw a pinpoint of light ahead, and as she watched it grew steadily bigger and brighter. Soon she could see it was the end of the tunnel. She could smell salt and sea ferns in the cold wind that rushed to meet them. The boat gathered speed now that its destination was near. The water roared and the boat began to jostle and bounce uncomfortably, as the river current fought its way into the stronger currents of the open ocean. Spray splashed over the bow, misting her hair and making her eyes sting. She grasped the side of the boat and looked ahead.

"Hold fast," the seaman advised. "The bay be treacherous here—even at low tide."

"And impossible at high tide?" Chetek queried.

The man nodded. "See the dark markings on the rock walls there? More than the height of a tall Rhodaru above the low-water level, they be! That be the difference in the marne at high tide and low—the monster we've reined to our purposes."

Though she didn't understand much of what was being said, Sivell knew a strange exhilaration at the man's words. It was as if he spoke of a different kind of magic, one that came from the human mind, a neutral magic whose secrets were open to any who looked for them, a magic that could be understood if she were willing to try hard enough. And it held out a promise for the future.

"There be the harbor," the seaman said, pointing to the right.

A cluster of low brown buildings hugged the foot of the cliffs along this unfamiliar coastline. She could see docks and the masts of fishing vessels. They were over the turbulence of the river's mouth now, and the sailor turned the bow to let the sail catch the wind. Canvas flapped in confusion for a moment, then filled and began to pull toward the harbor. It was calmer once the wind had control of the boat.

"And there be the *Marne-Queller*," the man said. "She'll be taking you down the coast."

Sivell shaded her eyes against the glare. A fishing boat rocked gently at anchor, tiny against the vastness of gray sea and gray sky.

CHAPTER FIFTEEN

The small boat bumped against the lee side of the *Marne-Queller*, rising and falling against it while the seaman attempted to throw a rope to the bigger boat. Several hands helped make the rope fast. Sivell looked up at a group of fishermen in woolen hoods, peering down at her from the gunwale. Someone held a hand out to her, indicating she should climb aboard swiftly.

"We part company here," Chetek said. "The *Marne-Queller* will sail as soon as you're aboard."

"Will I see you again?" It seemed she'd known this Rhodaru all her life, for the few days they'd shared had been so crowded with danger and new experiences.

"Perhaps."

A red-faced man leaned down to the small boat. "Hey! Be you ready to board or do we miss the tide?"

There were so many things she should say to him—she was oddly reluctant to leave without Chetek. But the words didn't come.

"Let it please the Great Shaper to look favorably on your journey home, Chetek," she said finally.

"On yours also," he said, looking at her intently. In this subdued marine light his eyes were a cloudy amber, his expression sad. "May we both find what we hope to find."

For a moment, she thought he too wanted to say something else. But he closed his mouth and kept his thoughts to himself.

With Chetek and the seaman pushing and the red-faced Ganu seizing her wrists and pulling, Sivell climbed aboard the *Marne-Queller*. As soon as she was safe, the small boat cast loose. She watched while the seaman used an oar to shove himself away from the shelter of the fishing vessel. The little boat's sail caught the wind and it began to speed over the waves to the harbor mouth, the figures in it getting smaller and smaller. Chetek waved to her once.

Now she was totally alone with Ganus for the first time in her life, surrounded by colorless faces and pale hair. She drew her jacket closer around her.

Treng came out on the deck, draped in a cape of some slick gray material that covered him from neck to mid-calf. "Get below into the cabin. You be not attired for wet weather. This be no Liani picnic cruise we undertake today. The marne be running high and the squaller threatens to blow."

He disliked her almost as much as she disliked him, she thought. "I don't mind a little spray. I'll not spend the journey below!"

"Please yourself. But at least fetch a cape."

This sounded like good advice, so she made her way to the cabin's entrance between the two masts, carefully stepping over the sill and down the three shallow steps. Against one side she saw an open hamper full of dark garments. She made a face at the selection of colors they presented: black, gray, and dark brown. What perverseness possessed the Ganus to prefer such drabness when there were so many brighter dyes to use?

As she bent over the hamper, she heard a rumbling, and the sound of metal grating on metal. Vibrations spread up from the wood beneath her feet to set her teeth chattering. She pulled out a cape and managed to get it around her shoulders, stumbling as the boat lurched under her feet. There was a muffled thud, then silence. The *Marne-Queller* seemed to be turning slowly. She could hear the dull sound of ropes running over pulleys, and the squeak of canvas. One side of the cabin began to rise and the other dipped, and then she saw waves running past the round window on the lower side. She felt urgent movement forward; they were under way.

It was more difficult to make her way back on deck than it had been to enter the cabin while the boat rode at anchor. She managed well enough until she was almost to where Treng indicated she should sit. At that point she lost her balance and fell against him. She heard the laughter of the fishermen. Heat flooded her cheeks. Looking up, she saw not anger but contempt in Treng's eyes. With as much dignity as she could manage, she removed herself from his lap and looked at the horizon.

After a while, still looking at the line where the leaden sea met the iron sky, she spoke. "Last night, in your father's palace, someone tried to kill me."

He gave no sign of being surprised. "There be many Ganus who have no love for the Lianis."

"One of *your* men."

"How do you know?"

"His name is Hathor."

"Hathor be Bor's pledgeman. He joined my party only to accompany us to Goron. I be not responsible for my brother's pledgemen." Treng turned away to speak to the helmsman.

Fuming, she realized there was nothing she could do about it right now.

She gazed over the gray water. Already she was farther out than she'd ever been. Even in summer the Lianis rarely ventured far on open water. The Ganus, however, ranged over the sea, summer and winter, in search of fish. Yet even they were reluctant to sail this coast in winter because of the treacherous passage past the jagged outcropping of rocks that made up Kri's Necklace.

They'd already left the little harbor of Goronway far behind. The red-faced man was at the helm of the *Marne-Queller*, and it appeared that he was following a course not parallel to the coast, but headed out toward the horizon. She watched as the hills at the sea's edge sank down, and the trees that covered their sides vanished from her view. Soon the coastline was only a blur between sea and sky.

"Have something to eat." Treng held out one of the

small loaves of sour bread the Ganus were fond of. "It'll help later when you be sick to have something to lose."

At that the fishermen laughed again.

She controlled her anger. Did he have to be so deliberately objectionable? "Thank you. No."

"Hunger doesn't help. It only makes the stomach hurt more later," he said, his tone gentler this time. "And even these men, used to the marne and its ways, be not too proud to try to avoid the marne's sickness if they can."

She took the bread without looking at him and picked at it. It was crusty and fresh, and soon hunger took over. She finished it, and didn't refuse a second when he offered it. Nor did she turn away from the cold corli eggs a fisherman offered. Then Treng held out a flask. At first she shook her head, for she saw that in the absence of goblets, her lips would have to touch the rim where his had been. But the wind was icy, and the spray that came flying over the bow from time to time was green and cold as tears, and a sip of wine would be a welcome warmth.

She took it and sipped, trying not to think who'd used it before her. Fire burned its way down her throat. Red-eyed, coughing, she turned to Treng and found him nodding, amused.

"Fishermen drink a heartier brew than dancers," he said.

The waves were higher now, and the *Marne-Queller* began to pitch and toss, working her way up the face of a wave only to plunge headlong down the other side, spray flying. Even with the cape around her, Sivell felt wet and utterly cold. She gripped the side of the boat and stared at the coast, appearing and disappearing as huge waves rolled past. The men shouted at each other, and there was a great deal of changing of the angles of the sails. Treng spoke to the man at the helm, and no one paid any attention to her.

She was watching the rise and fall of the walls of water going past, the appearance and disappearance of the coast, when she noted a vague uneasiness, a slight sourness at the pit of her stomach as if the bread didn't sit well with her. She took another sip from Treng's flask, glad of its warmth. This time her throat seemed to hesitate as she swallowed. She fixed her gaze on the sails standing out stiffly from the masts.

"We'll soon be within sight of the Necklace," Treng said.

She had difficulty hearing him, as if the spray had blown into her ears too, plugging them.

"When we pass the rocks it'd be wiser for you to stay below. There've been others, like yourself unused to sailing, who've been swept overboard at that point. Old Kri still adds to his necklace!"

"I'd rather stay up here."

"You may regret that!" he said. But he turned back and resumed his conversation with the helmsman.

The *Marne-Queller* was having difficulty making headway now. Her timbers shuddered and groaned as she fought her way through the sea that grew increasingly surly with each minute. The fisherman's wine flamed in Sivell's cheeks, and she held on to the side of the boat with fingers that seemed to belong to another for all she could feel them connected to her arm. Then the *Marne-Queller* began to climb the vertical wall of another wave. In the cabin, the hamper took a notion to change sides, and it slid across the floor, coming to rest by the cabin's door. On the table, a collection of knives and plates did likewise, not stopping at the table's edge but tumbling over each other in their eagerness to join the hamper on the floor. Sivell stared at them, unable to think clearly enough to understand what had happened.

At that point the *Marne-Queller* reached the crest of the wave, paused briefly to gather her strength, then plunged down the other side as if she were determined to carry her crew straight to the bottom. She hit the trough of the wave with a wrenching thud that jarred every bone in Sivell's body. Then she seemed to stop dead before traveling on.

In that uncanny pause, the *Marne-Queller* shuddered like a living thing. Sivell leaned as far as she could over the side of the boat and gave the sour bread and the corli eggs and the fishermen's wine to the sea.

When it seemed that there was no more to be rid of—anything else would have to be her stomach itself—the spasms ceased. She leaned weakly against the side, feeling nothing, drifting in a twilight world between waking and sleeping. After a while she was aware of the pressure of a hand on her shoulder.

"Here," Treng said. She turned her head listlessly and saw that he held out another small flask. "Sip this. It'll calm your stomach and soothe your head."

She wanted to shake her head but the effort was too great. Instead she reached for the flask with unsteady hands, and he guided her so that it reached her lips. This liquid was unlike the other, cool instead of fiery, and slightly bitter, distilled from unknown tree roots that grew in unknown forests.

"Now you feel better," he said, smiling.

"If you knew that would happen," she said after a few minutes of savoring her calmed stomach and the head which had returned to normal size, "why did you offer me food earlier?"

"Because it had to happen at some time," he replied, corking the little flask and setting it aside. "Better now than when we pass Kri's Necklace. Nobody'll have time to help you then."

What an odd man he was—aggressive and surly one moment, the next, surprisingly thoughtful toward someone he considered his enemy. It was a difficult puzzle. She glanced at him when she knew he was looking away, but found no answer in his proud face.

She turned her attention to the jagged mass of Kri's Necklace directly in their path. At first it seemed their course would take them straight onto the rocks, but later she began to see that the helmsman knew his job. The rocks would be cleared safely. Yet as she saw the margin the helmsman allowed for their passage, she became aware of the strong current that ran counter to their path, pulling them off course, directly toward the Necklace.

The fishing boat began to shudder constantly as she not only fought her way up and down the waves, but also battled a current that would have her slide broadside into the rocks. The wind too had increased, and when the *Marne-Queller* wasn't climbing a wave or plunging down, she rode on one side so that Sivell felt she was standing upright even when she was sitting down with her feet braced to hold her in place. All the while, the wind sang a terrifying song in the sails.

Steadily the Necklace increased in size. She'd never been so close to these rocks, and despite her fear she couldn't help marveling at their majesty. They rose out of the water like defiant giants. At their feet, the sea raged, great pillars of foam rising in tribute to these haggard monarchs whose heads were crowned with wheeling sea birds.

Men's voices shouted into the wind, ordering, commanding, cursing, encouraging the *Marne-Queller* to pass the Necklace and not heed the lure it spread. Sivell closed her eyes against the spray that stung and blinded her. If only there was some way to be done with this nightmare voyage!

She was determined to think of something else, something happier. She thought of summer nights under the twin moons, shiftdancing in the meadow with Parvey's help, together outdoing the best efforts of the most gifted Lianis, even Kela—

And immediately she knew what she'd never thought before: Parvey's ability to take her with him when he shifted was more than the superior ability to be expected of one of royal blood. It was the gift of his wizard father— a Venn.

Think about the Venn, Mordun had counseled. But she couldn't see very far into the puzzle yet.

They were close enough to the Necklace now to see veins of lurid orange running diagonally across the black faces, and the misshapen nests of sea birds clinging to narrow shelves just out of the reach of the sea. It seemed that the *Marne-Queller* couldn't possibly survive the battering of the waves or the current's incessant drive to the rocks.

Sivell had never in her life experienced fear such as

this which seized her, clenching her heart so that its
beating became a pain-filled struggle, clawing at her
lungs so that every breath seemed to draw blood. In her
ears she heard Kri's siren song of death. If the *Marne-
Queller* were only to give in and dash them all on the
rocks, at least it would be over! Why didn't Sivell
unclench her fingers that were gripping the boat and
slide down into the water instantly, instead of waiting for
it to claim her in the end, as it surely would?

But she didn't let go. And the *Marne-Queller* continued her defiant battle.

Suddenly, it was over. As if on some secret command,
the waves reduced their height, the current ceased to
pull, the rocks began to slip away behind. Shouted
curses gave way to laughter, then to a song, the first
she'd ever heard on Ganu lips.

"The worst be over," Treng said, looking down to
where Sivell still clutched the boat's side.

"She's a very great boat to have brought us past the
Necklace without mishap," Sivell said. "I thought I was
destined to be the next jewel around Kri's neck!"

Treng smiled. "Not without cause be she named
Marne-Queller!"

The sun broke through the clouds that had hidden it
all morning; it had passed its zenith and appeared
directly over a low white mark on the coast. Her heart
leaped up at the sight—Tia-ta-pel! She went up into the
bow of the *Marne-Queller* to watch her city grow. Soon
she could make out the spires of the city and the hump
that was the castle. After a while, the east tower itself
became visible above Sorway Cliff, gleaming like polished marble in the sunshine.

Treng joined her, glancing at her cheeks that were wet
but not from spray. "You be glad to be going to your own
herth."

She nodded, unable to speak of it at that moment.

He too was silent for a moment. Then he said,
"Passing Kri's Necklace be a difficult voyage, even in
summer. You did well." He was staring at the coast and

wouldn't meet her eyes. "You surprised me. I hadn't thought a Liani—"

He stopped, leaving the thought unspoken.

Something passed between them in the awkward silence. Different as they were, enemies even, there was the promise of something else.

"Come with me to Tia-ta-pel," she said. "There must be friendship again between our people. Come with me and proclaim it."

"How can there be friendship with a race of witches?"

"But we're *not* witches! We're humans—like you."

"You have the magic of shifting."

"No magic! Just something we do. Like—like you know medicines and maps of stars and—"

"Sivell . . ." he began.

There was an expression in his eyes that she hadn't seen there before, a gentleness. Silence hung between them. She saw things warring in his mind—old suspicions about the shapeshifters jostling the genuine love he held for his nurse, Gera, a Liani, and his knowledge that this was Gera's daughter. Then it was gone. When he continued, it was a lord of the Ganus who spoke.

"Between your people and mine lies a gulf words cannot span. And if my father be right about the Venn—"

He went back to the stern, and spoke only to the helmsman for the rest of the voyage.

They came in sight of the mouth of the harbor that served Tia-ta-pel, cradled sleepily inside the sheltering arm of its sea wall. The wind had dropped, and the *Marne-Queller* drifted slowly toward the deserted quay.

"We won't tie up here," the helmsman told her when she came back. He seemed relieved she was leaving his boat. "We must turn back at once."

As the boat came level with the outermost quay, a fisherman sprang down with a line coiled about his arm. He pulled against her drift, stopping the *Marne-Queller* long enough for Sivell to jump off. Her legs bent under her as she touched ground; her bones seemed to have turned to sea water. The man steadied her. Before she could say any of the things that were in her heart, the fisherman had jumped aboard again and the *Marne-Queller* was already turning away toward open water. She watched as the boat left the quay. It didn't seem possible that they must face the rage of Kri's Necklace again, in darkness this time, yet she knew of no other place they could go.

The last thing she saw was Treng in the stern of the boat, watching her.

When the boat was a small speck far out on the shining water, she turned toward her city. For the first time she noticed there was no one about; the small boats moored at the quayside were untended, and nobody walked on the steps leading up to the city. She looked up at the towers of home, and their windows flashed blankly in the sun. She couldn't have said why, but instinct warned her to be cautious.

Closing her eyes, she allowed the almost motionless air of the winter afternoon to flow about her, through her, until it had dissolved all semblance of human shape. Then she opened the gates to the reservoirs inside herself, the places Askar had taught her to find where the subtler skills waited: the scents that deflected and bewildered the mind of those who looked at her, camouflaging her in their weakened attention, and the power that caught light and slowed the headlong rush of spinning particles, bending their path so that she appeared to be far from where she truly was, hiding her in a cloak of misperception.

She opened her eyes, and almost invisible, the queen of the Lianis returned to her city.

CHAPTER SIXTEEN

Sivell went up the smooth steps from the sea. Once, in happier times, she'd descended these steps to picnics on the water.

The light lay thick and sluggish on the stone, making no shadows. The higher she climbed, the more silence and loneliness pressed in on her. No voices sang in the streets, no bells chimed the passage of the afternoon. Even the birds flew past silently, as if they were reluctant to break the strange mood that had come over the city. At the top of the steps, the winding street that led up to the castle was deserted. The houses presented a row of shuttered windows like eyes closed against her.

What could have happened? She shivered, although the air was warm and still.

Something—a slight stirring of the air that grew into a sound—broke the silence. She heard the heavy tread of feet moving unnaturally in rhythm, marching.

But nobody *marched* anywhere in Tia-ta-pel!

She hesitated. The marching group rounded the corner directly in front of her. Now she knew that Askar's teaching had served a purpose, for she was certain they wouldn't have let her go if they'd seen her. There was something odd about the ten male Lianis, some of whom she'd known since childhood—their faces were immobile and somber, the dark fire of their eyes was smothered. With them was a stranger, gray bearded, with a face neither old nor young. He too stared straight ahead, but where the others moved unseeing as if in their dreaming bodies, he moved with eyes that had never been awake.

Sivell shrank back against the wall. The old people in Tia-ta-pel whispered that a Liani without sight could lose her way among the shiftshapes she made, for without seeing herself or others, how would she know? Sivell was not inclined to believe such superstitious gossip, but nevertheless she held her breath as he passed her, realizing that her shiftshape would not disguise her from one who used other senses than sight to know. Slowly his face turned in her direction, the blank eyes moved over the place where she stood. She strained every last bit of skill Askar had taught her, letting go, losing whatever remained of Sivell. She hadn't faced such a test since her Proving, but the blind stranger mustn't sense her presence.

After a few seconds' hesitation, he turned away and quickened his pace to catch up with the marching men. Sivell let her breath out in relief.

They were headed for the castle. She allowed them to get well ahead of her, then followed. At the gate, the group paused and the blind man went on ahead. As he did so, a sentry stepped out. The two conferred, then the sentry stepped aside, letting the group enter.

Never before, in all the long years of Ilia's history, had a sentry guarded the entrance to the castle. There'd never been a need. Sivell's stomach tightened painfully.

The men filed past the sentry and she followed.

Entering the castle after her stay in the Ganu palace, she saw as if for the first time the familiar sights of home: carved wood beams and banisters, window glass like translucent flamestones in the great hall, rainbow-bright rugs on polished floors. Somewhere in an upper room an aril sounded, and a high voice sang. It was the same as it had always been—yet it was not the same. She read the difference in the solemn eyes of passing serving girls, heard it in the sadness of the melody the unknown musician was playing, felt it in the chill of the empty hearth. Something terrible had happened in the very short time she'd been gone—but what?

The marchers halted in the great hall where Sool's body had lain on the fisherman's litter. Some sat and

some leaned against the wall, but none spoke or looked
anywhere but immediately ahead. The sightless one left
them there and took the corridor that led to the throne
room. Sivell followed. It was dark, but she needed no
more light than he, for she knew every inch of the way.
When he entered, he left the door ajar and she slipped
in behind him.

She was dazzled by the light in the throne room. Ganu
lamps were bright, but she'd never seen a Ganu lamp
that could fill a room with brilliance such as this. The
light pulsated out from the jade throne, and when her
eyes adjusted to it, she saw that a figure sat on the
throne, back turned to the door. She watched the figure
bend forward, and immediately the light sprang to the
area of the room toward which the figure's hand was
directed. It began to change color, throbbing from white
through shades of blue to indigo. That corner of the
room was bathed in an eerie glow.

The blind man made a small sound, and the figure on
the throne turned to face him.

Sivell jumped as if she'd been struck.

"You're late!" Kela said, closing her hand and extin-
guishing the light she'd been playing with.

For one fearful instant, Sivell thought she'd been
discovered.

But the blind man nodded. "Yes, Madam."

"Well? What did you find?"

"The Lianis are ready," he said. "Now we must wait for
the prince."

"Was there no sign of my cousin Sivell?" Kela was
splendidly dressed with jewels at her throat and on her
fingers; her golden bird shiftemblem crowned her piled
black hair. She looked like a queen, Sivell thought.

He hesitated before answering. "No."

"Remember, I rely on you because you don't rely on
eyes," Kela said. "This is why I summoned you here
from the Bay. Sivell may be poorly skilled, but she's
royal, after all. And I think you understand that you
mustn't tell Parvey."

"No indeed, Madam!"

"Good! Until that time, you take your orders from me."

"Yes, Madam Queen."

The words were a knife blade in Sivell's stomach. She'd known Kela was jealous of her, but she'd never dreamed her cousin was capable of trying to usurp the throne.

Kela left the throne and paced the floor. "Your Prince Parvey is likely to be too tender toward his sister. We, on the other hand, have no such weakness, do we?"

"No, Madam. We'll make Ilia strong."

"Remember the vision of what Ilia must become."

"In visions the unsighted may do better than the sighted," he said eagerly.

"Just don't make the mistake of forgetting who's queen!" Kela snapped. "And if anyone finds the ex-queen, bring her to me. You'll answer for it if they fail."

The blind man bowed, and turned to leave. Sivell, her mind in turmoil, hardly managed to care that he might sense her presence. But he appeared shaken by Kela's words and passed her without noticing.

Now Kela began to play with the light again, extending her hand and directing the beams with her fingers. Despite her shock, Sivell strained to see how this magical effect was done. She couldn't see a lamp—however small—in her cousin's hand. Before long, Kela stopped and frowned. Now the light became a slim white band which she directed on the sea-green throne itself. Around the base ran the lines of carved names of the queens of Ilia. In the peculiar light, Sivell read the names of queens in legends her grandmother had told her. Kela moved the band slowly across the names: grandmother's grandmother, grandmother's mother, grandmother herself.

Then the light picked out the next name, "Falina-Nolasdaughter," and finally, "Sivell-Falinasdaughter." At that name Kela paused.

The letters began to glow.

While Sivell watched horrified, her cousin burned her throne name off the throne.

When the black smoke from the burning name cleared away, there was an ugly scar across the base, but Sivell felt the burn on her heart. Kela tried to smooth out the scar with a wave of her hand and a broader band of light, but it remained visible. She gave up. Concentrating her efforts once more, she pointed, directing the light to the empty spot.

Then Sivell saw what her cousin was doing: Kela was writing her own name in place of Sivell's.

When she was done, Kela stepped back to admire it: "Kela-Tuellsdaughter."

But that too was not enough. One more time she bent her light on the names, and this time she burned out Sivell's mother's name, replacing it in turn with her own mother's name, Tuell-Nolasdaughter. Now the line was complete again from grandmother to granddaughter, and Kela turned away, satisfied.

Sick with horror, Sivell looked at what Kela had done. It was as if she and her mother Falina had never been queens in Tia-ta-pel. The new lettering was crudely burned into the stone, uneven and ragged, but the names of Kela and her mother, Tuell, Nola's second daughter, were clear enough for all to read.

Yet Sivell knew that what was worse than this treachery was the knowledge that there was a power unleashed in Tia-ta-pel, greater than anything the Lianis had ever known. She had no idea what it was, but no doubt whatsoever that it was evil.

Kela was pacing the throne room again. Sivell drew back as far as possible into the shadows. Once, her cousin had been the first to detect her shifted presence, and although that was a long time ago and Sivell was stronger now, she was tiring of the strain.

Then the door opened, revealing Parvey, his crowned jalu emblem trembling like a flame. Sivell trembled, too.

"Where've you been?" Kela demanded. "There's so much to do!"

Parvey walked heavily like one who'd gained a lot of weight suddenly, as the Ganus sometimes did in old age. Yet he was, if anything, leaner than when Sivell had last seen him. If anybody could detect her presence, Parvey could. His eyes roamed over the place where she was, but he appeared to notice nothing. He turned his back on his unseen sister and inspected the new lettering on the throne.

"That wasn't well done."

Kela pouted. "You didn't give me very many lessons on using this little trick!"

"It wasn't necessary to deface the throne names. If you want, we'll make a new throne for Ilia."

She came to him and put her arms around his neck, smiling. "You know how impatient I am! And this is such fun to play with."

Parvey didn't smile in return. "The *laser* is no child's toy, Kela."

"Call it any silly name you wish!" She broke away, her shiftemblem fluttering and flashing in her irritation. When he said nothing more, she asked, "Is everything ready in Tia-ta-pel?"

"We'll attack within the week."

The shock caused Sivell's control to waver. She felt an arm and a leg materializing, hair drifting on mist—she hastily restored control. Luckily, no one was looking her way.

"And Sivell? Has no one seen her?"

"No reports of Sivell," Parvey said.

"Better for her if she doesn't try to return," Kela said carelessly. "I've given orders that—"

"I know of your orders!" Parvey interrupted angrily. There was silence again in the throne room.

"You're being difficult, Parvey," Kela said. "When we've defeated the Ganus, you'll feel better."

"How little you understand what this is all about!"

Kela glared at him. Slowly she raised the hand that had controlled the magical light and pointed at him. But his gaze was steady in return, and after a while her hand faltered and she lowered it.

"Power is hard to get used to," he said. "Time to rest."

Parvey led Kela out of the throne room and the door swung closed behind them.

Sivell's knees went suddenly weak and she made a partial return from shiftshape. The ex-queen, Kela had called her. And Parvey had spoken of an attack. It must be an evil dream brought on by tiredness after her long voyage. Then she looked at the names burned into the base of the throne and knew it was true. For a moment she had the sensation of the floor tilting under her, as though she were still on the *Marne-Queller*. She clutched the wall for support. Whatever was she to do?

The door opened again. Parvey looked straight in the direction where Sivell stood.

"Sivell."

Tired, very frightened by what she'd seen and heard since her return, she shifted back.

"I knew you at once. You'll never be skilled enough to hide from me. But you're lucky Kela was busy playing with her new toy!"

"Parvey, what's happening here?"

"I warned you against going to Goron," he said in a voice thick with fatigue. "The people think you've betrayed them, going over to the Ganus."

"But why would they think that?"

"Kela told them you have a Ganu father."

Deeply stung by something she felt might indeed be true, she argued, "All that matters is that a queen pass her Proving. I won the right to the throne in spite of my father."

"I helped you, Sivell. Don't you understand? You wouldn't have done it alone."

Now a door opened in her memory and she remembered—a jeweled jalu—her will weakening—a sense of betrayal.

"You used magic on me?"

"You might call it magic," he said. "I wanted to help you. You weren't strong enough alone. Askar gave me the knowledge how."

"And you told this to Kela?" His silence was enough reply. "Why?"

"Because there are things about us and the Venn you

don't understand. But nothing can ever be the same once you know!"

The Venn. Think about the Venn. She felt her limbs turn to ice. "What is this terrible secret about the Venn, Brother?"

"They made us," he said simply.

"They helped the Great Shaper, yes, I understand that."

"No!" he screamed at her. "You don't understand at all! You're living in a tale, Sivell, *a tale!* Somebody made you up!"

"Then tell me the truth, Parvey!" she cried. "No more lies."

"They fashioned us for their own amusement," he said, calmer now. "This shiftskill we possess? A combination of altered DNA, mutable cell structures, and an ability to camouflage ourselves through disruptive coloration—Batesian mimicry—countershadowing . . ."

The torrent of unfamiliar words poured over her. She had no idea what they meant, but some of them she'd seen before, in the king's library in Goron.

". . . photophores and chromatophores to confuse those who seek us by using the weakness of the human visual sensory system against itself—pheromones to evoke behavioral response—"

"This is the *science* of which Askar spoke?" she interrupted. "Something of this I begin to perceive. But these words—"

"Of course you don't understand the words! How could you? How could any of us without their help?"

She felt as if the ground were dropping away beneath her feet. She felt the looming presence of a great and dreadful truth in his words. Yet she didn't have the time to deal with it now; she must think about her land, her home. *Concentrate on Ilia!*

"What has this to do with Kela calling herself queen, and men marching through the streets of Tia-ta-pel?"

"There'll be war."

"Why must this be so?"

"Because I don't know what else to do," he said simply.

She believed him. She looked at the face that had been so dear to her, seeing the lines of pain etched under his eyes, the new hardness about his mouth, the odd, swollen patches on his cheeks like a malignant growth. "And you, Parvey, what's happened to you?"

"Do you know what I am, Sivell? Do you know who my father is?"

"Yes," she said. "Our mother warned me."

He considered that for a moment. "I'm one of them, you see. But I'll use my powers to forge a strong Ilia. I'll harness the Venn's own power to defy them! But first, Sivell, I must defeat the Ganus."

She felt the pent-up fire of his power beneath the surface, capable at any moment of becoming an inferno in which both Ganu and Liani would perish. He paced the throne room.

Desperately, she tried again. "It can't be the Great Shaper's wish that its children become killers of men."

He spun toward her. "I'm not concerned with that beast's wishes!"

At that blasphemy, she hit out hard at her brother's face. He jerked back. Her hand and heart both stung with the pain of contact and the knowledge that Parvey was quite mad.

When he'd recovered from the blow, he said calmly, "Kela was always jealous of you. Now she's queen she'll try to destroy you."

You are destroying yourself, Parvey! she wanted to cry out. Instead she said, "What shall I do?"

He seemed for a moment to be the old Parvey, struggling with his love for her. She tried to catch and hold his gaze, but he glanced away.

"Your father—whoever he was—gave you gifts, too. Perhaps they'll help. Meanwhile, to be safe, you'd better leave Tia-ta-pel."

"I see I don't have a choice," she said heavily. "But there's something I must do first."

Tension drained swiftly out of his face; his shoulder muscles relaxed. "Name it."

"I'd like to visit Sool's grave. It must be somewhere in the city?"

Parvey shook his head. "Across the river, under the jil trees."

"It's better so. He loved the forest more than the city that could never forget he was only half Liani."

"We're all half-breeds! All of us—every last person in this city!" Parvey said bitterly. He turned away from her abruptly, standing before the dark windows, his arms folded tightly across his chest. "We've been seeking the magic that'll let us be more than we really are. We didn't know what it was we were going to find! Go now—before I change my mind and harm you."

"I don't believe you would, Parvey," she said. He was her dear brother, her protector, he couldn't have changed that much no matter who his father was.

"You know nothing about such power as I've found! It swells in me like a fungus growing in darkness. It may destroy me along with everything else."

"Then give it up now, I beg you." She laid a hand on his sleeve. "Before it's too late!"

"I don't control it, Sivell." He removed her hand gently. "It controls me."

It was midnight when she left the castle, and although the snow had already begun to melt from the streets, the air seemed cold enough to slice to the bone. Over the rooftops the stars burned like frozen tears. Canela rode alone in the eastern sky. The city had barred its doors and windows against her; she didn't need her shiftshape. At the edge of the forest the jil trees stood stiff and leafless. She walked beneath them not knowing what she might find till, on a bend of the quiet river, she came upon a stone slab set into the frozen ground. She passed her hand over it and felt the carved inscription: "Sool."

He'd deserved more honor from the Lianis. He'd been killed trying to save them from a war which neither side would win. And in return, they'd cast him out to lie under a slab that bore only his name.

She sat on the stone and gave way to a rising tide of

despair. Her tears fell on Sool's grave. Canela struggled up the sky a little way, never freeing itself entirely of the jil branches that ensnared it, then sank back down. Overhead, the stars Sool had charted came and went on their endless journeys, neither seeing nor caring that their observer's eyes were closed forever.

Almost a full year had passed since she'd sat in this meadow with Sool and spoken of the stars, yet it seemed only a day. She'd been happier than she knew then, for gentle Sool had been closer to her than anyone would ever be again. And Parvey had been her protector, the strong jalu whose wings sheltered her from harm. Now Sool was dead and Parvey hunted her, and the Venn she had believed were her race's friends had turned into enemies in a way she couldn't comprehend. All the joy she'd once known, less than a year ago, seemed a hundred years in the past. What was left but trouble and pain and the certainty of defeat?

We're all half-breeds! Parvey had said. But a half-breed wizard was too hard to fight. There seemed little point in going on. It was too much to expect of her. Maybe she should leave the throne to Kela and find somewhere to hide for the rest of her life. No one would miss her.

Night had long passed its turning point when sleep finally claimed her, blotting out her pain. She lay down on the hard earth, her head cradled on the stone that marked Sool's resting place, and slept.

The sun came up, pushing watery rays through the bars of the jil trees, breathing a little warmth onto the frozen earth. Sivell woke and sat stiffly, massaging the circulation back into cramped, aching muscles.

Downriver, two corlis argued over a scrap of food, ignoring a river teeming with fish. But for all the squawking and wing flapping, she saw they never touched beaks. As suddenly as they had begun it, they resolved their disagreement and floated side by side in peace, mirrored in the calm water. A lone gray feather drifted away on the light breeze.

She took it as a good omen.

Cold, sore, and hungry as she was, she felt better this morning. She wouldn't give up just yet. She'd go back to the Ganus and warn them. Mordun had treated her courteously. It was the least she could do in return.

She needed food. Water could be had from the river, but she must find food soon or become weak. The quickest path to Goron lay over the hills, that path Sool had taken to his death. She had no reason to doubt Bor still held the hills. If Kela's forces—she couldn't yet bring herself to call them Parvey's—were to attack first, then Bor would be under no restraint to treat her as anything but an enemy. Worse, he might be taken by surprise and defeated. Why had she taken time to sleep? She should've gone immediately to Bor.

Above Sool's grave, a branch of the jil tree had put out a frail blossom, deceived by the sunshine into thinking spring had come. She picked it, and laid it on the stone that bore his name.

Hati feet traveled swifter than human feet. It was a shape more suited to haste. She would let her shape drift into the gentle creature's contours and race across the hills to Goron. She felt the beginning of velvet softness, smooth flanks, and trim hooves shaping themselves—

No. Ever since Parvey had returned from visiting his father, something new and evil crawled through this power of shifting. Without knowing what it was, she had no hope of controlling it. And Parvey had said it controlled him. Until she understood what it was the Venn had done to them, she would not use this tainted gift they had given.

She turned unshifted eyes toward Goron.

CHAPTER SEVENTEEN

The path along the sea cliff to the hills was still icy, and patches of snow lay under the violet shadows of the trees. Sivell's progress was slower now, for the Ganu boots she'd been wearing since the day she left Tia-ta-pel with Chetek were rubbing her feet, and blisters were blooming around her ankles on her toes and heels. Yet without the boots she'd have gone slower still. How long since she'd worn soft shoes and delicate sandals?

She brought her attention firmly back to the path. Already there were signs of the coming spring. Small yellow buds stood up hesitantly here and there in the snow, and she saw the hard lines of tree branches blurring with the golden fuzz of new growth. Ilia's brief winter was already fading.

After she'd been climbing steadily for an hour, she saw silhouetted on a rise ahead a bush whose nuts were edible. She scrambled hastily up the bank. The bush wouldn't have very many, but its nuts were large as a fist, and soft inside thin, shiny shells. She was lucky, for in the tangle of thorny branches she saw one remaining nut. She sat beside the bush, chewing the tough meat, watching the sunlight sparkling on the roofs of distant Tia-ta-pel.

It might be a long time before she saw her home again, and maybe never, if her mission failed. She still couldn't believe what had happened. She went over and over the scene with Parvey in the throne room—surely, there was some misunderstanding? But she found none.

And suddenly she remembered what her grandmother had said to Parvey, so long ago now when they were discussing Sivell's Proving: *"Never think I don't know what lies in your deepest heart."* Apparently, everybody knew about Parvey's ambitions. Everybody except Sivell.

She discovered she wasn't very hungry after all.

On the other side of the gentle rise on which the nut bush grew, she saw the wandering course of a small stream; she was directly over the cliff it had carved in the soft earth. She lowered herself over the edge with care, but even so her foot slipped and she slid several paces before coming to rest by a tree root. She tried again. Several times her foot went through the soft snow into hidden holes underneath, wrenching her knees and tumbling her forward against tree trunks that bruised her cheeks and forehead in the process. The hills were full of potholes and hidden caves, and a wise traveler didn't wander overland for fear of plunging down into darkness. Some of the caves went all the way down to the sea far below, and had their openings in the pounding surf behind Kri's Necklace. It was a sobering thought, and she trod more carefully until she reached the little stream. The water was cold and sweet and she drank gratefully.

The sky was empty, a thin gray-blue; only the occasional cry of a hunting jalu troubled its silence. The path climbed steadily now, and she was soon out of breath. Then it crested a hill, revealing the dark sea far below.

She stood directly above Kri's Necklace. She could see the changing color of the water, rolling blue and indigo, with flecks of lighter green as it flowed over the underwater rock mass. Foam spread in a wide arc around the northern edge of the Necklace, where the current boiled against the rocks, but on the southern side, in the lee of the Necklace, was a crescent of calm sea. On this side, close in to the cliffs and caves of the shore, the rocks formed a sheltering arm. And cradled in this tiny, hidden bay, its mast rocking gently back and forth, was a Ganu fishing boat.

There was no time to consider this, however, for rising

up to her over the hill ahead came a noise like many boots crunching the snow. The path was exposed totally at this point, offering not so much as one scrawny bush for concealment. She should have traveled in shiftshape! Yet she'd made that decision and would not go back on it now. Since there was no alternative, she stood and waited.

Seconds later, the heads of a group of Ganus appeared, hoods flung back, cheeks red from exertion and cold, their hair pale in the winter sunlight. As they came over the rise and saw her, their hands went to the knives at their belts. They halted several paces before her. This close, she saw that most of them were very young, hardly even her age.

Then one who was not so young stepped forward.

"This be a prize find, certainly!"

She knew the speaker only too well.

"Take her!" Hathor commanded. The young Ganus obeyed him wordlessly. "She be a tricky witch, but this time she won't get away if you put the touch of silver on her!"

He held out a silver coin to one of the boys.

"What nonsense!" she cried. "But I seek your Prince Bor, and I won't use shifting if you'll take me to him. His father promised me safe passage."

She'd expected him to curse or argue, but instead he slapped his thighs and laughed, a coarse, rolling laugh that echoed hollowly back at them from the surrounding hills.

"Oh, rich beyond measure!" he roared. "Never fear, witch. You'll see Bor, for he seeks you!"

Hathor flicked his hand at the boys and turned away. At his signal, they looked for sturdy ground to sit on, staying close to the path. One, smaller than the rest, moved farther off, but a sudden collapsing of the earth under his hips brought him scuttling back on hands and knees. Another, who hadn't yet seated himself, tugged Sivell's arm, motioning her to sit also. She felt the lump of the silver coin he clasped in his fist against witchcraft. His eyes were wide and unblinking, but his facial

muscles twitched. It was a hard task for him to watch a
Liani witch. She smiled at him to put him at ease, but
this seemed only to make his discomfort worse. He
lowered himself beside her, staring ahead, his hand
remaining on his knee.

"Why're we waiting here?" she asked, when Hathor
was deep in conversation with the one older Ganu in the
group.

The boy pretended not to hear her. When she
repeated the question, he cleared his throat and spoke,
his voice high and shaky.

"We await the coming of Lord Bor."

"I won't hurt you," she said gently. "I'm not a witch
but a human, just like you."

The boy stirred uncomfortably, his eyes on Hathor's
back. "Silence now," he squeaked, "or I'll draw my
knife!"

She felt the ripple of awe that passed through his
companions, who would've been too scared to speak to a
witch. She smiled, turning her face from him so that he
wouldn't see she had no fear of him. They were all so
very young!

They waited for Bor, and the sun began to slip down
the sky. The cold was rising up from the ground again
before they heard the tramp of hooves and the complain-
ing bellow of a bad-tempered medwi. Up the hill came
another party of Ganus, seasoned hunters this time,
faces darkened by exposure to wind and sun, with
scarred cheeks and hard eyes. In their midst, two rode
medwis. One was Treng; the other she guessed from the
strong resemblance to Mordun was his brother Bor.

At their approach, the boys scrambled to their feet,
and the one who'd spoken to Sivell poked her shoulder—she should rise also. The riders reined in their
mounts, studying the boys and the prisoner. The medwis
puffed and blew through their nostrils.

Hathor came hurrying up. "Lord Bor! I've a pretty
prize for you!"

The older of the two riders frowned, and Treng leaned
over and spoke in a low voice to him. His eyebrows

arched suddenly up, almost disappearing under a thatch of hair the color of young tree bark. He dug his knees into his medwi's sides, urging it forward a few paces. Grumbling, it moved toward Sivell till she could feel its warm, moist breath.

"Why do you travel alone in these hills, Liani?" Bor asked. His voice was a dark rumble. He was a powerfully built man with broad shoulders who seemed much older than his brother Treng, for his hair and beard were already flecked with gray. His eyes reminded her most strongly of Mordun; they were as blue as the sea in the shadow of the cliffs.

"I came seeking you, Lord Bor," she said courteously.

"Does the prey come to the ferenti?"

"No. But when the jalu hunts, both hati and ferenti take refuge."

"Be you a jalu then?" A flicker of amusement came and went in Bor's eyes.

"This wastes time!" Treng cut in. "These things were said before in our father's herth, and we've seen how little the Lianis honor their oaths."

"That isn't true," she objected. "I told Mordun I didn't want war between our people. I haven't changed my mind or gone back on my word."

"Then you be not in command of your people," Bor said. "My scouts tell of an army gathering in your metros."

How could she deny the truth? She said nothing.

"There'll be war between our people, whether you want it or not, and Mordun himself will see the need."

"She be a witch, Lord!" Hathor interrupted. "This be only Liani trickery."

"You've no reason to trust me." She clenched her fists tightly at her sides for fear they'd betray her anguish. "But listen to what I have to say and judge for yourself the wisdom of it."

"Say what you came to say," Bor said.

The medwis began pawing the ground and snorting their impatience to be moving again. Bor slapped his

into silence, but Treng allowed his medwi to amble in a
slow circle, as if he didn't care to hear what she said next.

"The Lianis aren't your enemy. If they're guilty of
anything, it's only of thoughtlessness. My people aren't
accustomed to thinking much about such solemn matters
as bonds of needing and caring between one and
another. We don't marry as you do. We don't even feel
constrained to raise our offspring much of the time. So
how can my people understand they need the Ganus,
when they don't see they need each other? But we aren't
a quarrelsome people, and we have no desire for
bloodshed."

Bor leaned forward in his saddle, watching her face as
she spoke as if reading the truth of her words—
something she might have done, she realized. Treng had
halted his medwi and seemed to be paying attention.

She continued, more slowly now. "I have seen—
someone—in Tia-ta-pel, dangerous to both Ganus and
Lianis." There was no way to tell this and avoid the pain
she felt in the telling. "He uses the power of wizards—
for he's wizard born!—to control my people and lead
them against yours."

Both brothers looked at her from their seats high on
the medwis, which appeared now to be half asleep.
Neither allowed any reaction to her words to cross their
faces, sitting as still as stone carvings in the winter
sunlight. In the hush, she heard again the cry of the
hunting jalu, a discordant scream. The medwis raised
their heads in answering mutter.

"It be just possible that what you say be true," Bor
said after a while. "Those who've watched the Liani
preparations say there be something odd afoot. They say
the Lianis walk as deadmen through their metros. But
what be the Venns' purpose in this?"

"I don't know," she said. "I don't know if there's any
logical purpose in it at all, or if there is, if it's the purpose
of all the wizards, or only the madness of the one who's
half wizard."

"And who be this mad one?"

She looked away, her eyes hot and stinging. "My brother."

"This be a trick!" Hathor interrupted. "Why would a witch bring us warning against wizards, being herself the same kind?"

"I've never intended harm to the Ganus!" Anger blotted out her other emotions. "I sent my own ambassador to keep peace between us, when it was said the Ganus intended to attack. But a Ganu killed him. A Ganu spilled the first blood. Then I came to Goron myself with my message of peace! If this hadn't happened, my brother would've never had the opportunity to seize power in Tia-ta-pel."

"If your ambassador died, it wasn't by my order," Bor said, his words as unhurried as if he spoke of preparations for the hunt.

Did nothing ever shake him, she wondered? He would make an implacable enemy, slow and patient as the rocks below, holding back the sea.

"But it was by your orders that there were outlaw Ganus in the hills above my city," she pointed out.

Behind her Hathor growled, "Enough, witch!"

He laid his hand roughly on her arm to pull her back. She whirled angrily on him.

"I take orders from no one. Remove your hand from my sleeve, you gatherer of medwi dung!"

"Why, you—" He raised his hand as if to strike.

She saw it coming and blocked the blow. Her hand caught in his half-open jacket, and as he pulled away, jacket and under-tunic opened, exposing his white flesh. Around his neck he wore a blue pendant on a silver chain. There was a jil blossom etched on the stone.

A great roaring filled her ears, and she felt suddenly cold. "This stone belonged to my ambassador. Where did you get it?"

"We took the gaud fair in battle!"

"Liar!" She threw herself at him with such force that he stumbled. She grasped the chain, not thinking what she did in this sudden, furious rush of hatred for Sool's

killer. The delicate links snapped, leaving her with the
pendant in her hand.

"Enough!" Bor spurred his medwi forward. "If this
man be the one who killed the Liani, he did so against
my orders."

"Not me, Lord! I didn't do it. Another—"

"By your command, then?"

Sivell moved out of the way of the great beast's hooves
that came dangerously close.

"He was a spy, Lord, a spy!" Hathor whined. He too
backed away. "We took him because he was a spy."

"You admit ordering this killing?" Bor asked, indiffer-
ently it seemed.

"Lord," Hathor pleaded. "I served the good of our
people."

"On whose advice did this include wanton killing?"
Bor edged his medwi closer as he spoke. Its hooves
moved as slowly, relentlessly as its master's words.

Hathor backed farther from the path. "You yourself,
Lord, said we must free ourselves from the Lianis."
There was a note of growing panic in the man's voice.

"You've listened too long to stories the Rhodarus tell
around the campfire," Bor said, apparently still good-
humored. "You believed the Ganus were like the
Rhodarus, always warring, always killing. That be not
our way."

"But, Lord—"

"What we do here in the hills be a retreat from
softness, a time for renewal of an older Ganu way—the
way of the hunter. Not the way of oldlings that hang on
Liani shiftdancing, but not the way of the murderer,
either. Well, we'll find this other one who forgot this long
enough to follow your command."

"Pity." Hathor's voice quavered. "Have pity, Lord."

"You disobeyed my orders."

As he spoke, Bor freed the heavy medwi whip from its
loop on his saddle and raised it above his head. It
whistled downward at blinding speed. Hathor screamed
and sprang backward.

A sudden rumbling underfoot—and the earth gave

way, opening a large chasm into which he slipped just as
the whip drew its line across his arm. A cloud of dust
rose to hang over the opening. Hathor screamed again
and clutched at the unstable earth, but it gaped wider,
swallowing him.

Then he was gone.

Sivell stood frozen, limbs and heart engulfed in ice so
she could neither move nor speak. Bor urged the medwi
carefully to the edge and looked down. The animal's eyes
were golden circles and it wheezed in fear at the
dangerous edge.

"A fast way to the marne," Bor commented. "But I
doubt he'll return from it."

The young boys huddled together, their faces gray.

Bor looked down at Sivell, standing with the jil
pendant in her hand. "You spoke of danger to both our
peoples from the Venn," he said. "Be there any way you
know of preventing it?"

"I don't know," she said, still shaking. "But I must try."

"I've never seen a Liani with such a fierce temper!" A
brief smile curled his lips. "Perhaps together we'll find
the way to deal with this mad brother. Tonight my father
will be here. We'll talk then."

He wheeled the medwi away. Then he stopped and
turned to her one more time. "You be safe, Queen of the
Lianis. Ride with my brother."

He galloped away. Sivell couldn't have said which
disturbed her more, Hathor's sudden death, or the
coldness of Hathor's lord. The young boy who'd guarded
her stepped forward and helped her mount behind
Treng. She could feel the suppressed excitement flickering through the boy as he touched her arm. The medwi
groaned at the extra weight, though it was such a
powerful beast it could've carried two Sivells without
noticing. But it too was shaken by the smell of Hathor's
death. Treng kicked it forward; he seemed preoccupied
with his thoughts. As soon as she'd settled herself, she
put the jil pendant safely into a pocket in her inner tunic
and fastened the jacket over it.

This time she was too tired to enjoy the sensations of

medwi riding. It seemed that her head grew heavier by
the minute. She felt as though she were moving through
a mist full of dim shapes and figures and muted voices,
and which were real and which nightmare visions she
couldn't say. Once she jerked awake, aware that she'd
fallen asleep with her cheek resting against Treng's back.
She sat upright, avoiding contact with him as much as
possible. But soon drowsiness set upon her again and the
rhythmic gait of the medwi worked its hypnotic effect,
soothing her into sleep. Her eyes closed, and she
thought of letting them rest for only a minute.

It was her last thought until the medwi came to a
standstill.

The group had come to a natural bowl in the hills,
directly before a cliff face in which yawned the entrance
to a cave. The hollow was dotted with scrubby trees, and
more climbed the dark slopes. To one side of the cave
she saw a little pool, fed by a stream that plunged down
the side of the rock and drained away in the shadows at
the far side of the clearing. Hunters in leather tunics
entered and left the cave, and a group of medwi tethered
to one side lifted their heads and bellowed a welcome to
the newcomers.

"We dismount here," Treng said, sliding off.

From the way her cheek stung with furrowed markings she knew she'd been sleeping against his rough
jacket for some time. A hunter detached himself from
the group that surrounded Bor and held out his hand to
help Sivell down. She took it gratefully; she was so stiff
and clumsy at dismounting. The sun had set, but the
area was lit by many lamps strung from the trees. Here
and there the light struck an answering sparkle from
snow still tangled in the branches higher up the slopes.
Somewhere there must be a cooking fire; she couldn't
see it, but the mingled scents of wood smoke and food
reached her nose.

Bor was unbuckling the saddle of his medwi and
listening to an overweight Ganu who puffed like a medwi
as he talked. When the man fell silent, Bor spoke.

"There be a force massing in Tia-ta-pel. My scouts've

watched for two days now. This day they moved toward
the gate leading to the hill path. This night I think we'll
see their faces." He gazed at Sivell. "For now, eat and
rest."

He walked away, solid as his medwi which lumbered
off to its own kind as soon as he released it.

She followed Bor into the cave which was as large and
as brightly lit as the great hall of the castle in Tia-ta-pel.
In the center, a fire licked at the big logs with which a
boy kept it fed. Suspended over it was a huge black iron
pot from which came the smell of vegetables simmering.
Sivell's stomach knotted in anticipation. If only there'd
be no flesh in the pot! The herbs the Ganus used were
unfamiliar to her, and she couldn't identify the subtler
odors in the mixture.

Bor's entry was the signal for serving to begin. The
hunters gathered around the pot, bowls in hand, and
another boy dipped out steaming portions for them. A
man stood to one side, cutting hunks of bread off a long
loaf with his hunting knife and passing them around. No
one took any notice of the Liani in their midst, so she
stood in line and waited her turn. When it came, she
found she was supposed to provide her own bowl.

"Here."

The Ganu in line behind her pushed his bowl into her
hands. She turned to thank him and saw the young boy
who'd been with Hathor. He avoided her eyes. Her bowl
was filled with the broth, and she was given her slice of
the slightly stale bread. She looked for somewhere to sit
away from the hunters, and found a ledge along one of
the walls, half filled with shadow from the jutting roof.
She dipped her bread into the soup and raised it to her
nose. There was no telltale odor of flesh in the soup.
Encouraged, she tasted the bread, and found among the
unknown herbs and vegetables the sweet, satisfying
flavor of fresh-caught winter lengu. She ate hungrily,
wiping the bowl clean with her bread as she had first
seen Chetek do.

Some of the Ganus went back to the line for more.
Sivell joined them, and that bowl too she cleaned. Even

if she hadn't been so hungry she knew she'd have found it good. The Ganu eating custom was the same in this rough cave as it'd been in Mordun's palace; everybody ate in silence. Only after the food was gone did a boy pour wine for the diners, and the hubbub of voices began immediately.

There was no sign of Bor and Treng, and none of the other hunters paid her any attention. After she'd finished her wine—one glass only, for she found it very strong and rough—she unlaced her boots and released her painful feet. The floor of the cave was cool and pleasant after the tight confinement of the boots. She went barefoot to the mouth of the cave. The air was fresh, and the night dark for the lamps had been extinguished. From the near distance came the comfortable sound of falling water and drowsy medwis shifting their weight. The ground was icy, but that too was a rare pleasure. She smiled, thinking that for a pampered, delicate queen of the Lianis, she'd certainly changed a lot! No Ganu farmer could be dirtier than she was then, nor tireder, nor smell any worse. But she was warm and well fed, and for the present she was safe. At least, if Bor and his hunters weren't exactly her friends, they didn't seem to be enemies, either.

Odd thoughts—for a Liani, she realized. Yet she felt a clean, hard *rightness* to them, like the economy of bone that lay under the surface of the gaudiest bird's wing. Was this what Mordun had meant when he told her she couldn't see the truth if she thought as her race did? If so, it was tiring to think this way! She would need to get used to it a little at a time.

She stuffed her hands into her pockets, putting worries about the coming morning away from her, and touched the jil pendant. It seemed another, younger Sivell had given the stone to Sool, and one to Parvey. So many terrible things had happened since then. She stood at the dark mouth of the cave, feeling the cold, hard purpose growing in her heart.

CHAPTER EIGHTEEN

The shadows of evening crept up from the sea and embraced the islands. A few birds chirped sleepily, winging their way back over the water to roost in the mist-shrouded trees. Then the surface of the water parted and the servo'd sea dragon mounted up into the twilight in a shower of gleaming drops. Reaching the wide bay on the largest island, Koril dismounted and gazed across the still water to where the shadowy mass of the continent lay on the dark water. Koril smoothed his black jodhpurs and adjusted his gold-studded belt and waited.

The twilight over the sea lightened as the first of the moons rose. Now nothing moved in the islands, no leaf, no feather, no wisp of air. Koril's sea dragon stood motionless as if it too knew a need for sleep.

After a while, Askar came walking across the sand, wrapped in a full-length crimson cloak over a pearl-gray velvet tunic with a golden sash.

I have one more move, Askar informed Koril.

True, Koril replied. *But I fear the consequences of your move.*

They can't go back now, so they must go forward.

He can't hold the power you gave him. His life's too brief to assimilate the immensity of such knowledge. It'll shatter him like glass, and they'll all bleed from his breaking.

Askar gazed on the darkness. *We'll see.*

Lute music sounded faintly over the island, rippling through the valley between the dark mountains. Streams began to flow in dry stream beds at Mirandil's approach.

She came robed in burgundy damask over an underskirt of rose silk, the bodice laced with a golden cord, the sleeves and hem caught up and decorated with a heavy froth of cream-colored lace. Her unbound hair cascaded white and luminous as snow over her shoulders; silver tendrils caressed her brow. As she walked, soft lights kindled in the shadowed valleys. On her finger she wore a single ornament, a golden circle set with enormous rosy flamestones.

There's one of my dancing ones who's stronger than we planned, Mirandil told them. *Askar overlooks her in his doing.*

Too little and too late! Askar replied. *But I won't debate this. I've work to do.*

Without speaking of it, they each set foot on the inlaid path that glittered at their feet. A sparkle of dust—a swarm of tiny lights—and they vanished, only to reappear outside a vine-covered building. The door stood open. The shattered chords and antique dissonance of a twenty-first-century piece played on vibragong, cloudharp, and synthabell crashed out to greet them. Mirandil winced.

Tagak looked up from a workbench at their approach. She had exchanged her usual leather hunting tunic for a short white coat over bare legs. "Make your last move and be done, Askar," she urged. "I'm tired of this 'doing'!"

"Oh, Tagak! I too will bleed if he breaks," Askar replied over the clash and clang of synthabell.

"Well, don't worry," she said harshly. "He'll soon be dead, one way or another."

"There was no other way."

"No other way." Tagak's tone was sarcastic. "How irresponsible we've become in these times, giving power to one who can't possibly handle it, just to see what the outcome will be!"

Tagak became aware of the expression of pain on Mirandil's face and obliterated the vibragongs in midchord. Silence rang through the laboratory in their place.

This is all Askar's doing! Mirandil exclaimed petulant-
ly. *He plays with the lives of my dancing ones and
endangers them for his own amusement.*

"Since you bring up the subject," Askar replied, "who
was responsible for that idiotic piece of doggerel that
they're trying so hard to work around?"

Mirandil looked at him blankly.

"The so-called prophecy."

*But every city needs a prophecy on its foundation
stone,* she protested. *I'm no Shakespeare, but I did the
best I could! I thought it added a nice mystery for them
to think about.*

"They're thinking about it all right, Lady! The odd
thing is, they're trying very hard to make it come true."

Tagak ignored this exchange. "Once we placed a
priority on our ethics. But I suppose we've also forgotten
what that quaint word means."

She turned away from their blank stares and looked at
the laboratory, its once sterile vats and tanks now
covered with dust and crisscrossed with the tracks of
small animals who'd sought shelter inside. One area
showed signs of having been recently swept clean. Here
the faint velvet of moss grew in the grooves of brushed
chrome surfaces of 'scopes and analyzers. Rust banded
the steel of centrifuge and sterilizer; it speckled the long
rows of once gleaming instruments, clamps and laser-
knives, forceps, lances, and probes, mute evidence of
long centuries of disuse and neglect.

Askar turned his attention to the main computer; the
others paid no attention. His fingers played over the
command pad, tentatively at first, then with gathering
sureness. Lights sprang into being; color rippled on
display screens overhead.

"I almost forget how we did it," Tagak said. "Can you
believe that we would come close to losing the knowledge that was once so precious to us that we chose exile
rather than give it up? Now—I hardly even remember
why we thought it was so important!"

"What would you do if you could remember?" Koril
asked.

Tagak looked at him oddly. "Maybe make a child."

Askar glanced up briefly; then his fingers jerked over the command pad again.

"Perhaps you're right," Koril said. "Humans don't do well playing god."

"We don't do well living forever," she replied.

Askar spun from the computer he had been querying. "Where is it?" he asked in a hoarse voice. "Tagak—what've you done?"

"You would've used it, John," she said. "You would've stooped to that abomination, too."

"You've hidden it!" he challenged.

"No. Safer than that, my friend. I've destroyed it."

"That's impossible! There were built-in safeguards—"

"Donald taught me a lot before he left," Tagak said. "You may remember we were lovers briefly? And I've had a long time to work at it!"

"What's this all about?" Koril interrupted.

"I don't believe it! The formula for Ed's immortality serum—Gone!"

"Believe that it was to prevent you from making a worse error than you've already made, John," Tagak said.

"I can't forgive you for this," he said. "It was none of your business."

Tagak replied in a gentler voice. "You would've given it to him, and that would have made a bad situation so much worse. Don't you see that?"

"Gene splicing," Mirandil said unexpectedly.

They all turned to stare at her.

"There was something about starting early enough—and mystery genes that seemed to have no function. No—that's not right."

Tagak nodded, her eyes filling with tears. "Yes. That's where you worked, Miranda, with the early-starting genes that lay down the basic architecture of the body and brain. That's how you formed your colony."

"The only way you could alter human stock to become metamorphs, something caterpillars and polliwogs did without thinking about it on Earth," Koril added, "was by starting at the very base of the chain."

"The glorious tangled hierarchies of the code that split open like oysters, spilling genetic pearls under our fingers, I remember them," Mirandil said slowly, savoring the words. "The triple-jeweled nucleotides matched each to their golden amino acid, bearing the secrets of creation. Life itself heaped like a king's treasure under our microscopes. It was magnificent!"

"Only it never worked as well as you'd hoped," Koril said. "You had to augment it with illusion-making pheromones and camouflaging tricks."

"It was a puzzle," Tagak said. "A contest of minds, a game to pass the time."

"Oh—but it was hard work! And there were lots of false starts," Mirandil protested.

"Mistakes, yes." Tagak shrugged. Her words were meant for Mirandil, yet the sense of them was for Askar, pleading with him to accept, to forget. "We all made mistakes. But oddly enough, I think I had the most setbacks, working later in the chain to intensify visual range and hearing acuity in my group."

"Tricks," Askar said scornfully. "Wasting time on tricks when there was so much else to be explored!"

Both Mirandil and Tagak made fists against him.

"Perhaps because you also tried to select for a behavior pattern, Elena?" Koril said, leading them gently away from the holocausts they seemed ready to unleash on each other. "Psychoengineering proved a less reliable laboratory science than bioengineering."

Tagak smiled. "Well, it doesn't matter now. The damage has been done. The rats have escaped the lab and are running wild."

Mirandil looked horrified. "How can you say such terrible things?"

"The words aren't as terrible as the reality," Tagak said. "But the question now is: what can we do to minimize the pain?"

"Tagak may think she's won," Askar said. "But that remains to be seen! She may come to regret that I was

forced to take my third move in a way I hadn't planned."
He strode through the door, a swirl of crimson satin on
the dark night.

What can he mean by this? Mirandil wondered.

"Nothing constructive, I'm afraid!" Tagak said.

Can we do anything to prevent him?

Enough's been done already, Koril sent. *Better that we
refrain from further action.*

Tagak reverted to the link. *I thought at first it was
Askar's first move that disturbed this pretty little world
we made, that he was the guilty one. I could feel
righteous about that! If only he hadn't meddled in the
experiment! But the guilt was ours from the first day we
started to build this lab.*

A flute began to whisper a plaintive lament through
the laboratory.

Koril's thought was comforting, like the repetition of a
mantra. *We're observers. We'll wait and observe as we've
done for so long. Darkness is as much part of the design
as light; paths go down as well as up. And even we,
immortal and godlike as we've become, don't have all the
answers.*

The flute was joined by a shimmer of strings.

*But Tagak, I still can't understand why you destroyed
Ed's formula,* Mirandil sent to her.

Tagak chose not to reply.

Together, they left the building and sat outside on the
grass, watching the second moon rise, a silver-blue
bauble. The wheel of the galaxy turned overhead, and
somewhere in the white fire of its rim the tiny spark of
Earth's sun still burned. But they'd long ago forgotten
where to look.

CHAPTER NINETEEN

She didn't know how long she'd been sleeping when an urgent voice spoke in her ear.

"The king be here!" the young boy told her.

Her body was thick with sleep as she dragged herself up. The cave seemed to be filled with twice as many people as before. She heard the clank of weapons, the thud of boots coming and going on the hard-packed earth floor, the murmur of voices that now and again rose to an angry snarl. Mordun had brought a sizable force with him from Goron.

She pulled on her boots and fastened her jacket, then pushed her way through the throng, seeking a glimpse of Mordun. She came upon him at last in a smaller cave, opening off the bigger one. Bor and Treng were with him, standing at opposite sides of a large unrolled map. All three were booted and armored in leather and steel mesh. Echoes of a hostile exchange hung heavily between them.

They looked up at her approach.

"Youngling," Mordun said, extending both hands to her. "You haven't been harmed?"

Behind his father, Bor shrugged.

"I hadn't looked for you to return so soon," Mordun said. "It can only mean our agreement came too late."

"I'm no longer queen in Tia-ta-pel. My cousin sits on the throne in my place. But it's wizard power that controls the land."

Mordun kept her hands cradled in his. "How can this be?"

"Something has changed Parvey."

"No son of the Venn could ever have been wholly Liani," he said gently.

"He was so beautiful!" she said. "When he shift-danced, all the young girls of the Twelve Oldest Families wanted him for a partner. But he would take me, who could hardly shift at all. And I never thought it odd that he alone of all the Lianis could shift for two! He was my dearest brother, and I—"

She couldn't continue.

"And so he was, Youngling. But Venn blood be an unquiet legacy, working its corruption on lesser minds. You mustn't turn the knife in this wound. Think now of Ilia. Lianis and Ganus the tween need you."

He released her hands and turned back to the map. "It be well I've come, though my coming was to prevent battle, and my staying be to fight one!"

"We'll position the men you brought here." Bor pointed to the map. "Mine will be here. We'll do better fighting them in the hills which we know well."

"I can't say I be glad you be at home in these hills," Mordun said, "for that would be to condone rebellion. But strange times call for strange alliances."

"Majesty—" Treng began.

Mordun waved him to silence and leaned over the map, peering, screwing his right eye tight to hold the silver-framed crystal. "I wish we had more men. But against Venn power, no force be ever large enough."

"It be not number that'll rule today," Bor said. "It be cunning. And I hope we have plenty of that."

"The men be ready," Treng added. "They be our best."

Mordun glanced up at his sons. "Hunting strategy be a poor underpin for a battle. Yet we have nothing better! It'll have to suffice."

"There's only one Liani you need to fear."

Falina stood in the entrance to the small cave, wrapped from shoulder to knee-high boots in a silver Ganu cloak that matched the silver in her hair. The Ganu hunters made room for her, their movements courteous and respectful. Sivell noticed the tender glance Mordun gave Falina as she took her place by his side.

"I bear the blame for what's about to happen," Falina said.

"Nay," Mordun said. "This evil began long generations before! Shall the victim be held guilty for the crimes against him?"

"Nevertheless—" Falina broke off.

Her mother's pain was at least as great as her own. The bitter feelings Sivell had been carrying for so long drained away in that realization.

"I for one don't fear this Liani!" Treng exclaimed. "No matter how he be sired, Bor and I'll teach him respect for Ganu ways!"

"You be always ready to act before you've planned, Youngling!" Mordun said. "Well, we may need some of your ill-advised courage before the night be over. But don't make the mistake of thinking you can overcome Venn treachery by force. Your brother be wiser than you in this."

"Something Parvey said," Sivell began slowly, thinking it out, putting the pieces of the puzzle together at last. "The Venn shaped us—not the Great Shaper."

She stopped, feeling that she stood at the edge of a chasm such as Hathor had faced.

"It be not a comfortable thought, Youngling. If you don't wish to go on . . . ?"

But she had to go all the way with it now. "If this is true, why would they lie to us?"

Mordun said nothing.

"Perhaps there is no Great Shaper?"

The enormity of that thought stopped her. How could there *not* be a Great Shaper? All her life she'd believed in the beautiful story of the Shaper dancing the dance of creation in its garden, and of Kirili, first-shaped—

She suddenly felt very cold.

"The one you call Shaper was the Venn's teacher," Mordun said. "No spirit, but a human like us, a molder of people. And we, their creatures, be an exercise in what he taught. The Ganus were made to show what humans be like, the Lianis to explore what humans could be."

"Then we are not— The Lianis are not—"

"Shaped in his image? No, Youngling. That be the Ganus."

Sivell swallowed. She felt as if Hathor's chasm had claimed her after all. Every comfortable belief, every solid law on which her life had been built, was gone in those words. She closed her eyes. There was a great, empty roaring in her head.

After a while, she said, "Then the Venn are our keepers?"

"Our masters," Bor agreed.

"Our enemies!" Treng spat.

She opened her eyes and saw as if for the first time these earnest-faced hunters. Stolid men, lacking the poetry and vision that the ability to slip between the shapes bestowed. Men whose shape resembled that of their makers more than her own could ever do.

Cold fury filled the place where pain had been a moment before. "We must destroy them."

Treng nodded. "We make a beginning by holding off the Lianis they've enslaved."

"It has to be done," she said.

"Unfortunately, Youngling," Mordun agreed, "it has to be done."

"I be ready to lead my hunters out," Bor said. "Treng, take your men and ride to the head of the valley."

He looked at his father. The old man nodded.

"Gera and I'll go with him. He may need Liani counsel." Mordun glanced from mother to daughter. "It be never easy to fight family."

"I have family on both sides," Falina said.

Mordun adjusted the bronze buckle on his sword belt without speaking. When it was done to his satisfaction, he looked up. "Stay with Bor, Youngling. He be not so foolhardy as his brother. We may yet have cause to be thankful he knows these hills as well as he does!"

Sivell deliberately wiped her mind clean of all but the most ordinary thoughts—the hardness of the packed dirt underfoot, the chill, damp night air, the smell of sweat and leather, the rub of her boots against her ankles.

The great cave emptied rapidly. Outside in the gray light of Canela, she watched Bor saddle the medwi with unhurried pace. Beast and rider were the hub of a slowly revolving wheel of activity. Ganu hunters emerged from the cave, saddled their mounts, passed their leader to take up their positions, all without exchanging words with one another. There was an air of urgent orderliness about this circling, as if they performed some solemn rite of battle. Bor alone seemed untouched by it, taking time to fondle the medwi's head, reassuring it.

"It be soon day," he remarked to her. "And then it'll begin."

As if in answer, the medwi pulled its head up sharply, its eyes wild.

"Whoa, Duhrn! Whoa boy!"

She watched his hands move over the medwi's flanks, soothing. It helped to think about the medwi. They were often bad-tempered, but not insensitive to their riders' moods. This one scraped the ground with its large hoof and rumbled a complaint.

"Have you seen battle before?" Bor asked. "No? Then you'll be no worse off than many of my younglings. Some of them've hunted nothing more ferocious than a hati."

"I thought Ganu children were raised from birth to be hunters?"

He finished buckling the harness, and stood holding his medwi's head, ready to mount. "In times past, that was true. Our herths be warmer now in Goron, as the oldlings say. Will you ride with me or alone?"

"With you."

He mounted swiftly, making it look easy, then gave Sivell his hand and pulled her up behind him. The beast lumbered after its fellows.

"Some of us still teach our younglings to hunt when they be old enough," he said as they passed the mouth of the cave. "But our natural prey be the ferentis that live in the Kai-weh mountains. It be not wise to take younglings on such a hunt."

"Why not?"

"Rhodarus."

"I thought the Rhodarus visited Goron in friendship?"

"They be not the kind to place much value on friendship. We've learned as much from them skirmishing in the woods as from polite conversations in the king's herth!"

She tasted bitterness. "How to fight Lianis, you mean?"

"We would break ties with you, not spill your blood. But if it be necessary, we will fight."

"If only I knew why."

"Men come to hate what they can't have."

"Perhaps now that we have a common enemy . . ."

He made no reply.

They made their way up a steep path winding between tangled bushes and scrawny myot trees. The medwi blew through its nostrils from time to time, a shrill whistle that was answered by one of its kind ahead or behind it on the trail. Though it was dark still, she knew from the contact the medwis kept with each other that Bor's mount was neither first nor last in the chain. The way became narrower, at times hardly more than a narrow shelf of rock skirting a sheer rock wall. These hills weren't very high, yet she didn't want to look down to the base of the wall. The medwi seemed unconcerned and plodded forward, whistling from time to time and grumbling when sharp bends in the path caused it to make extra effort.

After a while they reached the top and the medwi halted. She could see perhaps twenty animals on level ground between low branches of full-size myot trees. The air was rich with the aroma of myot needles and soft earth. The Ganus leaned forward in their saddles, gazing over the edge into the darkness of the little valley below. Some spoke in low tones to their neighbors, but they hushed when they saw Bor. Canela had set now, and a few stars still burned in the winter sky.

Stars that once were the dancing ground of a god! she thought bitterly.

An icy wind poked at the valley.

Bor reined his medwi in. "My hunters hold the southern entrance to the valley. Treng and my father with your mam position themselves at the northern end. Through this narrow valley runs the road from Tia-ta-pel to Goron, and the Liani force must come along it. Without medwis, they can't come over the hills as we did. We'll watch as they enter the valley, then block their exit. My father'll block their way forward."

He dismounted, then helped her down.

She watched him moving among his men. His sturdy presence seemed to calm them; he spoke a word or two with each one, laying his hand lightly on the shoulders of the younger ones. In his wake, he left smiling faces and chins held higher.

She became aware of a figure by her elbow and pulled herself out of her depression. The young boy who'd been with Hathor stood beside her. Even now, after seeing her talk with his king and ride with his lord, the youth seemed to have difficulty looking at her.

"Good morning."

He acknowledged the greeting silently. He fidgeted for some time in the pocket of his jacket. It was obvious he wanted to be able to speak to her but hadn't yet found the courage. Then he straightened up and cleared his throat.

"Have you a weapon?" he asked, his voice high again in his excitement.

"No. Do you think I need one?"

"Of course!" Then he blinked as if afraid he'd offended her. "I mean, you'll need something if we fight the wizards close."

"I see. What do you suggest?"

The boy brought something out of his pocket. "Use this to defend yourself."

Lovingly cradled in his hand was something that resembled a Ganu hunting knife, except that it was smaller, thinner, with a curved blade that flashed in the starlight. Ice gripped her blood as she looked at the thing.

He turned it over for her, and she saw an unfamiliar script running down the blade on the other side.

"What is it?"

"It be a Rhodaru dagger," the boy replied, proud of his knowledge. "You use it so." He demonstrated an upward, spiraling thrust.

She trembled as she took the weapon from his outstretched hand. "Where did you get this Rhodaru weapon?"

"A Rhodaru hunter gave it to Hathor for hunting ferentis. They use it on big golden beasts that prowl their mountains—and on men! It be quick and clean. Better than our clumsy knives."

She knew he'd given her the weapon that had killed Sool. She closed her eyes as her stomach wrenched and turned. The weapon burned her cold palm. Her fingers refused to close over it.

"What be the matter? Don't you want it?"

She opened her eyes and saw his concerned face.

"Be you not well, Lady?"

She breathed deeply. "Thank you for the weapon. I'll—I'll take good care of it."

He smiled at her, and disappeared into the tree shadows again.

She buried the dagger in her pocket. If it came to using that to defend herself, she doubted she could. But the boy had meant well.

Bor came to stand beside her at the edge of the cliff. The early-morning breeze stirred the branches of the old myot trees.

"The sun be late rising," Bor said. "It should be up by now."

Sivell glanced at him, but his face was in shadow. "It's your own impatience for battle that makes it seem late."

"There be some who see this dawn who'll never see another. I think of them and I would hang on to darkness!"

She reached for the comfortable bulk of the medwi, twining her fingers in the coarse mane to prevent them

from shaking. "Perhaps it's time for the Lianis also to
move into the day. We've been dreaming long enough!"

He said suddenly, an urgent tone to his voice,
"Whatever this day brings, promise me you'll serve
Liani and Ganu the tween against the Venn."

Surprised, she said, "Do you fear I won't?"

"Always before now, I've been able to think what
might happen and make plans for my people. This time,
I see only darkness ahead."

He was standing close to the medwi and she could feel
the tremor pass from his hands through the animal's
flank; Duhrn moved in sympathy.

"You aren't the terrible rebel your father thinks you
are," she said. "You'll make a good king in your time."

"It be not given to most parents and offspring to see
the same land in the map," he said, and she thought he
smiled.

Then he stiffened, staring down into the valley. "They
be coming now."

At first she couldn't hear anything. Then she was
aware of a faint pulse of sound borne on the darkness, a
soft vibration in the air, and a counterpoint of voices.
She felt an answering vibration begin at the top of her
head and work its way down her spine and legs, rooting
her feet momentarily to the ground. Bor had already
mounted. He reached down for her. For a second longer
she stood there.

It was beginning. The horror she'd hoped was only a
nightmare was really here.

Then she tore herself free of the fear and grasped Bor's
hand. He pulled her up behind him. The Ganu hunters
stood at the edge of the cliff; their medwis pawed the
earth. The sound of voices advanced into the valley,
spreading like ripples in still water.

"We must wait till they be well in and slightly ahead of
us," Bor said. "Then we'll drop down on them. Our
descent will signal to my father to close off the northern
exit in the same manner."

Now she could make out shapes moving below like
sleepwalkers. There was still too little light to see the

figures, but their number was great. On and on they came, and still they weren't within the valley's walls. Where had such a large force been raised? There must be at least a hundred of them! And against them Bor had to send a handful of Ganu hunters, many young and untried. Mordun had scarcely more at the other end.

The Ganus murmured among themselves as they looked down on the advancing tide of the Lianis. The medwis raised and lowered their horns apprehensively. Seeing this nervousness in his men and their mounts, Bor rode among them, calling each medwi by its name, encouraging the riders with light jests. Sivell could feel the mutual respect and concern that flowed between leader and men. With bitter humor she recalled how she'd thought of the Ganus as being *unfinished*. It was the Lianis, she saw now, who still had much to learn.

The end of the column came in sight, moving with dull precision as if their bodies were no longer inhabited by minds.

"How can this be?" she breathed. "What has Parvey done to them?"

"There be roots we know of," Bor answered. "Crushed and steeped, they yield a drug that induces a trance much like this. But they never be used so—or for so many, or so long!"

"The Venn gave him this knowledge."

"Aye—to kill men with. We be not worth much to our makers!"

The Liani force was now fully within the steep walls of the narrow valley.

Bor raised his arm to give the signal.

Sivell held her breath.

Then his arm flashed down on the medwi's neck and the beast leaped forward, down over the cliff. The air shattered with the noise of Ganus yelling and medwis bellowing, hooves thundering on the rocky slope, taking loose clods of earth and stone with them in a landslide.

The Lianis at the head of the column turned, hesitating as if bewildered by this interruption to their progress. Bor spurred his medwi into their midst. He

stood up in the stirrups, roaring, swinging his murder-
ous long sword. Sivell clung precariously behind him,
seeing the fear this wild apparition sparked in the eyes of
the Lianis. It was still too dark in the valley to see far up
the road, but from ahead came the Ganu battle yells that
told of Mordun's entry.

Then the smell of medwi sweat and harness—the
violent lurching and thrusting—the noise of men howl-
ing—weapons shrieking through the darkness—all became a blur to Sivell. She couldn't have said if the battle
went on for an hour or two hours, or even three. She lost
the sense of who was attacking and who was attacked.
She couldn't tell who was Ganu and who Liani. It was all
a jumble—medwi riders and foot soldiers—thrust and
parry of weapons—screams of the wounded—bellowing
medwis, their breath steaming on the crisp dawn air—
the slip and slide of hooves on icy ground.

It seemed endless, a lifetime at least, as if she'd always
clung to this stranger's jacket on the back of a plunging
medwi, as if she always would.

It was like using a knife to slice mist. As the Ganus
pressed forward, weapons ready, the Lianis slipped their
shapes and melted under the edge of the blades raised
against them. Something had been done to them in
order to make them fight at all, but it had left them their
shiftskill. Time and time again, she saw a Ganu bear
down on his prey, certain of victory, only to find he faced
the empty air. And as he turned to find the elusive
enemy, a Liani would appear suddenly behind him and
attack his unprotected back. It wasn't an experience to
encourage men used to fighting nothing more devious
than ferentis. The strain was beginning to show on their
faces and in the rising note of panic in their voices.

Bor had worked himself up to the head of the column.
Sivell peered around, avoiding his arm swinging the
heavy blade. A path opened up before them as the Lianis
fell back before this onslaught. Shiftshapes wavered and
gave ground before the Ganu leader's approach. Ahead
she could see one mounted figure, alone among the
Liani foot soldiers, approaching them. There was a

strange glow around rider and mount, wrapping them in wavering illusion that was very hard to pinpoint.

From the waist down the rider was a man, but above the waist he had shifted to the scaly body of a monstrous beast, the like of which she'd never encountered in her worst nightmares. Fire flashed in his eyes, and gleaming fangs showed in his shifted jaws.

Bor's medwi faltered.

To Sivell's ears the battlefield fell silent. To her eyes all motion stopped, except the relentless advance of the demon rider. Instantly, all talk about Shaper and Venn lost importance.

It was Parvey.

CHAPTER TWENTY

The one thing Sivell hadn't anticipated was that Parvey would lead his force against her.

He had ambitions for the throne of Tia-ta-pel, she knew that. But she had never dreamed he'd consider harming her. And he knew where she'd gone; he must have expected she'd be here with Mordun's force. He hadn't given her time to try to avert war.

That meant Parvey wanted it as much as Kela did.

How could he have changed so terribly?

He had so much power over her feelings even now that she couldn't accept the evidence of her own eyes. She couldn't believe he wasn't the same Parvey she'd known in her childhood. Surely there had to be some mistake? Perhaps there was some little thing between them that had gone wrong—some misunderstanding that could be put right? He was her kind brother. It wasn't possible that he'd be her enemy.

But wasn't that what Mordun had warned her against—a kind of thinking that prevented her from seeing truth?

Very well. She would avoid it. She would reason it out again.

Parvey was part Venn. The Venn were the real enemy.

She'd begun to take pride in the fact that she didn't think like a Liani, but she'd been blind when it came to seeing Parvey clearly. She should've known he would come. It had been clear from the encounter in the throne room.

Bor turned in the saddle. "What be this monster who approaches so furiously?"

She struggled, reluctant to say what had to be said, and won. "It's my brother, Parvey."

She felt him start at the name, the medwi startled too, as though it had heard and understood.

"Then we must draw him at once into combat."

No! No! her heart wanted her to scream. But she'd made the decision; it had to be done.

Parvey hadn't seen her yet, nor had he identified Bor as his opponent. Around them, Ganus and Lianis clashed and it was hard to say who had the edge now, the fiercer Ganus who were recovering from their fear of sorcery, or the drugged Lianis who seemed unable to stop fighting if they wanted to. It made her remember bitterly the manner in which Parvey had taken control of her mind at the Proving. She had even less to be proud of than these sleepwalking Lianis. Parvey hadn't needed drugs to capture her.

The Lianis moved and fought as though they were dreaming, their faces solemn, their movements dull and heavy. They advanced on foot against the Ganus, in their own shape until challenged. On they came as if they saw and felt nothing of the terror of the battle. The medwis reared up at this strange behavior, reluctant to move against such unnatural warriors. The Lianis shifting in front of them, adopting ferocious shapes of nightmare and madness, didn't confuse the Ganus as much as this somber, unhurried progress like an army of the dead.

The somber ones shall have their day.

So many meanings for an old prophecy, she thought. Like wizard gifts, they gave something other than they seemed to promise, leaving humans with only themselves to rely on at the end.

More Venn treachery, she saw now, for who else had given the Lianis the prophecy in the first place?

Thoughts raced through her mind, blade-sharp— asserting, challenging, contradicting all the comfortable things she'd once believed in. Was this what Mordun had meant her to do? She knew it was.

Then she saw a Liani—half-shifted, projecting a wavering, fiery shape—hesitating at the moment a Ganu sword rose to meet him. The shiftshape shivered, blurred. The owner's face surfaced, fear in his eyes. Then down he went before the raw power of sharp steel.

He had known his fate before it destroyed him. Was this unknown power that held them wearing off? The Ganus knew a drug, but hadn't known it was this powerful. Parvey had somehow controlled her mind at the Proving—one mind—but this was a whole army.

"Look to the flank there!" An older Ganu on foot slogged past Bor's medwi, puffing with strain, cheeks flaming. Sivell saw sweat glistening on his neck, dark patches staining the hunter's tunic. No struggle to take the ferenti had ever been this fierce for the man, yet he pushed himself back into the fray, over and over again.

Bor had worked his medwi through the confusion until now he was face-to-face with the other rider.

"Stop there, Lord Parvey!" Bor thundered, his voice rising above the din of the battleground. "I, Bor-Mordunson, challenge you to fight!"

A smile passed fleetingly over the beast's face. "The battle would be uneven, friend Bor. You are two to my one. I see you've converted my sister to your cause."

Sivell shuddered. This wasn't the Parvey she knew. His voice was deep, a growl like a wild animal. His face contorted into a snarl, revealing fangs.

Bor's medwi began to tremble, its eyes growing wide with fright. Parvey's mount was smaller, lighter than a medwi, an animal she'd never seen before. It greeted the medwi with a high whining which further increased the larger beast's discomfort. A hush fell over the narrow valley. Ganus and Lianis moved slowly back from this confrontation, till the two mounts and their riders stood alone in a cleared space.

"She shall dismount and I'll take you alone," Bor answered.

"No!" Sivell said urgently in Bor's ear. "Don't try to be a hero. You'll never take him without help. You'll never catch him if he shifts."

Parvey laughed—a harsh sound that made her grit her

teeth. "Let my sister stay. I have no fear of Sivell. She'll never hurt me!"

She closed her eyes, shutting out his words. He was probably right. How could she ever bring herself to harm Parvey?

At the far side of the circle Mordun appeared with Treng by his side, clutching swords and axes. The narrow valley, crowded with men and medwis, was silent now except for the soughing of the dawn wind and the shuffle of medwi hooves. The sky was at last showing fingers of lighter color through the branches.

"I'll make you a bargain," Parvey's voice rasped, his terrifying face turned toward Mordun. "If your son defeats me, the Lianis will acknowledge you the victor in this battle. They will return home and trouble you no more. But if I win, your warriors will lay down their weapons and accept me as their king."

Sivell expected Mordun to object immediately, but the old Ganu king sat impassively on his medwi.

"This bargain be not a fair one!" Treng exclaimed.

"As uneven as two against one," Parvey replied. "But see how fair I am. I will use only such weapons against you as you use to fight me. Sivell can bear witness to the powers I could use to blast you so that no trace of you would remain in this place." He glanced at her. "Remember what happened to the throne, little sister? Of course you do! I will agree not to use that power. Do you accept my terms, or must there be more blood spilled before we leave this valley?"

Sivell was aware of the wounded in the silent circle that surrounded them, the number of Ganu hunters that leaned on companions, no longer able to stand unaided, blood oozing from between fingers trying to stem it, and those from both sides who lay on the ground beyond. Her gaze returned to Mordun—and now she saw that one of Mordun's arms dangled oddly by his side. Mordun himself had been wounded.

The sight caused her a ripple of relief—*but I am untouched!*—then she was immediately shocked at this selfish reaction.

"Accept!" she urged Bor, her fingers gripping his shoulders. "This isn't the brother I once knew anymore. You don't stand a chance unless I help."

Bor closed his gloved hand over hers. "I accept your terms, Lord Parvey."

Around them, she felt the flutter of returning consciousness in the Lianis, the gasps of horror from minds that returned from the void to face the predicament they were in. So she was right; even Parvey with his Venn-knowledge couldn't control everything at once.

"Then be ready to meet your death!" Parvey spurred his mount forward.

Bor's medwi leaped hardly a second after that. They met with a bone-jarring crunch of sword against sword, the impact almost shaking Sivell loose from her position behind Bor. But they broke, wheeled and charged again. This time Bor ducked under the advancing weapon and Parvey's face slid past Sivell, close enough for her to see the blood-filled eyes of the beastshape he wore and feel its steaming breath. The medwi screamed in alarm and tried to shy away, but Bor held it in place, turning it to face Parvey's return.

Again and again they charged each other. Once, Parvey's sword nicked Bor's shoulder, ripping the jacket and drawing a thin red line across his arm. But Bor was unable to do the same to Parvey. For though Bor was the better fighter of the two, and his medwi heavier and more powerful than Parvey's mount, Parvey eluded them. He seemed to disappear just at the moment that Bor's weapon should surely have made contact. And the medwi was skillful at chasing ferentis, not battling people.

Sivell was panting with fear and strain. She felt something warm on her hand and glanced down. Bor's blood.

She heard him cajoling the medwi. "Come, Duhrn. Come, old friend. One more turn and we'll have the wizard by the gull!"

The medwi skidded around and prepared to charge

forward again, though it seemed only its affection for its rider propelled it onward.

But this time, instead of Parvey's mount being at the farthest point of its run, turning to advance on them, Sivell saw that the creature was already coming at them full speed as though this were its first charge. Sivell knew the thrust of real fear. For the first time she understood that she might be killed.

Bor cursed and spurred his panting medwi faster.

Not fast enough.

Parvey bore down on them as though they stood waiting to receive him, and the thrust of his sword took Bor clean out of the saddle. The medwi reared up, bellowing in rage and frustration. It threw Sivell off also, into a prickly mass of myot saplings which scratched her hands and cheeks, but she was out of range of the pounding hooves of both beasts.

There was no time to see how badly Bor was wounded. Parvey dismounted and advanced on them. She scrambled on hands and knees over the still-frozen ground to put herself between her brother and the man he intended to kill.

Parvey stopped, several paces away, his eyes glowing like the furnaces of Ganu tilemakers. "Get out of my way, little sister! I have such powers today as you have never dreamed of. I do what I must."

"Who says you must use them against us, Parvey?"

He didn't answer.

"Then you must kill me first," she said, getting her feet under her and rising. "Will you do that, Parvey?"

His voice rose to a nerve-tearing scream. "I warned you!"

The monster body grew taller and seemed to burst into flame, a pillar of fire out of which Parvey spoke. "I'll burn every tree in this valley to the ground."

She was aware of the frightened voices of the Ganus behind her, and the terrified snorting of their mounts. The lurid light cast by Parvey's shiftshape illuminated a ring of scared faces, mouths open, eyes wide. For a second longer she kept the thought that this was Parvey whom she loved. She couldn't quite bring herself to believe he meant her harm.

Parvey—son of the Venn who had made them and played with them like animals, denying them their humanity in a blizzard of lies.

Silence grew around her, a silence in which she could hear the blood pounding in her veins. Something stirred in her, something alien she'd never felt before, as if her blood remembered things her mind knew nothing of. Shifting was more than slipping the confines of the human shape; it was also an illusion. Who should know this better than she, who had once gone under to a jalu emblem? It was only a game played in the mind with the body's help—a child's game of Seek—but it was a Venn trick that could be used against them.

At the edge of the crowd, a small boy hiccuped, an innocent sound that shattered the spell of the silence holding them.

She lost all thought of Parvey and Sivell, brother and sister. She was aware only of a new hunger to fight.

She shifted, releasing her form, projecting an image of rain to counteract the hallucination of fire in which Parvey had clothed himself.

For a second, the real Parvey swam up out of the illusion and she saw shock that his face was pitted and pocked as if by disease. But he gave her no time to consider this for he vanished in an eyeblink. In his place stood a large boulder, as tall as a man.

The boulder began to roll toward the injured man who lay directly in its path. The illusion itself couldn't hurt him, but Parvey, within it, could.

She drew her watershape back together, her energy flying inward, and shifted again. For a second she was aware of the pounding of her heart. Then she assumed the throbbing energy of lightning which she darted at him.

The boulder split into a shower of little pebbles, falling at the feet of the wounded man.

Sivell felt as if she were momentarily fragmented in the air, her conscious mind shattered and floating outside her body. She struggled to regain control. This was an aberrant effect of shifting she'd never experienced before! Something was different.

Parvey again stood on the path in his own shape, with his jalu emblem on his tunic.

"Little sister," he said in a mild voice, "would you fight your own Parvey?"

He smiled and held out his hands as he'd done a hundred times at the shiftdance or when the game of Seek had been too much for her to bear. She looked into his beautiful face, like a carving in obsidian, and felt a longing to give up this struggle against him, to return to the protector of her childhood.

Sool's gone forever. Don't lose Parvey, too.

Surely, Parvey would never hurt her? Surely, she couldn't hurt him.

"Dear Brother—"

Had she already started to move toward the embrace of his arms when she saw it? The growing light in the sky touched his face and caught an answering gleam from his eyes. Venn knowledge had broken him beyond saving. It was a madness she knew he could no longer shake off.

He saw that she knew. He gave a fierce cry that echoed among the rocks and in the next instant he shifted—

And she lost him against the lightening sky.

Frantic, she searched left and right. If she didn't find him fast, he'd be able to reach Bor and—

Her heart pounded against her ribs. Her mouth was dry, her eyes stung. She had to find him!

Something—the touch of a light breeze stirring the hairs on her arm—a brassy odor, out of place in this valley of pine trees and dark earth and spring water—

There was a signature to shifting, the clue that children recognized instinctively when they played at Seek. It lay in the way she chose to see.

The disk of the sun was now visible on the horizon. Snow-filled gullies flushed rose and violet.

There—a tiny flicker—a ripple effect running over the

background darkness—vanishing as she looked straight at it.

She squinted. And she was aware that the way she *saw* had changed. Now she perceived the landscape as radiant topography. Waves of heat from cool snow through lukewarm boughs to the smoldering intensity humans generated assaulted her eyes with their layered brightness.

Parvey was over by an escarpment. She *saw* him as a hotspot on a cool background.

He knew she had found him.

"Sivell." His voice was a whisper that carried in the silence enveloping them. "Remember when we shifted together? Remember when my power took you, when it spread with yours like jewels against the sky on the day of your Proving? This is your dearest brother."

For a moment she thought—

But no. As she watched, hesitating, unwilling yet to accept the inevitable, he let his contours glide. The result was horrifying, and grotesque.

An enormous jalu turned toward her, stretching unwieldy wings. A cruel beak opened, talons flexed.

What could she do against Parvey's skill? He'd always had enough for two—

No.

So many things about her world she hadn't understood. This was another.

Hadn't Sool told her her brother's power had been in her own mind? *She* had given him any power he had over her. She could take it away.

The jalu lunged toward her.

She loved her brother, but he was mad.

She found herself shifting and went with the shape that came over her without knowing what it was. She sprang just as his outstretched talons brushed the wounded man, knocking the jalu sideways. She felt power in her rippling muscles, claws extended on the jalu she'd stunned.

He recovered and beat at her savagely.

"Acknowledge me master of Ilia!" the beast cried.

There was nothing in this mad voice remaining of the brother she loved.

"I have my father's power to compel your obedience! I command your life—or your death!"

She knew she would have to kill him.

No one was her master—not even the Venn who had grasped the flesh of her people with their bloodstained hands, wrenching them from their true human shape for Venn amusement. She would rather die than accept that humiliation.

"Sivell!" The beloved voice rang in her ears. Echoes of happier days stirred in her heart.

And then, so faint she wondered if she imagined it, "Too late for regrets! I cannot resist this power my father gave—I must use it!"

"Parvey! Askar isn't here— You're free—"

"No, little sister. Do what has to be done. Quickly!"

The solution didn't lie in pitting hallucination against hallucination. That was how the Venn wanted her to think. It was a way to keep her under their control. The Ganus knew a stronger way.

She felt something in her hand, though she didn't remember reaching for it. She lunged toward Parvey. The Rhodaru dagger that had killed Sool spiraled deep into Parvey's heart, but the wound it made didn't bleed.

At that wound, all shiftshapes vanished, and Parvey fell back on the ground. A silver chain that had been under his tunic slipped free, revealing blue fire. Trembling, her breath coming in great ragged gasps, she stood looking down at him. For one second she was jubilant—she had slain the monster! She had won!

Then as swiftly as it had come, exhilaration drained out of her. The knife slid out of her fingers and fell to the ground.

"Parvey?"

She knelt beside him, sick with horror. She'd wanted to save Ilia—the Ganus were helpless against this power—Parvey had gone mad—it was the Venn's fault—

But surely she hadn't meant *this*!

"Parvey! Brother!"

She'd had no choice. He would have killed her if she hadn't killed him first.

But he was her brother, and she'd killed him.

The blue stone gleamed in the wintry sunlight, catching her eye. Her mind fled away from the horror before her eyes. She took the pendant from him gently.

When she stood, her legs crumpled under her and she would've fallen to the ground if arms hadn't been there to catch her. She closed her eyes and fought the sensation of breaking up into a hundred pieces. It overwhelmed her and she gave way, slipping over into blackness.

Later, when she opened her eyes again, the sun was high over the valley. She was lying in the shelter of an outcropping of rock. Her mind was empty of thoughts.

Mordun bent over her. New lines had come to join the ones he'd carried in his face before. "The nightmare be over, Youngling. The Lianis be waiting to pay you homage as their queen. There'll be no more Venn trickery in Tia-ta-pel."

Memory flooded back and with it fierce pain.

"You were the only one who could've done it," Falina said, taking her hand. She too seemed older, grayer. "Their power destroyed Parvey, and would've destroyed us all."

"I'm not proud of what I've done," she said. In her heart she felt the cold clutch of a pain that had come to dwell there.

"None of us be proud, Youngling," Mordun said. "Ganu and Liani the tween be ashamed of what happened here this day. None of us will ever forget we shed the blood of brothers."

"I don't remember very much," Sivell said.

"You took the shiftshape of a karami," Falina told her. "It's the emblem of He-Who-Rules."

"But I've never seen a karami—only paintings in Goron."

"Your father is Rhodaru. Hadn't you guessed?"

"Rhodaru? I thought—"

Falina laid her hand on Sivell's arm. "You didn't want me to tell you the truth."

Chetek? She opened her mouth, then closed it firmly. It might be the last purely Liani thing she would ever do, but she wouldn't ask.

"The Rhodarus had a gift to give I believed you'd need someday."

"Blood lust?" she asked bitterly. "The ability to kill a brother?"

"We'll talk more of this later," Mordun interrupted. "For now, we'll take you back to the cave where you can rest and have your wounds tended."

Until he said the word she hadn't been aware of any. Now she felt the slow throb where her flesh was torn. She lay back and looked at Mordun and Falina without the strength to speak to them.

Treng appeared; memory sparked again.

"Bor?"

"Dead, too," Mordun said quietly. "As be many Ganu and Liani the tween— And there would've been more except for your courage, Youngling. Hold on to that!"

She saw the track of tears on his battle-grimed cheeks, and closed her eyes against her own.

"He'll be honored in Tia-ta-pel for as long as there are Lianis to speak of his bravery," she said.

Treng stood stiff in his grief like one who'd seen the sword of the angel of death descending all around him and he alone not taken. "We be waiting to hear your command for the Venn halfling's body."

She swallowed pain. "My brother shall be buried honorably in Tia-ta-pel, with no more and no less than our custom provides. He too was a victim."

Then she felt hot tears rushing down her cheeks and made no effort to stop them.

CHAPTER TWENTY-ONE

Falina kept Sivell confined to bed in the alcove at the back of the cave for three days. She passed most of the time in a deep, dreamless sleep, brought on by the herbal beverage Falina gave her several times a day. The Ganus knew many such herbal medicines, and while the sleep healed her mind, soothing ointments from roots and barks of trees healed her wounds.

Once, she dreamed of standing with Sool and Parvey, one at either side, on Sorway Cliff, looking out to sea at the rising sun. In her hand she held the assassin's knife. Sunlight caught it and it burst into flame. Then the flame went out, and in its place was a jil flower.

Sometimes, as she drifted between waking and sleeping, she was aware of hushed movement around her. Parvey's army had returned to Tia-ta-pel, but others had come from the city to see their wounded queen as she lay in Ganu care. They moved silently, solemnly past. The Lianis came without shiftemblem, a sign of great grief; they touched her hand, saying little. Occasionally, she recognized a face: Zil; Tye, the old counselor; Sool's mother. Zil brought news: Kela had fled the city and no one knew where she'd gone. Her grandmother, Nola, had come back from retirement temporarily to await Sivell's return.

When Liani visitors weren't present, Ganu hunters filed past. Their expressions were grim, but they too trod softly. And often, turning her head away from bitter thoughts that kept trying to push up to the surface of her mind, she found the young boy who'd been with Hathor keeping vigil by her bed.

On the fourth day she woke early to find sunlight streaming in the cave's entrance, setting the dust motes dancing. There was no one around. She sat up, her mind clear and still as if she were newborn. The Ganu boy was asleep on the floor beside her. She moved her feet carefully over the edge and let them rest on the hard-packed earth, still cool from the night. Then she stood, weak-kneed and shaky. She took a deep breath and set out slowly, each leg learning to walk all over again, toward the sunshine.

Outside, a fresh breeze brought her the sun-warmed scent of pine needles and spring flowers. Bird sounds and water sounds etched themselves freshly on her blank consciousness like the engravings on the blue stones. Everywhere there was a patterning of dark and light, sunlight and shade, bright flowers and brown earth, white rocks and dark water, warm earth and places where the night coolness still lingered, bird song and silence. It was a beautiful, new-made world. All the Great Shaper's creation seemed to take part this morning in this shiftdance of opposites.

Then she remembered there was no more Great Shaper for her or her people. She stood on a planet which the followers of a man named Venn had used as their playground, and she was their chosen plaything.

The stream splashed noisily over the rocks into a clear pool. Someone stood in the pool, lifting the water in his hands and letting the sparkling drops run over his shoulders. For a moment, a trick of sunlight reflecting off the water turned his white skin the color of honey. Something gentle stirred in her at the sight, a feeling she hadn't had in a long time. She moved toward the water-fall.

Hearing her footsteps, he turned.

"You be recovered, then?" Treng said.

He stepped to the edge of the pool and reached for a large, rough towel and began to dry himself. Now she saw, running diagonally down his chest, between the curls of water-darkened hair, the jagged red scar.

He saw her eyes on the scar, and said, without emotion, "We all be wounded."

Sivell sat on a flat-topped boulder at the edge of the pool and trailed her feet in the icy water. He toweled his hair. At the far side of the pool, where it disappeared in the tree shadows, a fish jumped, a flash of iridescent blue-green. She dipped up a little water in her cupped hands and sprinkled it on her bare arms. Her skin tingled and she shivered.

"You be cold," he said. "That tunic wasn't meant for outdoors."

She looked down at her short Ganu sleeping robe, then at Treng wrapped in the towel. "You're wearing less!"

"I be a hunter and used to cold." He picked up his cloak that lay on the grass beside him and slipped it over her shoulder. "And you've been ill."

"Thank you," she said.

For a brief moment their eyes met. Then they were both silent for a while. Treng finished drying himself and put on his tunic. Sivell gazed at the falling water. Once, she turned her head and found him staring at her. He looked away quickly, but made no move to leave.

Something quivered in the air between them, something so fragile the wrong words spoken too soon would break it. Yet she had to say something.

"You'll be king someday," she said.

He acknowledged this without replying.

"And I'm queen in Tia-ta-pel."

It wasn't what she wanted to say, but she didn't have the right words for him just yet. He didn't reply. Two brilliant blue and scarlet birds flashed across the pool and vanished. They watched as if seeing the birds at play was the most important thing on their minds. She sensed the tension in him as he waited for her to go on.

"Liani and Ganu have much in common."

"True."

"Once they were friends. They must be friends again. Alone, we're weak and vulnerable. Together we can defy the Venn."

His eyes were bluer than the pool's water this morning. "Going back be not easy."

"Not going back. Going on."

They listened to the waterfall's voice again. From the branches of a nearby pine tree, one of the birds began to sing. She thought she recognized the impulse that gave vent in this wild, ecstatic praise of life, the freshness of morning, and freedom.

"How will you persuade the Lianis that the Ganus be not unfinished?" Treng said.

"How will *you* persuade the Ganus that the Lianis aren't foolish children?"

This was really too difficult! He was as stubborn as all his race and wasn't helping at all. Yet she knew he felt it too, this odd feeling she'd had when she'd found him bathing.

"You and I must be a symbol of union for our people." Surely that would be clear enough to him? A Liani male would have understood what she was trying to say long ago!

"How so?" He trailed his hand carelessly through the water, apparently indifferent to her message. But she saw a nerve jump in his neck, betraying him.

"We must start a new race in Ilia, people that are both Ganu and Liani by blood." She waited for his answer, her own nervousness making her shiver. "It might be the only way we can defeat the Venn's purpose for us."

"If they still care! My father be of the opinion that was all long ago and the Venn have lost interest."

"I'm too proud to remain one minute longer what they had planned for me, whether or not they even remember," she said. "Help me tear down these bars, Treng. Even my brother—"

She stopped, the pain too intense to continue. But she had to continue, had to say the thing that had haunted her since the battle. "I think Parvey wanted me to kill him."

"How so?"

"He too didn't want to live in their cage. But he was too weak to do it by himself."

"But to let you kill him!"

"He had a Venn power in Tia-ta-pel that burned stone at a distance," she said. "I saw it. Askar called such power *science*. If he'd used that, we never could have taken him."

Treng stared thoughtfully at her for several moments. Then, abruptly, he stood up. "I can't live in your metros."

"Nor do I ask you to," she replied. "I can't live in Goron. This isn't easy for either of us, but we must free our people and heal the scars of captivity. And only we can do it."

"The Rhodarus who came to Goron told tales to our hunters. Bor—"

He broke off. She reached up and touched his hand gently, letting touch say the things she couldn't put into words.

"At first guilt stuck in my gull like a bone," he said. "I lived and he—so much more worthy than I!—had died. But now I know I be allowed to live because there be things to do that he—he would not have done." He controlled the emotions that threatened to spill over and spoke calmly again. "My brother long thought we were wrong to serve the Lianis, honoring them for their shapeshifting. He sensed there be something unnatural with that, something the Venn had meddled in. Bor listened to the oldlings who said we be no more than creatures in the Venn's own garden. The Rhodarus showed our hunters a way of life more suited to men!"

"The Rhodarus acknowledge no lasting allies and keep no leader for very long. Chetek told me this."

"They have a strong leader now. Our scouts tell us the warring clans have put aside their quarrel."

"This is bad news for us, if it's true!" she said.

"The new king has much to do before his realm be secure. It may take many years till he looks beyond the mountains for other conquests. But he will. And then there'll be war."

"How wrong I was to think the prophecy referred to the Ganus!"

He frowned. "What prophecy be this?"

She told him, adding, "Now I see it could mean the Rhodaru king and his warriors."

"We'll need more than prophecies and shiftskill against them!" He stood looking down at her, the sun setting fire to his pale hair so that he seemed crowned in gold. Then he frowned again. "They too must be products of Venn tampering with human stock! What theory be they meant to prove?"

He jerked away from her and slammed his fist viciously into the rock so that she feared he'd break the bones. She waited while the fury and the pain ran its course. His shoulders rose and fell. There was nothing she could say or do that lessened the anguish they both felt. She had proposed the only way they could cleanse themselves of this sickness that knowledge of their true origins had brought.

After a while he turned back to her, his eyes glistening. She saw a muscle twitch at the corner of his mouth. "I'll agree to what you say on one condition."

"Name it." She held her breath. Surely she hadn't been wrong about him?

"The Lianis take many mates and discard them quickly again. The Ganus take only one. Though I rule in Goron and you in Tia-ta-pel, ours must be a Ganu union."

She let her breath out slowly. "I'll share my throne with only you."

"But Tia-ta-pel—" he said. "The metros of shape-shifters!"

"Is that what stands in your way?" she said incredulously. How could he let such unimportant details block the future? She loved her city, but her mission against the Venn was paramount. "We don't have to stay there! We could meet anywhere—Donil's Bay, the summer cabins, right here in the hills if you wish!"

He absorbed this silently for a moment.

"When shall we do this?" he asked, gazing at the mist rising up the sides of the sunlit hills.

"As soon as we enter Tia-ta-pel. Afterward, you should return to Goron. I need to live alone for a while."

Now it was his turn to look startled. "For how long?"

"A month—a year—I don't know. But I *must* do this. I must think about what happened. I've spilled my brother's blood!"

She broke off, afraid she would break down and cry in front of him. He wouldn't understand such weakness. He wouldn't respect a queen who wept.

Treng took both her hands in his. "So be it, Sivell."

But his own eyes, when she finally looked up at them, were glistening, too.

Mordun, when he heard of it, was full of misgiving. Seeing that Sivell had recovered, he gave orders for the Ganu hunters to return to Goron. He himself planned to accompany Sivell on her re-entry into Tia-ta-pel. Falina excused herself from this, pleading a mourning period for her son. She kissed her daughter on both cheeks, and embraced Treng, and went with the hunters. Sivell thought she understood her mother's reluctance to return to her people after so many years.

Mordun sat in the warm afternoon by the cave's mouth, his injured arm strapped by his side, while the remaining Ganus gathered the packs the medwis would carry to Tia-ta-pel in the morning. Treng was off in the forest, exercising his medwi that had grown skittish with the prolonged inactivity of Sivell's convalescence.

"You haven't made a good bargain with my son," Mordun said. "He be hot-tempered and proud. There be little tolerance in him for Liani ways."

"I don't ask for any," Sivell said. "Only that he father my child so that we can unite our people against the Venn."

"As for that," the old man replied, "he'll do well enough!"

"Sometimes, when I was still sick," she said, "I dreamed of killing the Venn!"

"What would that solve?" Mordun asked. "Revenge be a cold meat to serve."

She had no answer for him.

"A greater concern be whether to tell your people the truth about themselves."

"But of course they need to hear the truth! Surely you're not suggesting I lie to them as the Venn lied?"

He shrugged. "Truth be a knife with two edges— freeing and also destroying. Even many among the Ganus don't want to hear this truth."

He'd opened up a new concern, one she knew she'd have to ponder before she made her decision. The whole fabric of Liani life hung on the pole of the Great Shaper. If she tore that down, who could tell what might fall with it?

After a while she asked, "Why are you so good to us? You gave to us before you took for yourselves. What did we ever do to deserve it? You must have known. Through all our careless treatment, you knew the truth."

"You needed us," he replied simply. "We be ordinary human stock—even though the Venn brought us into being. But you they experimented on, leaving you weak and vulnerable. Without us, you might not have survived."

"And see how we thanked you!" she exclaimed. "We knew no better than to despise you."

"We expected nothing else. We judged you not ready to hear the truth."

Something else she would have to live with, then, this knowledge of debt.

A few insects, encouraged by the warmth, whirred by her ear. Movement under the trees distracted her, and she glimpsed the disappearing form of the boy who'd been her silent companion through her illness.

Mordun noticed her glance. "That one's taken a liking to you."

She smiled. "He's gentle, and reminds me of a dear friend of my childhood."

"He be not like his father, then."

She looked at him for an explanation.

"He be Bor's bantling, but he doesn't know. Why should he? It will be of no use to him. Better to grow up not knowing." Then seeing the question in her eyes, he explained. "With us, a union be acknowledged only when it was made according to the old custom, and only the offspring of such a union be recognized as heirs. Bor never made such a union with the youngling's mam, but he saw to it the youngling was cared for."

Sivell listened to his words, watching the shiftpatterns of sunlight and shadows under the trees.

"How will we ever reconcile the differences they built into our people?" she said at last.

"I don't know, Sivell. But you be the only one who might do it, for you be unlike either."

She returned to the earlier conversation. "It'll be the first marriage in our tradition."

"Much good may it do you! To our minds, a union of man and woman be a refuge against loneliness. But my son be too wild, and you'll stay lonely."

"Perhaps," she said, thinking of the moment by the pool. "Perhaps not."

Treng burst out of the forest and clattered down the hillside, his medwi wild-eyed with excitement, prancing in place as he reined it in. Mordun narrowed his eyes, watching his son.

Treng lifted an arm in salute, then cantered off again.

Mordun grunted. "Tomorrow morning, then! We'll set out at dawn."

"Thank you."

"I'll send a messenger ahead to tell your people how their queen wishes to be received."

She nodded. "I have a particular request to make of them."

They went back into the cave.

It was noon when the little procession reached Tia-ta-pel. Sivell rode alone on Duhrn, the medwi that had been Bor's. It was the only one that would allow her near it without a Ganu nearby. Some kind of bond had been forged between them in the shared dangers of the battle, and Duhrn accepted her as its new owner. She wore a white robe that had been brought for her from Tia-ta-pel, fastened with a golden girdle, and her shiftemblem blazed in her free-falling hair. Treng rode by her side in a green tunic, his hair in the sunlight as gold as her girdle. Mordun was cloaked and booted in black, but wore the crown of the Ganus, a thin silver circlet set with flamestones. Behind them rode six Ganu hunters. Except for Sivell, none of them had ever set foot in Tia-ta-pel before.

At the western gate of the city they were met by the Lianis. Like their returning queen, the Lianis wore shiftemblems, but no jewels. As she entered Tia-ta-pel, little children came to her—hesitantly because of Duhrn—and gave her posies of spring flowers. They gaped in awe at the hunters bold enough to ride such fierce-looking beasts. The Ganus stared back at the Lianis.

Now she could see the towers of the castle, rising above the rooftops of the city. So many memories warred in her at the sight—joyous times, sad times, dances, festivals, quiet moments with a brother who'd never walk in the city again.

She turned to find Treng riding close by. He smiled at her. Mordun was wrong about his son, she thought. Wild and hot-tempered he might be, but not unfeeling. He'd be a good one to have at her side when she knew how she was going to oppose the Venn. She smiled back.

All at once, a huge flock of freed songbirds lofted into the air in a joyous confusion of vibrant color. She shielded her eyes against the bright sky and watched them wheeling overhead, her own little pet among them. There would be no more caged birds in Tia-ta-pel.

Bells rang out from the steeples, and banners lifted in the breeze. Sunlight turned the stones of Tia-ta-pel to gold. Sivell turned the medwi up the lane toward her castle.

CHAPTER TWENTY-TWO

(EPILOGUE, ILIAN DATE: 529)

The wind coming in off the water was brisk and laden with the tang of salt, sea fern, and fish. In another hour it would've blown away the fog that still lay on the water, under the cry of seabirds. The waves lapped the shore, foaming at the edge where they licked the footprints laid down before them. A brightness out at sea showed where the sun rose slowly through the fog. Even now a shaft of light was touching the highest towers of the still-sleeping city on the top of the cliff. The woman walking on the sand at the edge of the water didn't look back at the city.

At the foot of the cliff was a jumble of rock sloping down under the white-capped waves, but a little farther along the shore the rocks had pushed out into the sea forming a narrow jetty perhaps twenty paces long. The woman paused here, lifted her ankle-length white cloak so that her feet weren't encumbered, and climbed up. Cautiously she stepped over the jagged edges, the slick sides and the dark spaces between the rocks where the water fretted and boiled. She made her way out to the end of the natural jetty.

In winter the sea raced in over this impertinent tip of the land, submerging it even at low tide. But on this spring morning the waves rose and fell about the shell-covered sides, splashing the woman's feet. She listened to the suck and gurgle of the water, the hiss of foam slipping back from the rock, and the plaintive cry of the fishing birds. Alone in the landscape of foggy sky and gray-green water, she stared out toward the horizon, where, if there were islands, they weren't to be seen.

She reached in her cloak and drew something out. She looked at it closely for several minutes, as if reading a legend written there. Then she threw the object as far as she could out to sea. Attracted by the sudden movement, a seabird swooped down to investigate, but seeing only a dagger with a thin, curving blade, let it fall through the water undisturbed.

The motion of her arm caused her hood to fall back from her face, revealing dark hair. At that moment, the fog lifted enough to allow a ray of sunlight to shine full on her face, striking brilliant blue fire from the pendant earrings she wore. She turned back to land.

A small, dark man waited for her on the beach. She stepped off the natural jetty and stopped before him.

"I underestimated you, Sivell," he said.

She looked at him calmly. "Did you indeed, Askar?"

"You shouldn't have been strong enough to defeat your brother."

"After you'd armed him with some unholy Venn weapon, you mean?"

"It was a gamble I took in order to prevent a far worse fate from overtaking you!"

"Poor Askar!" she mocked. "For despite your meddling, Ganus and Lianis will live in peace."

"You've learned a lot about the Lianis and the Ganus, and the shaping of both," Askar told her. "But you don't know it all. How could you, being our creation? You can't know what was in our hearts—what high motives we had! And later, what despair."

She listened quietly, her hands hanging loosely at her hips. He began to speak faster.

"We'd been given the chance to settle a centuries-old question: which makes the difference over the long run, genetic heritage or societal environment? We could manipulate both! You see the physical differences we gave you. But you don't understand the reasons why."

"I understand you taught us to revere a lie."

He scowled at her.

A crystal boat rose up out of the waves, catching the sun's rays and fracturing them into a thousand rainbows. It bobbed lazily in the shallows. Askar seized the painter and motioned Sivell to board. She did so cautiously; beneath her feet she could see the green depths where fish swam.

"You turned your own teacher into our god," she said. The crystal boat moved silently out to sea, a ghost moving over dark water. "And more—a god whose only message was 'Seek pleasure' even in the midst of obvious distress."

"Would you have wanted Miranda to tutor you in the skills of making war? We did think of that! But it wasn't for you."

"Why did we need a god?"

"Because humans are born with a need to invent gods just as they are born with a need to invent language!" he shouted. "If you hadn't found your Great Shaper waiting for you, you'd have made up somebody else—and maybe worse!"

The offshore mist now flooded with violent color, then just as suddenly paled to silver. Images of armored warriors loomed over the boat, spears aimed at her head.

"We could help you," Askar said, calmer now. "Oh, very well. I admit it. We're responsible for this pain you're wallowing in! So perhaps we can even the score a little. Alone, you're nothing. A race of metamorphs with a dubious origin. But together—with our skills—"

Shapes more ominous than the armed warriors crowded the sky above her head, angular things of metal and fierce light. She was surrounded by gaping jaws; steel-tipped talons reached for her. Her heart beat wildly.

Then she remembered images conjured up, a long time ago it seemed, on the castle lawn. Illusions she'd put her hand through.

"No."

"Don't decide so hastily! There're hard times coming for your people. Do you suppose you'll survive un-aided?"

"You don't know us anymore," she said "*We* are the

humans now. Your race has abdicated their exalted status. Being human is more than just physiology. It involves being *humane*. The Venn have forfeited their claim to humanity."

His voice rose shrilly. "You have no idea what you're facing! The skills Elena gave the Rhodarus—"

Blood ran down the sky. Now she could hear voices shouting; screams mingled with the thud of weapon crashing into bone. Her stomach lurched at the sound. She gripped the sides of the transparent boat with trembling fingers and forced herself to stare boldly at the images.

Science, he had called it; something that humans did.

"You spoke of gods," he said. "You should know what the Rhodarus came up with, when Elena gave them the opportunity! An angry god for a warlike people. Or is it the other way around?"

"You don't frighten me. I'm half Rhodaru by birth," she reminded him.

"Ha!" he mocked. "And what good will that do you?"

"There'll be a day when all three merge in defiance of your plans. Liani, Ganu, and Rhodaru will become *Ilian*."

He gazed at her for a moment as if struck by a new idea, a new line of inquiry. "It wouldn't be easy to absorb the Rhodarus—Elena saw to that! Nor would it be accomplished quickly."

"I can be patient, too."

Askar grunted. "You won't see it in your lifetime!"

But the images and the horrible sounds faded, leaving only the waiting mist.

"I carry a child who's three races in one," she said. "I'll dedicate my descendants to the task of unity."

"My advice to you, Sivell, is build walls!" Askar said earnestly. "What's begun in blood will go through fire before it's clean again. The Rho colony will attack before the century's out. Even with the controls—the Gans— you'll be in trouble."

The boat nudged up against the sand, and Askar stepped out, leaving her to fend for herself. He paced about on the beach for a few moments, the green water licking at his feet. The crystal boat drifted out a little way then sank back under the waves. When he turned to her again his expression was melancholy.

"Your people, Sivell, your happy people playing all day, dancing in the meadows in moonlight, not a single care in their minds. What will you tell them?"

"I shall tell them we're human—no matter what you did to us—and that happiness is not the ultimate goal of those who are human."

"Kant's argument—centuries ago," he snapped. "But we didn't teach you that!"

"We'll do what we have to do, whatever the cost," she said. "But we'll stay free of the cages you built for us."

"And this *freedom*—this word that you cannot possibly truly understand!—it's worth so much to you that you'd give up the comfort of the mythos we gave you? Where will you ever find its replacement? What do you have to offer your people in return for the Great Shaper?"

She looked away from him for a moment to the sea, for this had been the hardest decision she'd made. Her people loved their Great Shaper; their security was the knowledge that they were shaped in its image. How would it hurt anything to let them go on believing in a benign mythology?

"Think, Sivell," he said, his voice sad, his eyes brimming with pity. "Instead of the cool dance of an eternal spirit in its lofty garden, you'll be giving them the bloody hand of the vivisector in their gut. Can you do this to them?"

They might never understand why she had to take away their beautiful dream. They might very well rebel against her for robbing them of something precious. But she knew it had to be done.

If they believed a lie, they would never be free.

"I'll give them the truth," she said.

"What do they matter to you?" he demanded. "These hedonists—sleepwalkers through life—they would've thrown you out and crowned your cousin queen and never wasted a moment's thought on the matter! You owe them nothing! Why should you love them?"

"It doesn't matter if I love them or not," she said simply. "It's still my duty to take care of them."

"Fine words!" he snapped. "But I am out of patience. You speak of things you have no understanding of. Very well, then. You shall learn them! You—our creation—lay claim to your humanity. Humans have the right to choose their actions. You have chosen. Now you must abide by the consequences."

Askar walked away from her, moving rapidly over the sand. Then he was suddenly gone in a brief flash, a sparkle like dust motes in a shaft of sunlight.

She retraced her steps to the path that led up the cliff to the city and found the boy waiting for her. His colorless cheeks and wide eyes told her he had seen Askar's terrifying images over the water.

But he'd stood his ground. It was a good beginning.

She put an arm around his shoulders and tousled his fair hair. "Why didn't you return with your king and Lord Treng to Goron this morning?"

"Let me stay with you," he pleaded. "Don't send me away. I can do anything you need. I be strong. I'll fight your battles!"

"Don't be so eager to kill. Some blood never washes away."

He gazed at her seriously. "I would only fight your enemies when you told me to."

She smiled. "I must prepare myself for the birth of my child. I need to do this alone."

He started to protest, but she stopped him. "I'll do this now, Tevun, but you may stay close by."

They climbed the path from the beach together, and the last shreds of fog blew away. The sun turned the sea to sapphire as bright as her earrings.

"After that," she said, "you and I and Lord Treng will have a great deal of work to do."

Whatever might come in the future, of agony or exultation, they would owe it to no one. That was what it meant to be human.

She took the boy's hand in hers and pulled him, laughing, up the path.

ABOUT THE AUTHOR

SHEILA FINCH, born in London, England, came to the United States in 1957 to do graduate work in medieval literature at Indiana University. The author of five science fiction novels and numerous short stories, she also teaches fiction writing and the literature of science fiction at El Camino College and runs a workshop in writing science fiction in the San Jacinto (California) mountains every summer. A resident of Long Beach, California, since 1967, she has three daughters.